'Offers a convi... ...he Second World War and a devastating account of the culture in which male entitlement to sexual and emotional comfort was a given.'

'*Ike and Kay* sets the backdrop for an important time in history brings to life controversial romances and characters that shaped history during the twentieth century.'

Buzzfeed

'An epic piece of historical fiction... the danger of war and the uncertainty of survival is conveyed through MacManus' in-depth research... a relatable, and compelling story.'

The Lady

'With keen eye for historical detail and strong narrative voice, MacManus has expertly and artfully painted an intimate, authentic portrait of love, duty and sacrifice against the backdrop of the greatest events of the 20th century. Masterful!'

Pam Jenoff author of *The Orphan's Tale*

'This portrayal of the long relationship between Eisenhower and his driver Kay Summersby uncovers a corner of the war's emotional texture not found in the grand narratives of history. MacManus weaves a touching, involving story of duty and heartbreak.'

Annie Murray, author of *War Babies*

'Two people thrown together by war... so much more involving and heart-wrenching for being a re-telling of a true secret history. I loved the drama of the setting and the fresh perspective on the momentous events leading up to the Allied assault on Nazi Germany; and I found Kay totally engaging, believed in her, wanted the best for her. *Ike and Kay* is an utterly compelling read.'

Margaret LeRoy, author of *The Drowning Girl*

'Thoroughly researched.'

Irish Independent

'While it is a fictional account... *Ike and Kay* is historical fiction for those who prefer the emphasis on the history... unusual and intriguing.'

Historical Novel Review

IKE

AND

KAY

James MacManus

DUCKWORTH

First published in the United Kingdom by Duckworth in 2019
Duckworth, an imprint of Prelude Books Ltd
13 Carrington Road, Richmond,
TW10 5AA, United Kingdom
www.preludebooks.co.uk

For bulk and special sales please contact
info@preludebooks.co.uk

A catalogue record for this book is available
from the British Library

Printed in the UK by Clays
ISBN 9780715652954

For Emily, Elizabeth and Nicholas

I

May 1942

They had waited three days for the train, stamping their feet against the cold on the platform at Euston Station, peering into the fog that descended on London like a shroud. You could hardly tell the difference between night and day in the blanket of grey vapour that slowed traffic to a crawl, stifled sound and left pedestrians groping their way along streets like the blind.

Charles Dickens would have known this fog, she thought. "London particulars" he called those days when the miasma rolled up the Thames from the Essex marshes and slithered into the city, clinging to buildings, drifting like smoke through open doors or windows clutching at people with slimy hands as they stumbled through the murk.

She slapped her gloved hands together, tightened the Sam Browne belt around her official issue khaki overcoat, and looked at her watch. It was 6.45 a.m. Three times now they had been ordered out of their beds in the pre-dawn darkness to meet the distinguished American visitors on a train that never arrived.

The other drivers, including her good friend Charlotte Montagu, had gone into the station for a cup of tea. It was against orders to leave their official cars, which were parked neatly in a row outside the station. But the train was finally due in fifteen minutes and in the fog no one could see whether the drivers were with their cars or not.

The Americans hadn't wanted to take the train. They had waited impatiently at Prestwick Airport in Scotland for the weather to clear. Only reluctantly had they been persuaded to take the overnight sleeper from Glasgow.

She found the girls happily seated with their tea in the warmth of the crowded café. They waved to her and shifted up the wooden bench to make room. Kay always called them girls, but in fact they were mostly women in their late twenties who had wearied of clerical or nursing work and wanted to do something more interesting.

Kay was conscious that she was the eldest at thirty-three, not that it made any difference. They were a cheerful lot, she thought, and they had every reason to be. They had been assigned three- and four-star generals, the most senior commanders in the growing American military presence in London.

The newspapers had treated the generals like film stars and carried long, admiring profiles: General George Marshall and General "Hap" Arnold were the favourites, and fan letters had already begun to arrive at the American Embassy in Grosvenor Square. It was May 1942, five months after Pearl Harbor had brought the US into the war.

Britain had yet to win a battle in a war that was being lost in the Atlantic Ocean. German U-boats were exacting a rising toll among convoys laden with food and fuel for a beleaguered nation.

Rationing had reduced bacon, butter, decent bread and anything but the scraggiest cuts of beef to a memory. Beer was watered down, and gin, whose provenance was often a bathtub rather than a brewery, was the only spirit available in public houses. Now the Yanks were finally coming, and London was eager to see what they looked like.

The BBC had broadcast the news that another military delegation was due to arrive in London that morning. The American ambassador, John Winant, was somewhere at Euston Station too, although they hadn't seen him. They were Motor Transport Corps drivers and their orders were to collect their assigned generals and take them to the embassy. Each driver had been given a name and a small photo for identification.

She had arrived late the day they handed out the assignments and the other drivers had got the most senior officers – and the best looking. They teased her about her American, not even a full general, a two-star major-general with a suspiciously Germanic name no one had ever heard of.

Kay squeezed onto the bench and watched gratefully as tea was poured from a chipped enamel pot into a mug.

"Any toast?" she asked, looking at a Formica tabletop bare of any suggestion of sustenance but for a bottle of HP sauce streaked with its own contents and small wooden salt and pepper pots. A brimming brown enamel ashtray sat in the centre of the table. Everyone was smoking.

"Toast's off – no bread," mimicked one of the girls, nodding towards a thin whey-faced woman in a stained apron behind the counter.

The girl, her friend Charlotte, offered Kay a cigarette and flipped open a silver lighter. It looked expensive and had entwined initials engraved on the side.

"Where did you get that?" asked Kay, inhaling deeply.

Charlotte smiled and shook her head.

Charlotte and she had been friends since both had sat nervously waiting for an interview to join the Motor Transport Corps a year earlier.

The corps had been formed at the start of the war to provide drivers for military top brass and important foreign visitors. There was no pay and the girls even had to buy their own uniforms – except for the standard-issue Sam Browne belt. They were mostly recruited through recommendation, a quiet word here and there in London's clubland or in the higher echelons of the Foreign Office.

The result was that the MTC began to be regarded, and widely derided, as a wartime finishing school for young women who wanted a role in the war effort without the boredom of a desk job.

It had been the American embassy's idea to form a special section of the MTC to drive their senior staff. All the major street signs in the centre of the city had been taken down in 1939 in case of an invasion and no one had yet put them back up. No American could find his way around town, and any able-bodied Londoner who could drive had been conscripted.

The vetting for the embassy job had been minimal. The main requirement was a good family background, a clean licence, the ability to drive a large American Packard anywhere in London at a moment's notice, and what was called "a pleasing appearance".

They all knew what that meant: good looks, a shapely figure, something to put a smile on the face of a weary American officer in bombed-out London.

Kay had no idea who had recommended her. An Anglo-Irish family clinging to the remnants of a rundown estate in

County Cork was hardly the required social background, judging by the other girls in the corps. They were all daughters of dukes or generals.

Charlotte's father was "Sir Somebody in the Foreign Office" and her mother was a lady-in-waiting to Queen Elizabeth at Buckingham Palace. They lived in a flat in Eaton Square which Charlotte said was the smartest address in London. There was a large country house in Yorkshire and a scatter of titled uncles, aunts and cousins.

"We're all hons, frightfully grand, but frankly it's a pain," she'd said to Kay after their interview. "The gossip columns never leave a girl alone. You're lucky not to have been saddled with all that. I rather envy you."

They were drinking gin and tonics in the Red Lion pub off Whitehall. Kay had described her childhood in southern Ireland where what had mattered to her parents was whether she could handle a .410 shotgun and take her pony over a dry-stone wall at full gallop.

"It was fun, but we were given precious little time or encouragement to learn anything," said Kay.

"Fancy being given a shotgun when you were twelve!" said Charlotte. "All I got was a bloody bicycle. That and a governess who taught us deportment and a ghastly woman who showed us how to dance with a young gentleman without treading on his toes."

Charlotte got up and began to dance around the pub with an imaginary partner, twirling around and saying in a loud voice, "If while dancing the waltz in close proximity with your partner you become aware that he is becoming aroused, you must leave the dance floor immediately and offer him a glass of water."

Kay burst out laughing and then covered her mouth as she saw people around them beginning to pay attention.

"She didn't say that!"

"Cross my heart, doll. I was fourteen and had no idea what she was talking about. I think Mummy thought we were too posh to be told the facts of life."

Charlotte had raven hair which was swept back in waves from a high forehead according to the fashion of the day for those who could afford it. Kay was a little jealous. Waves meant a perm, and that in turn meant the expense of a hairdresser. Like most women she made do with pinning her hair back beneath a headscarf.

Charlotte was not good-looking in the conventional sense; in fact there was nothing conventional about Charlotte at all. She was an inch over six feet tall and defied the drab wartime dress forced on most women by rationing. Charlotte's colourful silk scarves, linen blouses and long pleated skirts told the world that she had no need of clothing coupons.

What Charlotte liked was attention. She dressed, talked and acted to attract. She addressed her friends as "doll", explaining that it was a nickname her nanny had given her in the nursery. Her high cheekbones, well-rounded figure and a smile made more suggestive by lurid red lipstick had certainly attracted the attention of almost every man in the Red Lion when they'd walked in.

No one spared a glance for Kay. Not for the first time she reflected that the pale good looks and slender figure that had won her a modelling contract at the Worth fashion house two years earlier were not what men looked for in a woman.

Charlotte sat down. Everyone in the pub was now looking at her. She leant over to Kay, glancing around with comic exaggeration, and whispered, "They drink sherry at eleven o'clock in the morning, you know."

"Who?" asked Kay.

"Who do you think? Then they move on to gin and Dubonnet. The Queen is often squiffy by lunchtime."

"No!"

Charlotte put a finger to her lips, sat back, raised her glass and then laughed. She was always laughing; she never seemed to take anything seriously. Kay liked her the moment they met.

After the third gin Charlotte had said, "You may be an Irish peasant, but I'm going to make sure you get this job. I need someone like you around – the rest of them are so bloody dull."

Charlotte probably had used what she called her posh connections because they had offered Kay the job. For a woman in London in 1941 it was a chance to give up the squalor and horror of work as an ambulance driver – all broken bodies and blood everywhere – and do a job that was just as useful. At least that's what she told herself. It certainly sounded more fun.

Three blasts on a high-pitched whistle told the drivers their train was arriving. They drained the last dregs of their tea, ground their cigarettes into the ashtray and fished compacts from their handbags for a quick dab of powder onto pale cheeks. Lipstick and nail varnish were forbidden but, as Kay noted, the regulation did not seem to apply to Charlotte.

The drivers trooped onto the platform and lined up as the train arrived. The tall, gaunt figure of the ambassador pulled back the sleeve of his coat, looked at his watch and stamped on the platform to warm his feet. A crowd of journalists and film crews jostled for position behind a roped-off area.

Kay smoothed the skirt of her uniform while the others fussed with their belts and peaked hats. A crowd of passengers were coming down the platform with the Americans in front, four generals with peaked caps showing rank in the stars sewn onto their shoulder epaulettes. She recognised her man immediately from his photo, shorter than the rest with that wide mouth and ears that stuck up either side of his cap.

There was a moment of confusion as the officers paused to shake hands with the ambassador. Other passengers trudged past the group, anxious and weary after the overnight journey. When the crowd had cleared, the drivers looked around.

The platform was empty. The journalists were following the ambassador out of the station and crowding around his large limousine as the generals got in. Amid a burst of flashbulbs they drove off into the fog.

The girls walked back to their cars, laughing at the absurdity of a three-day wait for just a glimpse of the men they were supposed to be chauffeuring around London.

"What a charade," said Charlotte. "I hadn't even finished my tea. Anyone want another cuppa?"

The other drivers shook their heads and walked briskly back to their cars. Charlotte looked enquiringly at Kay, who also shook her head and said, "I think we should get to the embassy."

Kay followed Charlotte's tail lights until she lost her somewhere near Marble Arch. The only way to drive with any safety in the fog or nightly blackout was to keep close to the pavement where the kerb stones had been painted white. She wondered how their generals were getting on in the ambassador's car. The embassy had insisted on an American driver for security reasons. The man knew nothing about the wartime streets of London, many closed by bomb damage, and had probably got lost on his way back to Grosvenor Square.

Kay liked her job. The big American car drew admiring looks on the streets. She told herself she was making a contribution to the war effort. Traffic accidents in major cities had soared since the imposition of the blackout and the mindless decision to turn off traffic lights at major junctions. Her duty was to deliver anyone the American embassy designated safely and on time to their destination.

It was straightforward, easy work and, if she was honest, for all the status conferred on a young woman by a wartime uniform, it was rather boring. There were times like this, kerb-crawling through the fog, when she missed the excitement of driving an ambulance with bells ringing and lights flashing. The danger of driving through streets engulfed in fire wasn't the reason why she'd given up ambulance work. It was because she found she spent more time driving body parts to the mortuary than the wounded to hospital. She had become one of the horsemen of the apocalypse, delivering death rather than saving life.

Kay looked at her watch and worked out she would be at the embassy in a few minutes. She would be introduced to her general and given movement orders for the following day. The drivers were never told how long their charges were staying in the country. They were given a schedule for the next twenty-four hours and no more.

Where the American visitors went and who they saw was a secret. Kay, like the other drivers in the Transport Corps, had signed a document pledging on pain of death not to reveal any details of her work. It had made them all feel very important to start with, but the fact was that most of their work involved waiting for hours on end outside offices and military camps.

And that was what her life amounted to now. Driving and waiting, night and day, through blackout, fog, rain, hail or whatever weather the capricious English climate chose to summon from the heavens.

It was a good way, if not to forget, then at least to take her mind off her guilt and regrets.

Richard was overseas with his regiment somewhere in North Africa. He was an Irish American from upstate New York, a dashing officer well over six feet tall with warm brown eyes and minty chewing gum breath. To the fury of his family he had gone to Canada to join an armoured unit. It was his way of getting into the war, he'd said. He had hardly put the engagement ring on her finger before she'd found out through an anonymous note from "a well-wisher" that he was married.

He had wept real tears when he'd confessed. He swore that the marriage had been a sham to please their parents, that he was almost divorced and that she, Kay Summersby, was the only woman he had ever really truly loved.

Kay wondered whether men were born bastards or their mothers made them that way in revenge on the testicular tribe. Either way, she knew that women were born to forgive them. And she had forgiven him, or rather she had fallen in love with him, which was almost, but not quite, the same thing.

That had been a year ago and the awful thing was that she could barely remember what he looked like now. It had all been so quick. A few months of hurried kisses in darkened doorways, stolen nights in country pubs with creaky beds, a proposal on the steps of the Albert Memorial beneath the forbidding gaze of Queen Victoria's adored husband and then discovery, confession, forgiveness and a final night of redemptive lovemaking in a mildewed room near Victoria Station. Then he was gone. She well knew the truth of the popular saying at the time: *A quick fling, a diamond ring, then you wait for the phone to ring.*

And the phone never did ring. She got letters, of course, all spidery handwriting crammed onto the regulation two pages of thin army-issue blue paper carefully folded into envelopes stamped *Read By the Censor.*

He was in a tank somewhere in North Africa with his Canadian unit and talked of the heat, the flies, the endless desert, the stars at night scattered across the sky like sequins on a velvet cushion, anything but the war itself.

She smiled when she read the line about the stars. He said his Irish side gave him a love of words and poetry. There had been two or three letters a week to begin with, but they had dwindled recently.

She swerved to avoid a drinker who had emerged into the fog from a darkened pub and walked straight onto the road. She blew her horn, breaking another wartime regulation. Drivers were not supposed to sound their horns at any time of the day or night. Much of London slept by day as people got little enough sleep most nights with the air-raid sirens and the bombs.

In truth she didn't miss Richard's letters. They had just made her feel guilty. She had written back, of course, but doubted that the carefully phrased words of love ever reached a tank unit somewhere in the North African desert.

She didn't even know for sure he was in Africa. She just knew there had been a lot of fighting in the desert that spring. She looked at the announcement of casualties in *The Times* every day, but he was only a junior officer. She wasn't sure they would carry news of the death of an American second lieutenant who had somehow managed to join the British Eighth Army in the desert.

In fact she wasn't really sure of anything about Richard except that he loved her in that careless way that men do and that she had fallen in love with him, or rather with a pair of warm brown eyes and kisses that tasted of mint.

Charlotte had told her it was just another wartime romance and to forget him, which was probably good advice. After all, what could any woman mean to a man about to leave for an unknown destiny in a distant war?

Kay swerved again and swore as a creature, a cat or a large rat, ran into the beam of her dimmed headlights. Richard had said he loved her, he would miss her and that he would marry her when he got back. But every departing soldier said that, didn't they? It was written into the script of every wartime romance, and it was a lie. What young men really wanted was the freedom to enjoy the adrenaline rush of living with danger and delivering death. That was what it was all about, wasn't it? And where did that leave the women left behind?

In her case it left her driving a large car through the darkened streets of London on the way to meet an unknown two-star American general. It could be a lot worse, she thought.

She had been up since five a.m. and she was hungry. She parked her Packard, painted in camouflage khaki, in front of the embassy in Grosvenor Square and found a nearby café for a sandwich and a cup of tea.

She felt a pang of guilt that she hadn't found her general. The other girls had probably met theirs and were even now driving them across London to important meetings.

She couldn't see that it really mattered. Her man would be deep in briefings in the embassy with that strange ambassador by now. And a girl needed to have breakfast. It was the only memorable advice her mother had given her.

There were baked beans with fried tomatoes or liver and onions on the menu. She chose the baked beans. There was no knowing where the liver came from. The beans were barely warm, but she finished the dish quickly and split open a stale roll to mop up the juices. *Waste Not, Want Not* was the battle cry on the home front.

As she walked back to the embassy, she saw through the clearing fog the outline of two American officers standing on the pavement by the Packard. They were looking up and down the street and across the square. One was shorter than the other. They had small suitcases. They were looking for her.

She ran as fast as her long skirt would allow, flying down the pavement, skidded to a stop and saluted.

"I'm sorry I'm late… I think I'm your driver."

"And you are?" enquired the taller one.

"Summersby, Motor Transport Corps."

"You know where Claridge's Hotel is?" he asked.

She nodded. Of course she did. It was two blocks away – it would have been quicker to walk. He hadn't introduced himself but she knew he was General Mark Clark. And the shorter one was her general.

She ran back to the car, drove rather too fast the few hundred yards to where the generals were waiting, and braked hard, scraping the kerb with the hubcaps. Before she could get out they had got into the back without a word.

She checked in the mirror on the five-minute drive to the hotel. He had taken his hat off and she saw a broad forehead, thinning sandy hair and that wide mouth. And there were two stars on the shoulder of his uniform. Major-General Dwight Eisenhower. What a strange first name. Dwight. Where did that come from? And a half general. Just her luck.

2

May-June 1942

She was at the hotel at nine a.m. the next morning. She held the door open as Eisenhower and Clark climbed into the back of the car carrying bulging briefcases. They said little as she drove, burying themselves in the paperwork, occasionally muttering an oath as they passed a sheet of paper to one another.

She delivered her two generals back to the hotel at one a.m. the following morning. That set the pattern for the next three weeks. It was the same early morning pickup, then a drive to a government office or one of the many army or air bases around London. She would wait for hours in the canteen drinking stewed tea and trying not to chain-smoke, then maybe drive them to another base and finally back to Claridge's long after dark.

She could see her general was growing weary. His ruddy complexion turned sallow and the bags began to droop under bloodshot eyes. There was always someone in the car with them, usually another American general: George Marshall, Carl Spaatz or George Patton, names that were becoming familiar to the British public.

The Americans gave no interviews and refused to answer questions tossed at them by trailing journalists, but their photographs were always in the newspapers and their faces on the newsreels. Londoners found that very reassuring. The Yanks really had come and, as the song said, they would not be going home until it was "Over, over there".

At first Eisenhower and his colleagues whispered in the back, but as they got used to her they talked openly and she heard a rising tone of frustration and irritation: training was delayed, supplies had run short, orders had been misinterpreted, ships with vital equipment had been lost at sea – the list of problems grew in the weeks after they had arrived.

It was nearly the end of June and Hitler's invasion of Russia the previous year had placed the Wehrmacht well on the road to Moscow. Kay could hear the anxiety in their voices as the generals assessed Hitler's next move. If Moscow fell before the winter snows it would be Britain next.

Her general was always polite, thanking her courteously at the end of the day and asking her, rather than ordering her, to return the next morning. He called her Kay and made sure she was offered something to eat and drink when they vanished into their endless meetings.

He seemed quieter than the others, listening carefully to what was said around him, chain-smoking, making notes in a large foolscap pad that he carried in a leather attaché case. She watched him in the rear-view mirror, the broad forehead wrinkled with concentration, the blue eyes closed as he leant back to consider a problem, the face opening into a brief smile when someone suggested an answer then turning to a scowl when the idea proved impractical.

The rear-view mirror was her window into their world. She quickly learnt that her general was finding little to his liking in the military arrangements in Britain. As May had given way to June and the days grew lighter and longer, frustration had turned to anger in the back of the Packard. She had watched nicotine-stained fingers jabbing into documents, seen comments scrawled angrily across secret memoranda and heard muttered oaths give way to open cursing. It was like watching lava rise to the lip of a volcano. She waited for the explosion.

It came the morning she drove him to visit Lieutenant General Montgomery at a base in Kent near London. Monty, as he was known to all, had agreed to brief the American general but made it clear from the outset that he had little time or inclination to do so.

Eisenhower obviously knew all about Montgomery: the coming man in the British military, destined to lead the Eighth Army in North Africa. Known to be abrasive, self-righteous, a rigid tactician who openly espoused the creed of caution in battle, Montgomery was not popular with his peers, although liked by his troops.

Kay knew the day had not gone well when she saw the general walking across the parade ground to the car. Eisenhower never hurried anywhere. Patience was his trademark. He let others make speed around him while he moved slowly, ever watchful, waiting for the right moment to speak or act. Now he was hurrying to the car so fast that Mark Clark could hardly keep up with him. There was an unlit cigarette between his fingers.

It was just before six on a sunlit evening and the chestnut trees that lined two sides of the square had put forth their white candle-shaped flowers. They gave the trees the appearance of exotic birthday cakes, green creamy leaves rising like icing to a peak lit by the flames of white flowers.

The trees were one of the enduring images of an early English summer and Kay had planned to point them out as they left, but quickly changed her mind as she held open the rear door. Eisenhower sank wordlessly into the back seat, put the cigarette into his mouth and leant over to take the offered light from Clark beside him.

"Sonofabitch," he said as they drove through the camp gates.

She could see him in the mirror, white-faced with anger, the veins throbbing in his temple, fists tightly clenched. Drawing deeply on the cigarette, he wound the window down and expelled a long stream of smoke.

"Limeysonofabitch."

Clark joined in the parade of insults and Kay listened as the two men discussed their encounter with Montgomery. Their anger turned to disbelief as they repeated the story to themselves. The British commander had been briefing his American visitors in a crowded meeting room when he had suddenly stopped and barked out a question: someone was smoking, who was it?

There was silence in the room while everyone looked around. Eisenhower dropped his cigarette, ground it out beneath his shoe and said quietly that he had been smoking: was that a problem?

Of course that was a problem, Montgomery had snapped. Smoking was a disgusting habit and banned while men were on duty. Never do that again in my presence, he said.

Eisenhower was livid. He had been openly rebuked in a schoolmasterly manner in front of British officers very much his junior. Rank, status and emblems on a uniform were the lifeblood of any army and, although Montgomery outranked him, he, Eisenhower, had been placed in charge of pulling together the Allied military effort in Britain by none other than the president of the United States. As such he merited Montgomery's respect, not a public rebuke.

The anger in the back of the car turned to rueful laughter as Eisenhower told Clark how Montgomery had said goodbye to him. Realising that he may have gone too far in his rebuke, the British general had drawn Eisenhower aside and tried to smooth matters over. He had complimented Eisenhower on his promotion and promised co-operation in the difficult tasks ahead. Eisenhower had listened politely, shook hands, and was about to leave when Montgomery lowered his voice almost to a whisper and said, "My men smoke a lot too, you know. Rationing is very tight. I don't suppose you have any spare packs of Lucky Strikes, do you? Good for morale, you know."

Montgomery had not bothered to get briefed on his visitors. That much was obvious to Eisenhower. He knew from the start what Montgomery would only slowly find out: that the two men were exact opposites in background, temperament and training.

Kay delivered the men to Claridge's earlier than usual, at around eight p.m. She noticed the meeting with Montgomery had changed Eisenhower. He and General Clark turned their anger to laughter by mocking Montgomery's clipped, oh-so-English accent, his battledress beret and his habit of addressing everyone as if talking to imbecile schoolchildren. Both men relaxed. Eisenhower told Clark that he accepted Montgomery was a pompous prig, but he was also a master tactician who had laid out impressive plans for the coming campaign in North Africa. They would have to work with him.

Kay held the car door for the general while, as usual, a crowd of dirty-faced schoolchildren, little more than five or six years old, ran up with hands out, chanting, "Got any gum, chum?"

They should have been with other evacuees in the countryside. No one knew where they came from but they always seemed to be outside the hotel at the right moment to accost visiting Americans with demands for chewing gum or chocolate.

Eisenhower laughed while the doormen shooed the children away. Then he turned to Kay and said, "I guess the war can do without us for a few hours. You know a good place for dinner, somewhere where they don't serve cabbage or sprouts?"

Kay knew what he was talking about. She spent hours in a car every day with men who were served boiled cabbage or Brussels sprouts at every meal on the army bases they visited. She had heard him mutter more than once in the back to colleagues that this must be the fartingest war in history.

"The Connaught," she said. "Good food, just down the street and the tables in the restaurant are far enough apart for privacy."

"Good," said Eisenhower. "Give us ten minutes to wash up."

She drove them slowly the two blocks through evening streets still lit by the last of the sun. It would not get dark until ten that night, which meant they were safe from the occasional raid the Luftwaffe still flung at London. That wasn't the only reminder of the grim days of the Blitz.

Barrage balloons hung like spaceships in the darkening sky. Cables tethered these new London landmarks to parks and gardens that had been stripped of their iron railings. The streets were potholed, with missing houses and boarded up windows. She thought London looked rather better in the blackout than by day. At night, pedestrians with masked torches shone narrow beams onto the pavements, creating the surreal effect of walking among aliens.

Kay jumped out to open the doors at the Connaught, an ancient hotel dating back to the early eighteenth century that had changed its name from Coburg in the Great War, she told them as they got out.

"Why?" Eisenhower asked.

It was rather too German a name for its patrons, Kay explained. He smiled at that. She wasn't sure why.

The uniformed doorman stiffened, almost prepared, it seemed, to salute a man whose face and rank were becoming well known to Londoners. The general walked up the steps and turned. Clark went ahead into the hotel.

"You'll join us, Kay?" he said, posing the question as if it needed no answer.

Kay looked at the doorman, who was apparently struggling to understand what he had just heard. She wondered if she dared accept, and if she did, where she would park the car. The Packard flew the US flag on the bonnet and was known as an embassy car; there were very few like it in London. If she left it outside the hotel the police could hardly object.

But Motor Transport Corp drivers did not accompany generals to lunch, dinner or any social occasion; nor indeed were they supposed to talk to their charges beyond the usual courtesies. As she could see from the doorman's scandalised expression, Eisenhower was about to break a social taboo. She looked at her general. There was a smile on his face.

"I'd love to," she said, and walked past the doorman, knowing that he would probably earn half a guinea from the *Evening Standard* for the social travesty he had just witnessed.

They sat at a square table in a dining room strung with chandeliers and with a single rose placed in a small vase on the crisp linen of every table. The maître d' placed Kay between Eisenhower and Clark with a look that suggested he shared the doorman's disapproval. She liked Clark. He and

Eisenhower were like brothers, both career soldiers who had been rapidly promoted after the outbreak of war.

Their army talk in the back of the car was quick-fire, laced with expletives and coded with references she could not understand. But Clark was the one who would break off the conversation to admire a pretty woman on the street. Eisenhower would sigh theatrically, nod and pull the conversation back to the subject under discussion.

Kay was nervous and gratefully accepted a cigarette. Her hands shook slightly as Eisenhower held out the lighter. It was the first time she'd been face-to-face with her boss, the first time she'd looked him in the eyes, the first time she'd talked to him beyond saying good morning, good night and yes, sir, no, sir. Her world was the big Packard car and her job was to deliver her man throughout the day to meetings, lunches, dinners and back to the hotel at night.

She had begun to run errands for him as well, picking up the evening papers from the vendor on the corner or fetching cigarettes from the hotel porter. But that was all. In the weeks she had been driving him they had hardly spoken more than a couple of sentences. Now she was going to have dinner with him, and Eisenhower quickly made clear she was going to be very much part of the conversation.

Both Americans ordered sirloin steak, green salad and new potatoes, luxuries long forgotten by most Londoners. Kay thought it best to order the same and try and say as little as possible. Clark suggested a bottle of red wine. Eisenhower looked at Kay.

"Would you like some wine?" he asked.

She nodded and saw him smile. She decided there was nothing to be nervous about. These two men just wanted to relax, swap stories about the roller-coaster ride of their service careers and drink a lot of wine, and they wanted to do so in the company of their driver. That didn't seem to bother either of them, though the maître d' barely deigned to notice her presence. Kay was wearing her Motor Transport Corps uniform. Her rank and station were obvious to everyone in the dining room.

For an hour the war didn't exist. The Americans cracked jokes, each trumping the other's stories and both laughing out loud. She couldn't help but laugh too, not so much at the jokes, which she couldn't understand, but at the madcap way these two men enjoyed themselves.

They teased her about her slight Irish accent and the way she drove so slowly. They ordered more wine and smoked continually. The tradition in such grand restaurants was that one did not light up until coffee, but no one bothered to rebuke the American generals.

She had never seen her boss like this, never suspected that behind the military mask such a man existed. The grey face had recovered its colour, the eyes were blue rather than bloodshot. The grin got wider as the stories and questions flew across the table. He suddenly looked his age again, fifty-one, and not like the much older man he sometimes appeared to be after days and nights of argument and debate.

They asked about her fiancé and she made them laugh again by saying she was forbidden to say where he was or what he was doing.

Then Mark Clark asked, "You're Irish, aren't you?"

"Yes, born in Cork. Daddy has a small place out west by the sea. We grew up there, four kids running wild on horses every day."

"But Summersby – that's not an Irish name, is it?"

She looked down at the white starched tablecloth. No,

that wasn't an Irish name. That was the very English name of her very English ex-husband. They had married at the outbreak of war, thinking to seize a little happiness before the bombs fell.

Like all such marriages, and there were many like that at the time, it had quickly proved a failure. Summersby was a good-looking young publisher, although she never knew what he actually did. When he was called up and shipped out to a regiment in India they both accepted the parting as final. The divorce papers eventually followed.

She had told none of her friends of the marriage, although her family knew and had surprisingly given their blessing. Her mother had been quite open in hoping for a grandchild that would allow Kay to return to the family home in Ireland, far from the dangers of London. But Kay and her husband had agreed not to bring any children into a world of such tumult.

Instead they enjoyed the licence granted by a registry office wedding to spend a great deal of time in bed, which, as became clear, was all they had in common.

She remembered those pleasures with clarity as one remembers the look and taste of a good meal. Sometimes, at night, she would recall the intimacies they had shared and find satisfaction in such memories. After all, as Kay told herself, if Proust could find his past in a madeleine cake dipped in tea, why should she not find release and sleep in the recall of happy hours in the marriage bed?

They had arguments, of course, sometimes bitter fights about his drinking and her extravagance. But what he called "the sweet clemency of sex" always ended the rows. He used the phrase more than once. She liked it. He had obviously read it somewhere.

"Where did you get that from, the stuff about the clemency of sex?" she asked.

"I read it somewhere," he said. "You like it?"

"I might if I knew what it meant," she said.

"In sex we find forgiveness for our deceits and the betrayals," he said.

"What are you talking about? Who's betraying who?" she asked.

"We deceive and betray ourselves. All the time. We find forgiveness in fucking."

"I hate that word. It's vulgar. And I don't understand what you're trying to say."

He sighed and she knew he was going to patronise her because with his Oxford degree and smart friends in the literary world of London he was so much more intelligent and well-read than her. He never said or suggested that but he certainly thought it. She could tell.

"Let me put it this way," he said, "making love strips us bare. We go back to our beginnings. Before the fall from grace."

"What, you mean the garden of Eden, original sin and all that nonsense?" she asked, thinking she could forgive him his intellectual snobbery and sins, original or otherwise, because he was so good in bed. If that was the clemency of sex it was certainly sweet.

Now he was gone, swallowed up by the war like so many others. Someone was waving a hand in front of her face.

"Hey we've lost you – come back," said Eisenhower. "You were telling us about your family name."

"Oh, yes," she said. "Summersby was my husband's name. My ex-husband, that is. My maiden name is a bit of a mouthful – MacCarthy-Morrogh."

She watched them looking at her, thinking she didn't look old enough to have had a husband and now be engaged again. She had always looked much younger than her age and certainly didn't look thirty-three.

She had a clear, almost radiant complexion for which she thanked the Irish weather, dark brown hair, blue eyes, a bob nose and, as an early boyfriend had told her, "a smile that suggested a kiss on the lips". The boyfriend quickly went, as they all did at the time, but she liked the phrase so much she wrote it in her diary.

Her smile and a good figure had got her a modelling job in London when she managed to flee the rural solitude of the Irish west. Then came marriage, the war, the divorce and finally the job no one else wanted – driving an ambulance at a time when the long months of the phoney war meant there was little to do. But she had stuck to it, partly because it gave her wartime status in the shape of her uniform, but mostly, she knew, to put her whirligig past behind her and do something sensible with her life.

And here she was, having dinner with two very important American generals in one of the smartest hotels in London. The mention of her maiden name had suddenly made them curious.

"What did you do before this?" asked Eisenhower. She told him she had been driving an ambulance in the Bermondsey district of the docks during the Blitz.

She tried to stop there, but Eisenhower wanted to know more. The laughter at the table stopped as she gave a brief description of nights during the bombing when she would drive a vehicle with shredded tyres over smouldering rubble while a nurse in the back desperately tried to give help to badly wounded women and old men.

The young men were away fighting and the children had been sent to the country. It was always women and old men in the back of her ambulance. And they were usually badly burnt. The smell of cindered flesh was terrible, but she got by with the help of black market whisky. She never drove her ambulance sober in those days, she told them.

Eisenhower didn't take his eyes off her for a second as she talked.

"I want to go there," he said suddenly. "Tomorrow."

"Where, sir?"

"Bermond... whatever it's called. Down by the docks. Show me."

"Sir, you have meetings all morning."

"All right. We'll go when there's a break in the diary. How far is it?"

"About twenty minutes."

"Let's do that. You'll come, Clark?"

It wasn't a question. Clark nodded.

The Packard nosed slowly through what was left of the streets of Bermondsey the next day. The rubble had been cleared onto wasteland where once terraced housing had stood. The bomb damage across the river in Mayfair had merely left gaps in streets like missing teeth. Here on the south bank of the Thames, below Tower Bridge, acres of London had been levelled. Skeletons of buildings and warehouses stood forlornly awaiting the wrecker's ball. Old people were still picking through the rubble in a fruitless attempt to find belongings. As usual, small children who had escaped evacuation to the dubious attractions of the countryside were playing amid mounds of broken bricks.

The Americans said nothing as they surveyed the scene. They asked her to stop by a tea stall and got out. Eisenhower put his hands on his hips and looked around. There was still a smell of brick dust and burning in the air.

"You drove an ambulance here?" he said.

"Yes. They were going for the docks. Night after night."

"When was this?" asked Clark.

"The Blitz. A year ago. The bombing is nothing like that now."

"Poor people. Poor London," Eisenhower said.

The general returned to Washington not long afterwards. She drove him and General Clark to Northolt airport outside London where senior British commanders were lined up to bid them farewell. General Montgomery was not among them. Everyone was sheltering under umbrellas from a light June rain.

On the journey to the airport, Eisenhower and Clark were unusually silent. She knew what her boss was thinking. He had been alarmed by the state of the American forces in Britain. They were growing in number every week as men disembarked from troopships and planes, but they were far from ready for war. Soldiers, airmen, sailors, logistics staff, medical staff, cooks, engineers, an entire army was being assembled without being told of their mission.

Again and again she had heard him say in the back of the car that the senior American command in Britain was made up of men who had fallen asleep on the job. Idle and incompetent were words that had flown around the back seat of the Packard. She also knew that although Montgomery irritated the hell out of him, as Eisenhower put it, he valued him as a professional soldier.

In these last three weeks the Packard had become more a travelling conference room than a car. Sometimes Eisenhower had had three aides squeezed in with him and they had talked openly in front of her, even when it came to the code word "Roundup", the plan to take the fight to the Nazis in occupied Europe.

Eisenhower's mission, to assess and report back to the White House what was needed to mount a cross-Channel invasion, who should lead the Allied forces, and above all where and when the invasion should take place, had never been announced; indeed Kay sometimes wondered whether anyone in London beyond the prime minister realised what was being discussed in the back of her car.

Every now and then, after an intense session of argument and discussion about the complexities of the invasion and the difficulties of dealing with Prime Minister Churchill, General Montgomery and a host of senior British military and civilian personnel, she would suggest a drive into the country. In the rear seat, angry and exhausted, they would stop thumping fists into the leather seats. The aides would look at their boss. Eisenhower would nod.

She would take them to a pub on the banks of the Thames in Oxfordshire. The boss had loved those trips. Everyone called him Ike, but she preferred to call him the boss, and he seemed to like that. They all preferred gin and tonic to warm English beer, even if there was no ice and lemon, and they would try to play a game of dominoes on the bar while she persuaded the publican to provide plates and cutlery for the pork pies she had brought from the hotel. You could get almost anything to eat at Claridge's, but nothing in an English country pub.

Ike would sit on the pub deck on a weathered wooden chair looking at the river and talk about suddenly important questions such as Clark's idea to take a rowing boat for "a quick paddle on the Thames", as he put it.

Eisenhower retorted that it was one of the dumbest ideas he had heard since his father-in-law suggested he train as a Gaucho in Argentina and go into the beef business.

"Just think of it," he said, "two American generals with a real war to fight seen rowing on the Thames. That would be a great picture for the papers. What would people think?"

"No one will ever know," said Clark, "and it will be cool on the water."

It was indeed a very hot day that day. On the river, boats were being rowed by elderly men wearing blazers and ties while their ladies in cotton summer dresses lounged in the stern beneath white parasols. Ike merely smiled.

"Listen, dope," he said. "This is England, where everybody knows everything. You don't know the press here. They're like spiders, they get everywhere."

The two men had looked at each other, then back at the river. Then they had laughed, perhaps, she thought, at the absurdity of the waterborne costume drama in front of them. The traditional pastime of boating on the Thames seemed a very English form of defiance against the mad world over the horizon.

That was the memory she liked best of the whirlwind two weeks he had been there: Ike sitting by the Thames with his service cap placed on a wooden table by a tall glass of warm gin and tonic. His time in England had passed like a morning. Now she was taking him to the airport to report, not on a mission achieved, but on the huge task ahead.

She drove the Packard straight to the foot of the aircraft steps at Northolt, noting that the face in her mirror looked older, wiser and perhaps sadder than when he had arrived. The propellers of the plane were already beginning to turn. She got out, opened an umbrella and held it over the generals as they shook her formally by the hand, thanked her and began walking down the line of the dignitaries.

At the aircraft steps, Eisenhower paused, turned, and walked back to the car. He reached into the back seat and brought out a small box prettily tied in tissue paper and red ribbon. He handed it to her. "This is a thank you from both of us."

"Thank you, sir," she said and laid the umbrella against the car.

"Go on, open it."

It was a box of dark chocolates, a luxury that had not been seen since the start of the war.

He smiled. And then he was gone up the steps and into the aircraft before she could find the words to thank him.

She watched the plane take off and vanish into low cloud. She knew she would not be seeing her general again. He was going to be given a third star and promoted to something very important in Washington. They had talked about it in the back of the car. She had already been assigned as driver to another American general, this time one in the air force.

She took a last look up at the empty sky, got back into the Packard and put one of the chocolates into her mouth. She leant back, savouring a delicious, long forgotten taste, and then picked up another one.

3

June 1942

He had come back, of course.

She had read of his appointment in *The Times*. The announcement from the White House stated that General Dwight Eisenhower had been promoted to Commander of European Theater of Operations. The news was given front page coverage and was announced on the BBC in news bulletins throughout that day, 24 June 1942. She had ringed it in red in her diary. She knew exactly how long he'd been away because she'd eaten one chocolate a day from the box he'd given her. There were two layers, and when she ate the last one three weeks had passed.

She had been driving a very different American in the meantime, General Tooey Spaatz, commander of the US air forces in Britain. She loved the name, which made him sound like a mad comedian from the music hall era, but sadly Spaatz was a grimly silent character who never offered her a word of thanks. When he did speak, it was from the back of the car, and only to ask how long it would take to get to their destination. She would give an estimate and he would snap back, "Make it faster." She began to feel more like a fighter pilot than a staff car driver.

He had a suite at Claridge's which at any time of the day or night resembled the Hollywood version of a cocktail party – the smoke, the noise, the badges of high rank on the men's uniforms and the smart dresses of the women, many of them actresses who had come straight from West End shows, created an atmosphere completely at odds with his coldly impatient character. He would stride through the mêlée, shaking hands, making brief conversation here and there, greeting well known names from the stage, and then vanish into a small sitting room. She would accompany him, as was her duty, and for an hour or more she would sit there while he slumped into a chair at a desk, occasionally picking up a document to read and then sighing deeply. But mostly he sat back gazing at the ceiling. He would do this for what seemed like an eternity, and then he would look up, seemingly surprised to see her, and say, "Thanks, Kay, I guess I won't be needing you any more tonight."

The scene was repeated several times during the four weeks she served him, and she learnt to take books and magazines with her to fill the silent hours. She also understood that the long periods of concentration were the general's way of coping with the deaths of his young countrymen, whose names and ranks clattered into his office every day on the teleprinter.

The US Eighth Air Force had by then joined the RAF in large-scale daylight raids on Germany, and initially losses were high. Every week new planes fresh from factories across America arrived at British airbases, while ships unloaded the bombs, bullets and spare parts with which they would be armed and serviced. Young American pilots, bomb-aimers, navigators, gunners, aircrew, mechanics and armourers also arrived in their thousands.

They were young, fresh-faced kids with the minimum of training. Most of them had never left their home state before, let alone been abroad. She could tell he felt they were his responsibility, that too many were dying in the skies over Europe.

Then came one fine summer evening when she pulled up outside the hotel and General Spaatz flung himself into the back of the car almost before it had stopped. "Northolt airport," he barked. "And step on it."

She knew not to ask why, but drove with her hand on the horn all the way out through west London to the new airport that was being carved out of farmland. She understood the reason for the hurry the moment she arrived. A long line of VIPs were lined up beside steps alongside the runway. A B24 bomber had just landed and was taxiing slowly to the greeting party. It came to a halt, and scarcely had the propellers stopped turning than the doors were opened and a broad-shouldered figure with a big smile stepped out and down the steps. Eisenhower was back.

He had three stars on his shoulders now, she noted; he was commander of the "whole shooting match", as he put it later. He shook hands with the VIPs and then noticed her standing by the car. He came over straight away, trailed by Spaatz, who was his usual unsmiling self.

"Kay, how are you?" he said. "I gather Tooey here has been hiding you in the air force. You want to drive for me again?"

Spaatz spared her the embarrassment of a reply. "Now don't take Kay away from me," he growled. "She's the only driver I've found who really knows London."

Eisenhower just laughed.

"I have some fruit for you, Kay," he said and walked away.

The next day a basket of bananas, mangoes and peaches arrived on her desk. The following morning she was asked by a grumpy General Tooey to train a replacement driver. He seemed genuinely sad to see her go and shook her warmly by the hand.

A week later she presented herself at General Eisenhower's Grosvenor Square headquarters. She was late. A marine guard had refused her entry and then another marine on the reception desk made her wait half an hour while making several telephone calls.

The name Eisenhower may have been trumpeted across the nation by the BBC, but no one in the American embassy seemed to know where he was. Kay finally found herself outside a large oak door glistening with a coat of recent varnish. A stencilled notice carrying the words *Theater Commander* hung from a hook on the door.

She checked her face and hair in a vanity mirror and was about to knock when she noticed the varnish was far from dry. She gave the door a gentle tap with the toe of her shoe and entered on a barked command from within.

Eisenhower was seated at a desk from which smoke rose in a long plume from a cigarette smouldering in an ashtray. A cigarette between his fingers added to the hazy atmosphere. Even the windows seemed smeared with a yellow patina of nicotine. Beyond the trees on the square flaunted green canopies which swayed gently in the breeze.

The desk was piled high with box files on one side and two stacked wire mesh trays overflowing with correspondence on the other. A blotting pad lay between them. Eisenhower was staring at a noticeboard covered in green felt which stretched the length of one wall. Memos in paper of various colours, some typewritten, others handwritten in an illegible scrawl, were pinned to the board.

Kay coughed. "I'm sorry I'm late," she said. "I had trouble getting in."

Eisenhower frowned, looked at her and said, "Yeah, I know, it's chaos around here."

He took a drag from his cigarette, stubbed it out and looked at the wire trays. His frown deepened.

"Thank you for the fruit," she said.

"Don't thank me," he said. "I just want to know whether you can drive for me – for good this time."

"Of course I can. You just have to sign a document and…"

Eisenhower cut her short. He rose from his chair, picked up a wire basket and let it drop to the desk with a thud, sending a snowdrift of papers fluttering to the floor.

"I came here to fight a war, not sign bits of paper! Get the car and let's get out of here."

And that's how it started, in a smoky room with missives and memoranda of war scattered across the walls, the floor and the desk, while through the window the summer foliage of ancient trees murmured a rebuke at the smoky chaos around the new commander.

The war seemed like thunder from distant mountains that summer. The blitz of London and the big cities was not over but had lessened to a point where people accepted the raids as they did rationing – "just one more bloody thing to put up with" summed up the war-weary mood among the populace.

The newspapers were full of the campaigns in North Africa where British and German armies seemed to take turns to advance and retreat and the name of the garrison port of Tobruk became a symbol first of British defiance and then of another defeat.

Eisenhower moved through a daily routine that rarely varied: breakfast at Claridge's followed the inevitable complaint to the kitchen about the lack of strong, steaming black coffee; then to the embassy, on to the War Office and back to the embassy for a sandwich-on-desk lunch and more coffee. Twice a week red circles in the diary announced lunch or dinner with Churchill at Downing Street.

Kay drove him everywhere even on what would otherwise have been short walks. Eisenhower's face and uniform were by now well known to Londoners. Churchill had finally persuaded him not to walk the streets of the city. The prime minister insisted that there were enemy agents in London who would happily take a knife or a gun to the commander if they saw him.

"Complete nonsense," Ike told Kay, "but I've got to keep the old man happy."

Kay felt like a character in a play that summer in which her boss, as she called him, bestrode the stage and various players came in from the wings to take up their lesser roles.

There was Butch – Harry Butcher – very much the star of the ensemble, who handled the press. Colonel Ernest Lee from Texas, known to all as Tex, looked after the office, while "Mickey", Sergeant Michael McKeogh, was Ike's valet, personal orderly and part-time cook.

Ike called this his family and he treated them with the care, attention and occasional bad temper that he would his own children.

"And you're family now," he told Kay.

She was surprised and a little nervous at the designation. The others in the team would hardy welcome a mere driver and a half-Brit, as they called her, into their ranks.

"Thanks, boss, that's great to hear."

"I mean it," he said. "You're a member of the team. Where are we going, by the way?"

They were driving west out of London after a familiar explosion and the cry of "Get me out of here!" The reason this time was not any of the myriad military and political problems that flowed from the mysterious code word "Torch", but the pressure placed on the commander by London's society ladies.

London's society ladies, starved of eligible males and anxious for the prestige of transatlantic celebrity, showered the American embassy with invitations to luncheons, cocktail parties and dinners. Tempting inducements were handwritten on the margins of the stiff cardboard invitations: Noel Coward would be attending a cocktail party right across from the embassy in Grosvenor Square; a brilliant new actor called Laurence Olivier would be among guests at a very small dinner party.

Telephone calls followed and then supposedly chance meetings took place in the foyer of Claridge's. It proved too much. Kay suggested a move to the Dorchester.

"It'll be the same there. If I hear another Brit lady calling me her daahling general I'm going to explode. I've got to get out of town."

That morning late in July, with the sun doing its best to convey a sense of summer, she drove him west out of London, skirting the Thames.

"Look up there," she said, pointing to Windsor Castle. Ike was boyishly excited by the sight of ancient turrets and ramparts and the royal standard flying from the towers.

"Straight out of Disney," he said.

Kay too was excited. She was family. The others might not like it, but she had joined Eisenhower's inner circle of those he trusted best and worked with closely.

She deserved it, she told herself; it was a fair reward for the hours spent waiting in the Packard and the guidance she gave him about the hidden history of London and the arcane social habits of the English upper classes.

He had almost dismissed her as his driver when she told him that he could not smoke at formal dinners before the royal toast at the end of the meal. Every man Kay had ever known smoked cigarettes, pipes and occasional cigars, but she had never know a smoker like Eisenhower. Part of her duties lay in ensuring the day began with at least three packs of Marlboros in her handbag. By the end of the day he would always have smoked his way through them all.

The smoking rule at formal dinners, the forelock-tugging deference shown by Claridge's staff to guests, the importance attached to clothes according to the time of day or season irritated the "simple farm boy from Kansas", as Ike liked to call himself.

"Trouble with you Brits is everything is about class. Even the working class seem happy to be just that – lower than everyone else. They lack ambition. It's pathetic."

"I'm not a Brit, I'm Irish," she replied.

They were driving back to London past the playing fields of Eton. Kay decided not to tell him that the boys there still had to wear top hats.

"Let's have a drink. Take me to a pub," he said.

She swung the car off the main road and drove into Eton village. A large black bull swung from a board over mullioned windows. Above the door a legend in fake medieval script read: Rest here a while and drink in peace. They walked in. It was late morning. There was a group of old men at the bar hunched over half pint glasses of beer. Behind the bar a young girl barely in her twenties was reading a magazine. Ike took off his peaked cap and hung it on the back of a chair.

He was just another senior officer having an illicit drink with his girlfriend as far as the drinkers were concerned. No one paid any attention as he and Kay sat down with gin and tonics at a table in a window bay. Ike held up his glass and clinked it with hers.

"Funny thing is, I'm getting used to this without ice," he said.

"You can get used to anything, sir," said Kay.

"Not the war," he said. "Never that. And don't call me sir. We're off duty."

Kay was not off duty at all. She was sitting drinking warm gin with the most senior American officer in Britain. Such familiarity would have been unthinkable in the presence of a British officer.

The drinkers had separated into one group playing cards and the other dominoes. The men talked in low voices, hardly disturbing the solemnity of the room. Occasionally they paused to light pipes or cigarettes, glancing shyly at the strangers in the bay window.

The bargirl remained bowed over the pages of the magazine, raising her head from time to time to flick a damp tea towel at a fly. The clock behind the bar measured the minutes in metallic whispers.

Framed prints on the walls showed horse-drawn coaches pulling up beneath the Black Bull sign with a whip-waving driver on top and a man blowing a bugle beside him. Above and below these tributes to the romance of Victorian travel, posters warned that careless talk cost lives and urged people to eat more vegetables.

The timeless calm of the scene and the sense that nothing in the Black Bull had changed since the days of the mail coach eased the way for a second round of drinks. Kay could see the physical change in her boss. Everything about him loosened and relaxed as if he had submersed in a warm bath.

Kay knew that she was incidental to the pleasure he took in the calm of a very English pub. He had slipped away and returned to the early days in Abilene where daily life was made up of hour-long bible readings with his mother, wholesome food on the table but never enough for seconds, and frequent fist-fights with local boys.

Eisenhower finished his drink and lit a cigarette.

"You don't sound Irish to me," he said suddenly.

"I don't have the Irish brogue you hear in the films, if that's what you mean, sir," she said, "but I was born in County Cork and that's as Irish as you can get."

The Packard was outside. She was on official duty. She was careful how she addressed her boss.

"But you're not really Irish, are you?"

"How far back do you want to go? Daddy's family settled there generations ago. But you're right, we're Anglo-Irish."

He wanted to know more. Whether he was really interested or just being polite she could not tell. She told him of running wild with her two sisters as they grew up on a small estate in County Cork. The Great War had passed the children by except for the shadowy absence of their father, a distant figure they hardly knew and of whom it was said that "he was doing his duty in France". Then came peace and the teenage years. There were horses to ride, boats to sail and young men to flirt with as the girls grew older.

Kay stopped, aware that she had talked too much.

"Go on," said Eisenhower.

"We had the most wonderful childhood. We thought it would never end," she said. "We didn't know at the time how lucky we were. Looking back it was like a dream."

"That's the trouble with dreams – you have to wake up," said Ike. He got to his feet and put on his cap carefully, adjusting it so that the braided peak was at the correct angle to his face.

The drinkers in the pub turned slowly and stopped talking. The bargirl looked up. The peaked cap transformed the middle-aged officer with receding sandy hair, and a companion who looked young enough to be his daughter, into an image all too familiar from newspapers and newsreels. A babble of conversation broke the silence as Kay held the pub door open for him.

Eisenhower said nothing on the drive back to London. She knew what he was thinking. He had had a brief moment of escape. Everything about the Black Bull had pleased him. He would want to go back but that was impossible. The drinkers would talk, the visit would become the property of the newspapers. People would come and stare if he returned.

They drove past Richmond Park, where Kay remembered playing golf on the course in pre-war days. At the thirteenth hole they always saw a small house through a screen of trees, a Hansel and Gretel cottage that looked as if it had been lifted straight from a Disney film. It was called Telegraph Cottage and had once been a gamekeeper's lodging.

She swung the car off the main road and drove through the park. Ike had returned to his newspaper and did not notice the detour. She parked on a side road. Telegraph Cottage looked exactly the same as she remembered it.

"What do you think, sir?" she said.

Ike looked up. "About what?"

"You wanted a country place near London, didn't you?"

There was general dismay among Ike's team at his sudden decision to move from the luxury of a London hotel to what he called his "bolthole in the woods".

Telegraph Cottage was just a little doll's house. It was totally unsuitable for a commander of Ike's rank, too small and so far from London that nobody would ever find it. What would Churchill think? The answer was obvious: he would be appalled that the most senior American commander had chosen such humble quarters.

Eisenhower brushed aside such arguments. He loved the place. Kay had found a caretaker with a key. They had been given a tour. There was a cosy sitting room with a large fireplace, a dining room, a small kitchen and pantry on the ground floor, and three bedrooms and a bathroom upstairs.

A carefully kept garden fenced off at the rear gave onto a woodland path which led to the thirteenth hole on the golf course.

Telegraph Cottage became Eisenhower's weekend retreat, and, increasingly, where he returned at night during the week. Kay could make the drive in twenty-five minutes from Hyde Park Corner with the help of a US flag fluttering from the bonnet of the Packard. When Eisenhower finally relented and agreed to the installation of a phone at the cottage he ensured that it was a direct line only to his office in Grosvenor Square. He said Churchill would never be off the line otherwise.

That didn't stop the prime minster. He made an immediate visit and was given a guided tour of the house and the garden. Kay trailed the two men and listened with an astonishment that Churchill clearly shared as Eisenhower outlined plans to grown vegetables, especially his favourite runner beans, in the garden.

Churchill considered these plans while puffing on his usual cigar.

"Napoleon played chess to take his mind off forthcoming battles – and you are going to grow runner beans?"

He paused.

"Good," he said, speaking slowly, stretching the word out to emphasise wholehearted approval. He had come straight from the House of Commons and spoke as if he was still in the chamber. At the end of the visit the prime minister drew Kay aside.

"I hear you are responsible for finding this remarkable sanctuary," he said in a low growl.

"Yes, sir," said Kay, bracing for a rebuke.

"Good. Make sure you continue looking after our general."

Kay blushed, nodded and mumbled, "Yes, sir."

The move to Telegraph Cottage was accomplished within days. Butch, Tex and Mickey shared the two remaining bedrooms while Kay was given lodging nearby in a house owned by two elderly ladies.

Every morning at seven a.m. she drove to the cottage and began the day over breakfast, reading out to her boss the schedule she had typed out the night before. The rest of the staff ate in the kitchen.

Kay's elevation in Ike's family hierarchy was noticed and resented. She was a newcomer to an intimate circle, an arriviste seeking to profit from association with a famous man.

Worse still in the eyes of the "family", she was a woman, not young, stranded somewhere between youth and the lower slopes of middle age, but with that undefinable appeal to an older man.

It was not only Eisenhower's immediate aides who cast a cold eye on the new arrival in his team. Senior British and American staff officers invited to join breakfast meetings returned to London with exaggerated accounts of the informality of Telegraph Cottage and priggish comments about the presence of Kay Summersby at Eisenhower's side.

Those who queried Ike's absences from London were simply told that he liked it that way. He would tell people that he slept much better at Telegraph Cottage in the peaceful surroundings of Richmond Park than in the grand hotel rooms of Mayfair. During the day he found the peace to work and think denied him in Grosvenor Square.

Motorcycle despatch riders arrived almost every hour, but the phone rarely rang. Birdsong replaced the steady thrum of central London. The occasional roar of anti-aircraft guns reached the sanctuary of Richmond like the sound of distant drums.

Most days Kay still drove the boss to London for meetings, but he usually insisted on returning by nightfall. There were plenty of winks and nudges from the girls in the Motor Transport Corps and especially from Charlotte, who regularly appeared at Kay's side, as if by chance, in the ladies' lavatory.

"You're getting on very well with the big boss, aren't you, doll?" she said one evening, applying mascara to her long eyelashes from a bottle marked Revlon. Her bright red lipstick was real too. It was typical of Charlotte to produce such make-up as if it was the norm in wartime London, whereas most girls used burnt cork for mascara and beetroot juice on their lips.

"I'm doing my best – we all are," said Kay, accepting the offer of the mascara brush. Charlotte might be snobbishly inclined to mention her grand connections at Buckingham Palace rather too often, but she was also generous with the benefits that came her way.

"Oh, come on," said Charlotte. "He's mad for you, everyone can see that."

"Don't be ridiculous," said Kay, handing back the mascara brush. Charlotte handed over the lipstick.

"Has he kissed you yet?"

"Charlotte, behave yourself!"

"One of the girls swore she saw you two having a quick smooch in his office."

"And just who would that girl be?"

Kay was looking straight into the mirror while painting a delicate bow on her lips. It was a Friday night and there was the usual reception for the drivers and junior staff in the canteen that night. There would be thimblefuls of South African sherry served in tiny glasses, fish paste sandwiches and small talk with mostly married officers in the command staff.

The MTC drivers and assorted women secretaries would put up with that for the required hour, then escape to the local pub for watered-down beer, pork pies if they were lucky, and a game of darts.

"I can't reveal my sources, but come on, Kay – fair's fair. Do tell. You know I wouldn't breathe a word."

They both laughed then because Charlotte was known as radio Montagu.

"I'm helping an overworked man keep his sanity while planning to send tens of thousands of young men into a battle. Is that good enough for you?"

"He's a married man, Kay. Mind you, I don't think his wife back home is going to hear of a little wartime fling, is she?"

"Stop it. I do believe you're a little jealous," said Kay, handing back the lipstick.

"I'm not jealous. I'm bored. Funny, isn't it? In the middle of a war you find yourself working for the most stultifyingly boring man in the universe."

"What, that nice air force commander?"

"Nice? Huh, he won't even say good morning to me. Just grunts."

"You mean he won't make a pass at you?"

"Fat chance," said Charlotte. "Come on, let's see if we can get more than one glass of sherry tonight."

If Kay was completely honest with herself, and she tried to be, she rather enjoyed the scent of scandal that clung to her. She liked the turned heads and whispers that followed her in official canteens and coffee shops where the staff gathered. She also quietly enjoyed the glow of authority conferred by the knowledge that this great man needed her so much.

She knew why. He was lonely. Ike was not religious, but his loneliness in those months was like a communion with a higher authority. She knew he wrote regularly to the wife who waited patiently for him in a small apartment in Washington. She knew too that Mamie Eisenhower had complained that the apartment was too small and lacked air conditioning to cool the humid days of high summer.

The Pentagon offered little support for the wives who were left behind, while making sure that their senior commanders were given every comfort and professional assistance in the field.

Mamie Eisenhower wrote long letters to her husband every week, sometimes more than one, which he dutifully answered. Kay knew he regarded it as his duty to reply to each one within a day of receipt. He had once asked her to type a letter home straight from his dictation. That had been a big mistake. Mamie had been furious and made it clear she wanted handwritten letters from her husband or none at all.

The point was made in a brief letter that Eisenhower read sitting at his desk. Kay had been taking dictation for over an hour and the letter came as a welcome break for coffee. He sighed deeply, folded the letter and put it in a desk drawer. "Is anything wrong?" said Kay, putting coffee on the desk. She had guessed its contents.

"Yes, but don't let it worry you," he said. "Now, where were we?"

Later when she was alone in the office, curiosity overcame caution. She opened the drawer and took out the letter. Its brevity was brutal, the message cold.

Dearest Ike,

Never ever send me a typed letter dictated to that woman. If you have not the time to write yourself please don't write at all.

Mamie

So she had become "that woman", just as to many of Ike's staff she had become rather more than a mere driver. Jealousy feeds on rumour and the rumours had certainly taken wing across the Atlantic.

Kay shrugged. How did the old rhyme go? "Sticks and stones may break my bones but names will never hurt me."

She could see that Eisenhower didn't miss his wife or anybody else, even his son. How could he? The days were full, the nights were short, and in the words of a poem that Kay remembered from somewhere, "life slips by like a field mouse not shaking the grass".

"Who wrote that?" he'd asked.

"I don't know – an American poet, I think. It's just one of those lines that sticks in your head."

"Nothing sticks in my head. It's like a parade ground of facts and figures marching past – whole armies of them on the move up here," he'd said, tapping his forehead, and grinned, suddenly pleased with his own words.

The familiarity between them jeopardised the innocence of their relationship, but she told herself she was only doing her duty.

"Mind you look after our general," Churchill had said.

And that was all she was doing – obeying orders from the highest authority.

4

October 1942

Petticoat Lane proclaimed itself the oldest street market in London, and there on a Sunday morning Kay and Charlotte browsed among the traders, picking over second-hand clothes, books, suitcases, cheap jewellery and the occasional stall selling whatever fishermen could glean close to the shore at night, mostly cockles, crab and small flatfish.

The market described itself as the defiant heart of London's much-bombed East End, but in fact it lay closer to the city of London's business district and thus tried to attract wealthier residents with displays not just of clothes but of exotic pets.

It was among the fish tanks, caged birds and squawking parrots that Kay first saw the puppy. It was a black Scottish terrier barely a month old and obviously not well. The animal lay on a bed of fouled straw in an old bird cage, seemingly asleep.

Kay rattled the bars of the cage. The puppy raised its head, wagged a feeble tail and went back to sleep. Seeing her interest the vendor, a lady wearing a smeared butcher's apron with a cloth twisted around her head, lifted the puppy from the cage and stroked its back.

"Pedigree Scottish terrier," she said. "Comes with a collar."

"How much?" asked Kay.

The woman looked at her. Kay was wearing a brown skirt and a patched blouse. Probably an off-duty nurse. Then she saw Kay's black well-polished shoes. They were obviously expensive.

"Five guineas," she said.

Kay laughed in surprise, putting her hand to her mouth.

"Come away," said Charlotte, taking her by the arm. They walked off with the woman's voice floating after them: "All right, four guineas for luck, three fifty and cheap at that and I'll throw in the lead…"

"What on earth were you doing? You don't want a dog," said Charlotte.

"I do actually."

Charlotte put a hand to her friend's forehead.

"You're not ill, are you?"

"I want you to go back and buy that puppy. Don't offer more than two guineas and make sure she throws in a lead."

"What on earth are you to going to do with a puppy? It'll wee all over the place and cost a fortune to feed."

"I'll tell you later. Now please go and buy it."

Late that evening they sat in a pub with two half pints of beer on a smeared table. The puppy was straining at a lead tied to the table leg.

"Kay Summersby, you are a devious girl with a dark heart."

"Such harsh words," said Kay.

"I know why you've got that puppy."

"It will be a great little companion."

"Of course, but not for you."

"What do you mean?"

"It's his birthday soon, isn't it?"

"Whose?"

"You know perfectly well, you little minx. The mighty Ike."

"It might be."

"You're going to give it to him, aren't you, no doubt with a bloody bow round its neck?"

"Maybe."

"You little schemer."

"It's from all of his team, we all talked about it. Don't tell a soul – promise?"

"Fibber," said Charlotte, pointing a finger.

"All right, it's my idea but it will be our birthday present."

"It's from you and he'll know it. You're making it a bit obvious, aren't you?"

Charlotte was never one for the tactful approach or the raised eyebrow to convey a hint of disapproval. She liked to go straight in and speak her mind. Perhaps that's what made her a good friend.

"It will help to take his mind off things. He's so wound up. He'll love it. He used to have a dog before he went into the army, he told me," Kay said.

Charlotte pointed at the puppy.

"Oh, I see, this thing is to help us win the war, is it? Doll, I think you're hiding something."

The thunder from the mountains drew closer. The code word "Torch" became part of almost every conversation in the back of the Packard that autumn as Kay drove back and forth from London. Every time she looked in the mirror the display of medals, ribbons and gold braid on the officers around Eisenhower seemed to glow brighter.

Rumours of a cross-Channel invasion or some similar grand offensive against the German Reich had even penetrated the café near the American embassy where Kay took lunch while in London. MTC drivers were not allowed to eat in the embassy itself. The thin whey-faced woman behind the café counter was happy to tell anyone that an Allied cross-Channel invasion would be launched in the spring. When Kay reported this to Eisenhower he solved the problem in typical fashion.

"I am going to brief you on our operational plans. You need to know anyway given the cable traffic you will be handling. 'Torch' is the code name for the invasion of North Africa. We are going in next month, end of November. Now you know you will have to eat in the commissary like the rest of us. We can't have you out there with all those German spies roaming around."

He smiled with a quick grin that showed the boy beneath the man. Kay turned to leave. The windows of the office had been cleaned. The trees in the square were shedding their summer greenery and turning russet and gold.

Kay had reached the door when he said. "Just one thing…"

She turned, reaching for the notebook in her handbag.

"You'll need a travel warrant."

"What for?"

"You're coming with us."

It was a Friday at the end of the week when Kay, Butch, Tex and Mickey walked into his office. Mickey had glasses and champagne. Tex carried a plate of cheese carefully cut into squares and placed on biscuits and Butch carried a small birthday cake lit with a single candle and carrying the numerals 52 picked out in pink icing.

Kay put the puppy on the floor. Eisenhower rose, surprise written in the frown on his forehead. Mickey popped the cork. Butch placed the cake on the desk. The puppy produced a puddle.

"What the hell is that?" he said.

Everyone looked at Kay. This was her idea. The rest of the team wanted no part of it. A puppy for a general in the middle of a war?

"It's your birthday present," she said and gave the puppy a little push. The animal wandered hesitantly forward until it reached the desk.

Eisenhower looked down at the puppy and sighed. Then he looked across at Kay and sighed again. The pleasurable satisfaction among the rest of the team was almost audible. Kay had committed a grievous social blunder. They waited for a bellow of "*Get that dog out of here!*" Eisenhower bent down, picked up the black bundle, and put it on his desk. The puppy sat down. Ike patted it. The puppy put out a pink tongue and raised two dark eyes to the man bending over him. The two looked at each other. Eisenhower turned to the room smiling.

"We'll have to think of a name," he said. "Now let's have some cake."

As the others left after the celebrations he called Kay back. She was nervous. He was not paying any attention to the puppy which had begun to wander around the desk. It was going to fall off any second. Perhaps that's what he wanted. He wouldn't shout at her in front of the others, but he might well do so now.

"I will be flying sometime the last week of November. I want you to come on afterwards when we have secured a headquarters. I'm telling you this so you can make plans. Have you got the warrant?"

"Yes, sir. Erm…"

"What is it?"

"I thought you might not like your present."

The puppy fell to the floor with a soft thump and began chasing its tail. Ike scooped it up and held it high in the air.

"You're lovely, aren't you? Where did you come from?"

"I bought him from a street market. Scottish terrier. Pure pedigree the woman said," said Kay.

"Pedigree or not, he can't come to Africa with us. We'll keep him at the cottage. And we need a name."

"I thought of Topsy, sir."

"Topsy? Don't be silly. This dog needs a real name. I'll think of one. Now take him away before he pees all over me."

Ike handed the dog back.

"Thank you, Kay, that was very kind. I love the little chap." Ike petted the puppy as he nestled in Kay's arms.

"And Kay…"

"Yes, sir?"

"You don't have to call me sir when we're like this, one to one."

"Right, sir… I mean…"

They both laughed as he waved her out of the room.

Mrs MacCarthy-Morrogh had a mind of her own and admired herself for it. She regarded herself as a strong woman who had found consolation from the sadness of a long and failing marriage in the arrival of three beautiful children.

Every week on Thursday afternoons she left her small house in Surrey, rented for the duration of the war, and took the train to London. She would take a taxi from the station and arrive at the Dorchester Hotel in time for afternoon tea.

Kay always joined her, work permitting. Mother and daughter usually enjoyed these meetings, enlivened as they were by Mrs MacCarthy-Morrogh's talent for turning minor family gossip into high drama.

Recently, however, a strain had developed between the two ladies. Mrs MacCarthy-Morrogh had convinced herself that General Eisenhower would like to join them for tea and she intended to send him a formal invitation to do just that.

She was sure the Allied commander would like the brief relaxation from his tiring schedule provided by fine tea and light pastries. Her daughter had told her many times how stressed and tense he always was. Kay tried to explain to her mother that the idea was preposterous.

"Mother, I'm only his driver. I've told you he's far too senior and important to bother with the likes of us – even at the Dorchester."

"I thought Americans weren't supposed to be snobbish."

"He's not being snobbish; he's busy, besides he won't leave that puppy alone. He's besotted."

"Puppy?" said Mrs MacCarthy-Morrogh, eyeing the lounge for a waiter.

"I gave him a little Scottish terrier for his birthday."

"Good Lord," said her mother, who was minded to remark that if her daughter's familiarity with Eisenhower allowed her to give him a puppy she might also have persuaded him to come to tea. But she didn't. A waiter appeared.

"Tea, madam?"

Mrs MacCarthy-Morrogh looked at her watch. It was 4.45 p.m. During the Blitz the previous year everyone had felt able to drink whatever the hour. Even far from the bombs in the country glasses were raised to the embattled metropolitans well before the accepted hour of six.

Now old habits had reasserted themselves. But the bombing had not entirely stopped. Only last week a lone German bomber had flown up the Thames at low height and managed to drop a bomb on Buckingham Palace, causing considerable damage. That was the trouble with the war, thought Mrs MacCarthy-Morrogh, one never knew what was going to happen next.

"No. I'll have gin please, with tonic, a slice of lemon and plenty of ice."

"There's no lemon, madam," said the waiter.

They drank gin in tall glasses with plenty of tonic water and a sprig of mint and toasted the memories of friends and family who had died one way or another in the two years of real war. Kay's mother said nothing had happened in the first six months after hostilities had been declared in September 1939. The phoney war didn't count.

Her mother finished the first glass quickly and Kay ordered a second with rather more tonic water. Mrs MacCarthy-Morrogh sipped it, called the waiter and asked for an extra measure.

The tearoom was not crowded that afternoon but they leant forward to talk in whispers of Kay's fiancé, Richard, killed by a mine in the desert the previous year. Kay tried hard to mourn the loss of a man she hardly knew. She kept his ring on her finger and a small photograph of a smiling face beneath an army cap in her wallet, but such mementos did nothing to assuage her guilt.

She could find neither tears nor any real feeling of grief to mark Richard's passing. The brown eyes and the minty breath were memories that had faded like the photographs in a family album. His letters had been consigned to a trunk in the attic. That was the price of war, she told herself, though the realisation that she had never really known him was as shocking as the knowledge that now she never would.

By now her mother was quite drunk. She talked about the past. Old people are always happier with their memories than with the burden of the present, Kay thought. They retreat to the past for comfort and calm because that is where they know they are safe and where they really belong.

So Kay listened, as she had so often, to stories of Irish independence and civil war in the 1920s which ended the lifestyle of the Anglo-Irish families with their big houses, servants and horses.

"And then you left us," said her mother accusingly. "Just like that, you upped and went with hardly a goodbye."

Kay smiled and put a hand to her mother's cheek. The skin felt thin, like tissue paper. She held her hand there, feeling her mother pressing her cheek against it. She had indeed left suddenly because she didn't want the inevitable family arguments that would follow her announced intention to seek her fortune in the mysterious and alluring metropolis called London.

Her mother had followed a year later, the year war broke out. She had come to look after her daughter, she said. In fact she too wished to escape the loneliness of life in rural Ireland with the added incentive of fleeing a failed marriage.

Kay had been luckier than most. Her slender good looks were in vogue at the time. To the astonishment of her family, and especially her parents, Kay became a model for the Worth fashion house and appeared in *Vogue* and other fashion magazines in the spring of 1938 wearing the flowing gowns created in Paris for wealthy ladies of Europe and especially America.

It was the second idyll of her life; the golden haze of cocktail soirées, dinners in fashionable restaurants, weekend parties and a succession of affairs with amusing but hopeless men lasted until 1939.

The threat of invasion and the start of the Blitz had brought Kay a stark choice. Return to Ireland or find a job that would pay the rent of a one-room bedsit near Victoria Station. Life as a model had placed Kay on many a magazine cover but had earned her scant financial reward.

The only commercial skill she possessed lay in her driving licence. She had been accepted first as a hospital driver ferrying outpatients to and from their homes in South London, and then, when the bombing inflicted heavy civilian casualties, as an ambulance driver. Her mother had not been pleased.

Mrs MacCarthy-Morrogh was asleep, her head resting against the wing of the well padded armchair. A waiter removed the glasses, looked questioningly at Kay, and moved silently away.

Code names multiplied that autumn, confusing conversations as those concerned struggled to remember their meanings. "Torch" became "Gymnast" and then "Torch" again. "Challenger" was replaced by "Beaver" and then by "Bayonet", an unlikely name for a train, thought Kay, but what a train it was.

The camouflage-painted locomotive had just two carriages with a private sitting room, a dining room, meeting rooms and bedrooms for eight people. Every room was panelled in teak, the cutlery was silver, the crockery bone china and the glassware crystal.

This was Eisenhower's travelling headquarters gifted by Winston Churchill for the occasional long journey north of the border to Scotland.

"Where did Winston get this from?" asked Ike.

They were travelling north at speed aiming to get to the west coast of Scotland at midnight.

"It was part of the royal train apparently, sir," said Kay.

"You and your royal family," said Ike.

"I like our King, sir," she said.

Ike looked up from a document marked *most secret*.

"You're only Irish when you want to be."

"That's not fair, sir."

They were seated at a desk covered in a scatter of maps and papers as the countryside slipped past. The plan was to visit six beaches on the west coast between midnight and two a.m. to observe night-time landings carried out by American infantry.

Butch was passing papers across the table to Ike who studied them and handed them on to Kay for filing. Several aides stood in the background wondering, as junior staff do on such occasions, whether there was any reason for them to be there.

She spread maps on the table, trying to judge the route they would take up the coast later between beaches, some little more than coves, marked for the simulated invasion. The weather was calm. The moon would be no more than a silver sickle.

The conditions would be nothing like those of the African landings in a few weeks' time. But Eisenhower argued to himself that at least it would give his troops their first experience of trying to get themselves, their heavy weapons and light transport from a ship to the shore at night.

The train rocked slightly at speed, slowing only when passing major cities. After supper everyone leant back in their seats, allowing the hypnotic sounds of wheels pounding the track beneath them to summon a few minutes' sleep.

No one dared go to the sleeping quarters unless Eisenhower changed his mind and did so himself. He had given orders that no alcoholic drinks were to be served on the journey and no one was permitted to sleep. Everyone was to work through the night.

Kay stared at the reflection in the window. Everyone in the compartment had their eyes closed. Eisenhower too was looking at the window and caught her eye. Their reflections looked at each other, as if two strangers had entered the carriage. Ike leant forward. She turned from the image in the window to face him.

"Who's looking after the dog?" he asked.

"Mickey," she said, "at the cottage."

Eisenhower nodded, leant back and closed his eyes.

Several cars were waiting at the small station, heavy British Humbers entirely unsuitable for the work that lay ahead that night. Kay took the lead car and drove into pitch darkness with only her sidelights on and without so much as a white line on the small roads to guide her.

She slowed the car to a crawl. After fifteen minutes Eisenhower snapped at her to speed up. She dared not. Bog, thick heather and deep ditches lined each side of the road. The fingernail paring of a moon cast little light. The rest of the night dissolved into chaos for all concerned.

The inspection party arrived late at every beach and at every beach Ike blamed Kay for driving at the speed of a legless tortoise, as he put it. With great difficulty Kay resisted the temptation to point out that since the invading troops and the landing craft were nowhere to be seen on any of the beaches their arrival time hardly mattered.

She tried to explain that the roads, some no more than tracks, demanded caution, and it was better to arrive late than not at all.

"Don't argue with me," he had said in a clenched voice that betrayed anger at the shambles around him. "Just do as you're told."

"What, even if it means driving you into a ditch?"

She shouldn't have said that. Don't answer back was the golden rule for government drivers. He wheeled on her, pushing his face close to hers.

"You're going to be driving me in the desert soon. You'll be on operations. That means you'll obey my damned orders, understand?" Kay flinched. If it had not been so dark he would have seen mutiny in her eyes. He turned away and walked to a group of officers huddled on the sand dunes. Beyond lay a beach bare of the troops that were supposed to have landed there an hour earlier.

The group climbed back aboard the train at four a.m. Having vented his anger at what he termed "a bloody farce and an utter waste of time", Ike went to his sleeping quarters.

Kay and Butch looked at each other. It was obviously their fault. The next morning she drove her boss in silence to Telegraph Cottage. He spent most of the time in the back scribbling memos, muttering oaths, then tearing up the memos and starting over. No one dared speak. It was as if a storm cloud had settled in the car and was about to unleash lightning. Kay shared the general relief when they arrived at the cottage.

The front door opened to release a small bundle of black fur which flung itself barking at Eisenhower's legs. He handed a briefcase to Kay, bent down and patted the dog. He looked up and smiled.

"He's in great shape, isn't he? How are you feeling – OK?"

It was as close to an apology as she was going to get. Kay smiled.

"Fine, but I could with some sleep."

"We all could. First order of the day – everyone take a nap for an hour."

Mickey cooked the boss's favourite dinner that night: steak with fried potatoes and a green salad. The puppy bounded from room to room, getting under feet and causing general irritation to everyone but Ike.

Cards were produced afterwards and Kay, Ike and Butch sat down for a three-handed game of bridge bidding for the dummy. Mickey busied himself in the kitchen while Tex, who regarded bridge as an effeminate version of poker, read a newspaper.

It was on their first hand that Ike suddenly said, "I've got a name for the dog."

Everyone waited.

"Telek."

"What?" said Butch.

"Telek," said Ike. "Kay, what do you think?"

"How do you spell it?"

"T E L E K," he said.

Seeing the general mystification he rose and put the cards on the table.

"You work it out, fellas, I'm going to have a nightcap."

Eisenhower sent his staff to bed but called Kay back. This is how most evenings at the cottage ended. They sat opposite each other with Telek curled up on the carpet between them. Kay poured a weak whisky for him and a gin for herself. Ike sank back into the sofa, raised his eyes to the ceiling and started talking.

There was only one thing on his mind: Torch. The word burned like a flame between them. He was excited, confident and restlessly impatient to give the final command for the invasion.

He talked almost to himself, inviting no interruption, giving no details, but musing on the strategic victory within his grasp: eviction of the German army from North Africa. For once Churchill and Roosevelt were in complete agreement. This was the first step in the defeat of Hitler in Europe.

"You'll be driving an armoured Cadillac," he said. "Big one-ton beast."

"How exciting," she said. "When do we go?"

He raised his glass and she poured another whisky. He drank and said, "You'll be coming later by ship. Better that way."

Damn, thought Kay. Better for whom? Not for her. It meant a ten-day voyage in some troop hulk all the way down the west coast of Ireland, through the Bay of Biscay and into the Mediterranean. There were German U-boats in the Med.

"Any chance I could be with you on the plane, sir?"

The formality of the request was designed to make him see its logic. After all, he would need a driver the moment he set foot in Africa – and someone to take notes, fix meetings and pour the late-night drinks.

"No. I wish I could but it's not possible," he said.

Of course it was possible. He only had to issue an order. She was thinking how to make the point tactfully when he said, "You mustn't tell anybody, not even your mother."

"I've signed the Official Secrets Act, sir. You know I would never say anything to anybody."

"How is she, by the way?"

They talked about their mothers, a safe topic far from what Kay wanted to discuss. Ike's mother had died some years earlier.

"They never leave you, mothers," he said.

"Mine certainly never leaves me," she said, thinking of the weekly teas in the Dorchester for which she always seemed to pay.

"No, I'm being serious. What's that old saying? Every man dies alone. It's not true. Every man dies with his mother's hand in his. A mother is the first and last thing any man sees on this earth."

"That's very romantic," she said.

He laughed. "No one's ever called me romantic."

"And what about women – do they die alone?"

"Don't complicate things, Kay. Women are the mothers – don't you see? They never die."

There was no sensible rejoinder to that remark. Kay tried to think of a way of steering the conversation back to her transport to Africa. As if Ike guessed her thoughts and sought to deflect them, he suddenly rapped out a question.

"What do you think of Telek?"

"The name?"

"Yes."

"A lot of people are going to wonder what it means."

"Let them wonder. And you?"

"I think I've worked it out."

It wasn't difficult. Telek fused the first four letters of Telegraph Cottage with her own initial K. Ike said he found peace and contentment in his sanctuary in the woods of Richmond Park. Now he had chosen to acknowledge to those who could work it out the importance of Kay Summersby in his life.

The professional family around the general also worked it out very quickly. The thin tendrils of gossip about Kay and the Allied commander now clung closer to both of them. Kay never raised the subject because she knew Ike would pay more attention to a passing fly. The raised eyebrows and the whispered gossip behind his back never seemed to bother her boss.

After months of working on his staff and now about to accompany him to North Africa, Kay was no longer just a driver – she had become a personal assistant, mixer of cocktails, partner at bridge and hostess of Telegraph Cottage. She noticed that Tex, Butch and Mickey had kept watchful eyes on the way she had risen within the family circle.

She had heard them talking among themselves in the kitchen at the cottage one day. She had missed the start of the conversation but heard a voice, she thought Mickey's, saying, "They're closer than two coats of paint."

"You think she's getting it from him?" said another voice, Tex this time.

"Nah, he's too smart." Mickey again.

"I wouldn't bet your pyjamas on that," said Tex.

"Cut this talk, guys, it's not right." This was Butch, very much the senior member of the family. Kay knew he always spoke up for her. She knew too that it was not just Ike's family that referred to their relationship as being closer than two coats of paint. The worst of the canteen gossip had turned them into lovers at the heart of the Allied command while the mildest rumours suggested merely that their relationship was affectionate but chaste.

Kay did not ignore the rumours, she hardly could with Charlotte giving her knowing smiles and asking silly questions whenever they met.

But she denied them to herself, and to others by stating simple facts: General Eisenhower trusted her and appreciated her work. She was very efficient. If at the end of the day he asked her to join him for a drink long after the others had left, so what? They would sip whisky, exchange small-talk about the goings-on of the day, and occasionally laugh at the absurdities of military red tape.

That was her job and if it took them to the edge of innocence it did not take them beyond. This man would never love or need anyone more than the wife who waited for him jealously in Washington.

That's what Kay told people. But it was a lie. She knew it even if he didn't.

5

February 1943

The torpedo struck the *Strathallen* just after midnight in the Mediterranean, forty miles from the Algerian coast. Kay and two other women sharing the cabin were thrown out of their bunks onto the floor.

The wail of a siren signalled the order to abandon ship. They had been warned this might happen. The orders were simple: dress quickly in warm clothing, do not take luggage or pause to find any valuables such as jewellery.

The *Strathallen* was a converted liner shipping two thousand troops to the North African campaign. Kay had been ordered to join the ship and report to Eisenhower's headquarters in Algiers. It was just before Christmas 1943. They were only a day from port when under the starlit sky of a Mediterranean night the German U-boat struck.

Kay and her companions scrambled into a lifeboat as the ship listed heavily. Around her on a calm sea she saw other lifeboats filled with troops. There were many more in the water swimming for rafts, wreckage, anything to stay afloat. There were shouts from the ship as the angle of the list increased.

She should not have been on the *Strathallen* at all. It was against regulations for a Motor Transport Corps driver to leave London. Eisenhower had plenty of pool drivers to draw upon in North Africa. But he insisted that she, Kay Summersby, be at his side for what was proving to be a bitter campaign against Rommel's Afrika Korps. Ike had personally signed the movement order. No one thought to question it.

She spent the night and most of the next day in the lifeboat until a British destroyer picked them up and put them ashore at a small port on the Algerian coast. Hours later the voice of Tex came over a crackly phone line from the general's headquarters in Algiers.

"We heard about the *Strathallen*. He's been worried sick about you. Here he is."

And then Eisenhower was on the phone, the same old American twang synthesised through static into a voice from outer space.

"Kay, are you all right?"

"Yes, sir."

"Thank God. You had us really worried there."

"A lot of people didn't make it."

"I know. You worried the hell out of us. I'll send a plane to pick you up in the morning. Get some sleep if you can."

The next morning Kay walked into the St George Hotel in Algiers, once one of the most luxurious in North Africa. Now the marble floors were caked in mud as soldiers tramped in from the rain-washed streets outside.

She felt naked without a proper uniform. Her skirt was stained with salt. She wore a borrowed blouson jacket over a torn shirt and a headscarf over messy hair. Her stockings were in tatters and her shoes looked as if they had been dredged from the sea, which is exactly what had happened to them.

Everyone stopped what they were doing and looked at the drenched waif who had stepped in from the rain. Tex appeared, ushered her past armed sentries into Eisenhower's office, and left. Ike rose from his desk beaming and walked to her.

"Welcome to Africa, Kay!"

"Sorry, sir. I look a mess. I haven't got a thing left, it all went down with the ship."

"You look OK to me. Let me take a look."

He put his hands on her shoulders turned her around.

"Well, not much damage that I can see," he said.

And then he embraced her, holding her so tightly that she could feel the buttons on his uniform pressing into her chest. He stepped back, his face reddening with embarrassment.

"I'm sorry," he said. "I was really worried."

The gesture was so unexpected and the memories of the last forty-eight hours so fresh that she began to cry. Ike fished out a handkerchief and handed it to her. She blew her nose loudly. She had been torpedoed and survived. It had all happened so fast. One minute they were asleep and the next struggling up narrow gangways to the lifeboat stations.

The lifeboat had been overcrowded. They had not been able to pick up many of the survivors swimming around them. Members of the crew had used oars to fend off those trying to climb aboard for fear of capsize. She had lost all her clothes. All she had left was a lipstick and a comb.

"I'm sorry," he said again.

She dried her eyes, smiled and said, "What for? It wasn't your fault we got torpedoed. Anyway I feel I'm a part of the war now."

She fished a compact from the bag and looked in the mirror. "God. I look like a tramp."

"The Germans didn't leave much behind but there's a good tailor in town," he said. "I'll get him to run up a couple of new uniforms for you."

She sniffed. "Thank you, sir."

There was a knock on the door and Tex's head appeared. "Your ten o'clock is waiting, sir."

"I must go," said Kay.

Eisenhower walked back to his desk, sat down, frowned at the document in front of him, then looked up with a smile. "I'm glad you made it. I need you out here," he said.

The next day a tailor came to fit her for the new uniforms. Two days later she wore them to his office. Ike was pleased. He faced her, looking up and down, then put his hands on her shoulders and turned her around.

"Sleeves are too long and the skirt a little short but I guess the tailor can fix that," he said.

"I think it's fine, sir."

"Kay, if it's fine by you it's OK by me."

He was smiling as he gently ran a finger down the side of her cheek. Then he turned and sat down at the desk. It was as if the sinking of the *Strathallen* had awakened something in him that he had been unable to recognise on his own.

From that moment in 1943, in a mid-winter campaign that brought initial disaster upon the American forces, Eisenhower insisted on her presence at his side from daybreak to nightfall, whether at headquarters or at the front line with shellfire bursting not far away.

Kay felt far closer to him now than she had in London. She attended military briefings and visited hospitals with him to talk to the wounded. She trailed behind him taking notes of soldiers' names and addresses after he had talked to them.

"Every man I talk to or shake hands with gets a letter – got that?"

"Yes, sir."

Then the armoured Cadillac arrived with a bonnet that looked long enough to launch an aircraft and darkened windows. Then the Cadillac arrived with darkened windows and a bonnet that looked long enough to launch an aircraft. Camouflage added to the impression that it was a creature that had recently escaped from a zoo.

"It looks like a dragon," murmured Kay as Ike lifted the bonnet to show her the armour-plating over the engine.

"She's all yours," he said. "Take her out and drive her around."

The next day Kay drove the Cadillac close to the front line. It was a winter's day with cloud and mist shrouding the taller dunes in the distance and the desert churned to mud on all sides. The destination was the Kasserine Pass, where Rommel was attacking American forces in the first wartime confrontation between the two nations.

Sandwiched in a convoy of armoured vehicles, Kay drove the big car with one eye on the sky for enemy aircraft. Eisenhower was jammed between two officers in the back. They were also craning their necks skywards.

"If we get strafed I just want you all to get out of the car and run like hell – every man for himself," said Eisenhower.

"And don't expect me to hang around and open the door for you," said Kay.

She looked back in the mirror. Back in England she would never have said something like that. Now it was different. Ike flashed her a smile in the mirror.

"Every man for himself," said Kay. "Fair enough, but what about the women?"

"You do your best to keep up with us," he said.

"You won't see me for the dust in your eyes," she replied.

The battle for the Kasserine Pass was a disastrous defeat for the Allied forces. American forces retreated some fifty miles towards their rear base, cursing the name of Rommel every mile of the way.

Without sufficient supplies and with Montgomery's Eighth Army to his rear, Rommel was unable to exploit his success. But the battle sharpened Eisenhower's respect for the German. Intuition told him they would meet again on the battlefield.

The Kasserine battle also brought Kay the surprise of a late Christmas present. The festive season had come and gone a few weeks earlier amid the gloom of endless rain and the misery of military defeat. But when Ike finally assembled his staff for a celebration lunch at his villa in Tunis, he did so with style.

There was turkey on the table provided by the ever-resourceful Mickey McKeogh. There were Christmas crackers and carefully wrapped small gifts on every placemat. Glasses of champagne had already been poured and placed beside small candles.

Each guest in turn opened their gifts to find bars of perfumed soap, miniature bottles of cognac and silk scarves. Then it was Kay's turn. She tore the wrapping off her present to find a small wooden box carrying her initials. The room went quiet. Everyone was watching her. She suddenly felt nervous. She looked at Ike.

"It's not going to bite me, is it?"

"It might bite somebody else. Open it."

She did so and gasped. Inside, in velvet inlay, gleamed a silver pistol.

Eisenhower was immediately at her side, anxious to explain a gift that had silenced the room.

"It's a Beretta 418. Nickel plated. Semi-automatic. Fits nicely in a handbag. Pick it up," he said.

She eased the gun out of the inlay and held it with the barrel down. It was light and fitted comfortably in her hand. The grip was a brown grained wood, probably rosewood, she thought.

Tex led a round of applause at the table until Eisenhower raised his hand.

"Boss, that's wonderful," she said. "Thank you. But I don't know how to use it."

"You told me you were using a shotgun as a kid in Ireland."

"That was different."

"Same idea. You load, aim and pull the trigger. Here, let me show you."

He was at her side. "Hold your arm out straight like this."

He stood behind her with his right arm beneath hers, holding it out so that the Beretta was pointing at the door.

"Now use your left arm to support the gun arm."

He took her left hand and leaning into her placed it beneath her right arm.

"There, you see! Now close one eye and squeeze the trigger."

Kay was aware everyone was still looking at her. She and the boss were standing almost as one. She could smell the cologne he dabbed on his face after shaving.

"It's not loaded, is it?" she said, half turning.

The room collapsed in laughter.

"No, it's not," said Ike, "but it will be when Tex takes you on the range tomorrow."

She wanted to give him a kiss, even if only a peck on the cheek, but the watchful eyes were waiting for just such a gesture. Instead she held out her hand, shook his and said, "Thank you, boss. This is the best Christmas present I've ever had. What a lovely surprise."

"There's not a man here who hasn't got a sidearm. You're one of us. Why should you be different?" he said. Everyone applauded politely, although they knew that wasn't the reason for such an unusual gift.

The opinion among the staff, one that Kay shared, was that Ike had given her the weapon, just as he had ordered the two new uniforms, for a simple reason: guilt. He had had no right to ask her to join him in North Africa and risk her life crossing the Mediterranean on a troopship.

She was a Motor Transport Corps driver and should never have left London. Indeed the MTC had strenuously opposed her departure. Somewhere in the backwoods of bureaucracy there had been a row.

Kay had been summoned to explain herself and merely said she was obeying orders. Objections to her transfer were overruled because Eisenhower was the supreme commander and if he wanted his London driver beside him in the desert who was to question that?

Kay was delighted at the promotion. She also enjoyed Charlotte's jealousy.

"You've got your bum in the butter dish, doll, you are just so lucky," her friend said.

She had guardedly told Charlotte that she would be going overseas on operations. Failing to conceal her envy but anxious to trump this information, Charlotte said she knew all about Torch.

"You're going to be in the desert, doll, among all those sheiks in their tents with long daggers in their belts trying to get their hands up your skirt."

Kay couldn't help laughing. They were whispering across a greasy table in the Red Lion with the usual watery wartime beers. The smell of stale beer, cheap cigarettes and old sweat, a smell peculiar to every pub in wartime London, the drab

surroundings and the slanting rain outside did something to
Charlotte's imagination.

"He'll come riding out of the sunset, sweeping down a
steep dune on a white mount, bend low and sweep you onto
his saddle and spur his steed back to the tent."

"Who?"

"Rudolf Valentino, of course."

"Then what happens?"

"You get ravished, doll. You could do with a bit of
ravishing – mark you I wouldn't say no either."

Kay laughed again. "Someone should bottle you and sell
you as a tonic."

Charlotte looked around. "God, get me out of here. I'm
just so jealous."

"I wouldn't be. It could be quite dangerous. There's going
to be a lot of fighting out where I'm going."

"Dangerous, my elbow," said Charlotte. "You're going to
be in the five pound seats watching the lions eat the Christians.
I suppose he's going to fly that bloody dog out as well?"

Kay said Telek was not being flown anywhere. She did not
mention that her own transport was to be a troopship.
Charlotte would have laughed out loud at that. It was
annoying. At the very least she should have been given a seat
on a military plane out to join him.

But that would have meant authorisation, documentation,
signatures. And that would have widened the circle of those
who knew that Kay Summersby was receiving special
treatment from the Allied commander.

His immediate staff were all too aware of the way
Eisenhower treated his driver. He had broken regulations to
enable her to join him in Africa. He had quite openly given
her a fancy gun. He had replaced her ruined uniform with
two new tailored outfits run up by the best tailor in Tangiers.

Everyone around Eisenhower knew also that there were plenty of other drivers who could just as easily perform all the duties that Kay dealt with: his mail, the phone calls, the daily diary, and mixing the evening cocktail.

Later in her room that day Kay took the Beretta out of the box, held it up and aimed it at the mirror. She liked what she saw, a woman with a gun in her hand. It made her feel confident and strong.

He had given it to her in front of everyone at lunch that day. He didn't give a damn what they thought of the present or the way he had put his arms around her to show her how to use it. That was Eisenhower.

He could do that even if he couldn't look deep in his heart and admit she had been torpedoed because he had broken all the rules. Kay Summersby shouldn't be anywhere near the front line. Now he had given her a gun. That was probably against the rules too.

6

March 1943

Mamie Eisenhower could remember the exact date and time when Kay Summersby entered her life. She had picked up a copy of *Life* magazine after breakfast and sat down with a fresh cup of coffee to read it. A friend had told her the magazine had run a story about Ike which she should read.

It was 9 November 1942 and her husband had been away for almost six months. In that time she'd read many stories about him in the press and carefully kept the cuttings in an album to show him on his return.

Following his promotion to commander, European Theater of Operations and his third star in June of that year, Eisenhower had become a household name. For Mamie that meant not just stories in the national press but regular attention from the Washington press corps. They sent her bunches of roses, boxes of chocolates, anything to get into the apartment she shared with another army wife in the capital.

She knew what they wanted: human interest stories about the wife the general had left behind. She never let them into the apartment, but the gambit when they called on the phone was always the same and often from women feature writers.

"How are you doing, Mrs Eisenhower? We're all so proud of your husband doing a great job over there, and you must be very proud too, so would you care to share some thoughts with our readers about life with Ike – that's what we thought we would call it, a big two-page feature – 'Life with Ike' by the wife he left behind. Oh, and by the way, Mrs Eisenhower, we know army regulations forbid any payment, but we would make a handsome donation to a charity of your choice."

She turned them all down, but that didn't stop the calls, which became more personal and more hurtful the more she refused to cooperate.

It was male reporters now too, digging for dirt.

"Excuse me, Mrs Eisenhower, for mentioning this, but we would like to give you the chance to refute some unpleasant gossip going around. It is all rumour, of course, but we would like to give you the opportunity to nail this nonsense."

"What are these rumours, exactly?"

There was always a pause at this point in the conversation, of which there were several, all remarkably similar, as the reporter concerned tried to phrase his accusation in a way that would present him as a friend rather than an accuser.

"Well, Mrs Eisenhower, I am sure these are just nasty rumours and we would like to help you deny them, but people do say you quite like your cocktails in the evening and that you never attend official events at night or dine with friends because you are, how shall I put this…"

"Because I've had too much to drink?"

"Your words not mine, Mrs Eisenhower."

"That is despicable and I shall let the general know to what depths you people can descend. What was the name of your paper again?"

"Good night, Mrs Eisenhower."

It was true that she hardly ever went out in the evening, for the very good reason that when her husband was preparing to send young men into battle, perhaps to die, she didn't think it appropriate to be seen drinking and socialising in public.

It was equally true that when friends came over in the evening for games of mah-jong or just for cosy suppers, cocktails were generously provided. That was the American way and what was wrong with that?

She knew what Ike would say: *The hell with them all.*

She smiled at the thought of him taking a call from one of the reporters. She turned to the magazine, flicked through the pages, and stopped smiling.

The article was headed "General Eisenhower and his 'family' in theater". There was a large picture of Ike and a photo montage of those who worked closely with him, including Lieutenant Commander Harry Butcher, naval aide, Mickey McKeogh, orderly valet courier, and Kay Summersby, "a pretty Irish girl who also drives for General Eisenhower". That was how *Life* described their relationship.

It was the word *also* that jumped out at Mamie. She had heard vaguely that the Brits had given Ike a driver and thought nothing of it. Now she learnt that the driver was a pretty Irish woman who apparently did other tasks as well. That begged several questions.

The woman, Kay Summersby, was undoubtedly pretty, as the caption said, rather strangely, Mamie thought. She looked again at the photo, which showed an apparently young woman wearing military uniform facing the camera with a slight smile. She was wearing a service cap which concealed her hair, and yes, she was pretty.

The story had jolted Mamie. Why had Ike not thought to tell her about his driver? He must have known that

Summersberry, or whatever she was called, would feature in stories about his team. He had warned her to pay no attention to press stories, but the *Life* magazine story was cold, hard facts. He had also warned her not to expect him back until the war was over. And that could take years. Years he would be spending with his pretty Irish driver.

That had been nearly a year and a half ago, sixteen long months during which the Summersby woman had been at his side almost constantly. Her photograph appeared in newspapers and magazines with her standing behind him, sometimes at the wheel of the Packard as he was getting out, sometimes in official photographs, but always there at his side – always.

The woman had appeared with him again in *Life* magazine a week ago, this time on the front page. There she was, in full colour, on the cover of a magazine read by every woman in America, standing right behind him with that tight jacket and forage cap. She was wearing lipstick and what looked like eyeliner, and her hair had been carefully coiffured to look tousled. Kay Summersby, a thirty-five-year-old civilian driver, was wearing a military-style uniform tailored to her figure. Rumour had it that Ike had ordered it for her.

From the moment she had first seen her in *Life* magazine, Kay Summersby had not looked much like a driver to Mamie. Her army friends in Washington agreed, and so did every rumour that spiced conversations in the bars, restaurants and bedrooms of Washington DC that summer of 1942. It was a well known, if tightly held, confidence among the power elite that General Patton and others in high command had taken mistresses while campaigning abroad. It seemed an accepted military tradition for American commanders overseas. But General Dwight Eisenhower?

The gossips loved the fact, and it was a fact, because the papers had reported it, that Ike had taken his driver to North Africa after the Torch landings a year back in 1943 and introduced her to Churchill and Roosevelt. The story that Ike had lost his temper when General Marshall tried to exclude her from a lunch with the president circulated with relish in the salons of Georgetown.

To general amazement, not least that of King George VI, Ike had even insisted that she took her place in the line to meet the British monarch when he'd arrived in Tunisia to congratulate Ike and his generals. The King, mindful of the royal scandal that had resulted in his brother's abdication only a few years earlier, had ignored her proffered hand, which was, in any case, a breach of protocol. He had looked straight through her and moved swiftly on to the next in line.

That story had been discreetly ignored by the British press, but the American gossip columns had no such regard for the unwritten rule in Fleet Street that one did not embarrass the monarch. Newspapers from coast to coast and across a great swathe of America in between had carried almost identical stories. "King snubs Ike's Irish driver" was the common headline over a photograph showing Kay Summersby in a line-up of top brass with George VI some way down the line talking to a general.

The American papers described Summersby as "attractive", "bob-nosed" and "young". At the age of thirty-five she was hardly young, but in Mamie's eyes that made her all the more dangerous.

Her friends assured Mamie that the gossip about Kay Summersby was just that – the idle chatter of shallow people with little else to do but invent salacious nonsense about the lives of the rich and famous. It was not true and they all knew it.

Faced with such gossip and her friends' less than convincing attempts to persuade her that the rumours were groundless, Mamie often wondered whether the real Eisenhower had eluded her in their long marriage. The idea of her husband having an affair with anyone, let alone a bob-nosed Irish girl almost twenty years his junior, was so uncharacteristic as to be preposterous. But did she really know the character she had lived with for so long?

They had met at an army post in Texas where Second Lieutenant Eisenhower had been posted after graduating from West Point. He was officer of the day, a largely honorary title which gave him certain formal duties, and smartly dressed in olive drab uniform with campaign hat and sidearm. She had been visiting a friend, the wife of an army major.

It was October 1915. A distant war in Europe had hardly ruffled the surface of life at Fort Sam Houston. When talk turned to war, it was of the need for cross-border raids into Mexico to deal with banditry. Mamie was eighteen and Second Lieutenant Eisenhower was twenty-four. He was much taller than she and took himself very seriously; at least that was the impression he gave as he strode around the post with a slight frown. He looked hard at the men he passed and occasionally paused as if to allow the world to take notice of the sharply creased trousers, the polished boots and the shiny buttons on his uniform.

She knew he was trying to make sure that everyone knew he was officer of the day. She was small, vivacious and had what her friends called a slightly saucy attitude that seemed to reflect a carefree spirit not overly impressed by officers, or by the conventions of the day.

Her friend had whispered as Eisenhower approached, "Oh look, here comes the woman-hater of the post."

Mamie Geneva Doud was immediately interested. She knew how to deal with woman-haters. When they were introduced, the second lieutenant bowed, took her hand and tried to kiss it as he had seen in films, and since she had seen the same films, she knew to withdraw her hand just before the brush of his lips. She allowed him to show her over the post, and when she bade him farewell kept her hands firmly by her side. Then she found herself too busy to come to the phone when he called two to three times a day.

She finally relented when one night she found him sitting on the porch of the house her parents had taken that winter in San Antonio. They were Denver people, but the wealth from the meatpacking business allowed them to escape the harsh northern winters for the warmth of Texas. He wasn't just sitting there; he and her father were sipping ice-cold drinks while discussing the latest raids across the Mexican border by the bandit Pancho Villa.

America was staying well clear of the latest war in Europe, but taking a military interest in banditry over the border. To a second lieutenant anxious to put his military training to good use, Pancho Villa seemed the next best opportunity.

Her father agreed. He liked the second lieutenant, and so, in truth, did his daughter. He hadn't got a penny to his name, and his family came from the wrong side of the tracks in a hick town called Abilene in Kansas, but opposites attract, she told herself. He proposed and she accepted.

They set a date for the wedding, but Pancho Villa almost galloped right through their plans. Lieutenant Eisenhower was caught up in preparations for a retaliatory cross-border raid after the Mexican bandit murdered sixteen Americans near the town of Chihuahua.

It looked for a while as if the marriage would have to await a long military campaign across the border, but the army relented, they married on time, and the elegant, coquettish Mamie Geneva Doud, who had been raised in a mansion in the fashionable suburb of Denver, Colorado, settled down to life as a second lieutenant's wife in the bleak surrounds of Fort Sam Houston.

Looking back now, as her husband was about to command the invasion of Europe, Mamie could count twenty different homes they had lived in as he'd climbed the long ladder of military promotion. They were not really homes, merely addresses on army bases where the identical married quarters had clearly been designed by a man who did not understand that a kitchen needed to be somewhat larger than a walk-in wardrobe.

She had given birth to two children and lost one to scarlet fever. "We lost a child," was how she put it when people asked. It was a cold and emotionally neutral way of stating a fact without having to reveal the anguish and pain that lay behind it.

They had stood absolutely still at that moment in their lives, on the second day of the new year 1921, when their first child, nicknamed Icky throughout the three years of his brief life, died in his father's arms. She had not been there at the end; she had been in bed with suspected pneumonia. Briefly, at that time, he had lowered his eyes from the career peaks before him, and she had forgotten the mantra of all service wives: PHT – *push hubby through*.

When they resumed their lives after months of mourning, he was enslaved by the long hours required by a staff officer on the rise, and she was bound by the rigid social rules of life on an army post. Neither talked about their loss. They did not have to. Icky's death formed an unspoken conversation between them for the rest of their lives. It was as if a third person had entered the marriage.

Their second son John was now a twenty-one-year-old about to graduate from West Point. The ceremony would be in June, but she knew his father would not be there.

She was never told exactly where her husband was in England. Officially all they told her was that he was somewhere "in the European theater of operations". She did know, because he told her, that as a four-star general he had his own train, plane and personal staff in Britain. He had been given offices and offered large apartments. He lunched with Churchill at Number Ten and dined with senior British and American commanders in expensive restaurants.

She, on the other hand, was living in a small stuffy apartment in Washington. She had no servants, and for company the same coterie of Pentagon wives who met regularly for cocktails and dinner at which the same conversation about distant husbands played like a gramophone record. To relieve the boredom, Mamie took small jobs helping with war charities.

The distance between them was far greater than the three thousand miles of Atlantic Ocean.

Ike had come home after eighteen months' absence a couple of months ago for a ten-day furlough. This was the year when the war against Nazi fascism would be won. He would lead the Allies to victory and liberate Europe. He had assured her of this with a self-confidence she had found surprising. He had never talked like that before, always taking care not to promise what might not be achieved.

Now he seemed to be brimming with a self-confidence that lent urgency to everything he did. The old Eisenhower would move slowly and maintain a watchful silence while others rushed around him. He liked to say he boiled at a different temperature from men like Patton, Clark and Spaatz. She didn't like the change she saw in him.

He would break off conversations with her, look at his watch and rush off to meetings. She had given him that watch for his thirtieth birthday. Now it was being used to divide them. From morning to midnight he moved from one meeting to another: with the president in the Oval Office, with George Marshall at the Pentagon, with the Free French, the British ambassador, and so it went on.

To make matters worse, he wasn't supposed to be in Washington at all. The press thought he was still in London planning an invasion that would be launched in the first week of May, or so it was whispered in the corridors of Congress, but Roosevelt had secretly called him back for a final round of briefings and to make sure that Churchill's doubts about the perilous cross-Channel operation did not loom too large in his general's mind. So Ike wore civilian clothes and always left her apartment in the Wardman Park Hotel by the back entrance. They would occasionally meet for lunch or coffee in discreet restaurants like adulterous lovers.

When they finally managed a two-day break in White Sulphur Springs he had ruined it completely. Twice he had called her Kay, and then quickly corrected himself. He had spoken the name casually, once while asking for more ice in his drink, and the second time, which was much worse, in the bedroom. They hadn't made love, nor intended to, but he had called out "Kay" from the bathroom. She had been furious the first time, but stifled her anger. This time she had gone straight to bed without a word.

He had taken her in his arms and apologised profusely, kissing her and explaining that he hardly saw any other women in London but his driver, but that made matters much worse. Mamie kept back her anger, though, and suggested it might be a good idea if he got another driver.

He had shaken his head, sighed, lit another cigarette – he must have been smoking three packs a day, and this was supposed to be a relaxing break – and begun talking about his sorrow that he would be missing John's graduation in June.

He had smiled then, looked at her and said, "I shouldn't have even told you that. Crazy, isn't it?"

She knew she had lost her husband to the army. That was understandable. Her second lieutenant had become a four-star general commanding huge forces in a global conflict. No woman would expect to see much of her husband in such circumstances.

But she was not going to lose him to a woman he described as "just my driver".

When Eisenhower had taken the plane back to the coming battlefields of Europe, Mamie had gone to see him off at La Guardia airport. It was 15 January 1944, a date she had circled in her diary. She had hardly seen him in the ten days they were supposed to have spent together. Indeed she had hardly seen him for the last two years. The war had consumed her husband, and now "Overlord", the top-secret code name for the invasion of Europe, seemed set to spirit him away for the foreseeable future.

Mamie told her friends that he hadn't really been with her in Washington at all. He'd been back in London all the time, planning, talking to the troops, arguing with the British and allaying Churchill's doubts about the invasion. And all the time he was with that woman.

At the airport she had kissed him goodbye and said, "Don't come back till it's over, Ike. I couldn't stand losing you again."

7

June 1943

President Roosevelt was sitting in a high-backed cane chair reading a file of documents in the main room of a whitewashed villa when Kay entered. A fan turned lazily overhead. Eisenhower was the only other person in the room. Slatted shutters left the room in half-light. The president put aside the papers and looked up.

She immediately noticed his clothes. The beautifully tailored double-breasted dove-grey suit was matched by a tie and handkerchief peeking from the breast pocket. His face had a chiselled beauty about it, a face that was too large for the shrunken body below, a face that beamed the warmth of a personality that had been shaped and strengthened by paralysis, and most certainly a face that looked with evident interest on the attractive lady who had just walked into the room.

"Mr President, this is Kay Summersby, the British member of my staff you asked about," said Eisenhower.

Roosevelt leant forward with a slight smile and said, "I've heard quite a lot about you, Miss Summersby. I thought when I left the plane yesterday you might be there to drive me."

Kay blushed and stammered out words to the effect that the secret service would not allow it.

"Well, we will have to change that," he said and turned to an aide beside him.

"Miss Summersby will drive me on this trip," he said.

The aide nodded and made a note.

"Thank you, Mr President," Kay said.

"Good. That's settled. Tomorrow we have lunch in the desert."

The picnic with President Roosevelt, in fact everything about that extraordinary day, was a complete surprise. The boss always liked to surprise her with little things, a sudden change of plan, the opening of a bottle of champagne, a small gift, and then watch her face. But this was a surprise like no other.

The president's visit to North Africa had been a tightly held secret. He crossed the Atlantic on a battlecruiser, making landfall in Algeria before flying to a desert airstrip where Eisenhower had set up his forward headquarters.

The day before Roosevelt arrived, Kay was told about the visit in such detail that she became curious.

"Why are you telling me all this?" she asked.

"Because you will be driving the president. In my Cadillac."

"But surely he has a secret service driver?"

"Maybe, but he's asked for you."

"But he doesn't know me!"

Eisenhower smiled: "Just do as you're told, Kay."

The tide had turned in North Africa. Defeat of Rommel's Afrika Korps had opened the way for the president to visit his victorious general. The Pentagon, the State Department and the White House staff had all argued forcefully against the idea. No one dared say outright that a semi-paralysed man confined to a wheelchair simply could not make such an arduous journey. But that was what everyone was thinking.

Roosevelt listened to the arguments in the Oval Office. He smiled, nodded, put a cigarette in the holder and placed it between his teeth at the customary jaunty angle. This was always the signal for a decision.

"I am going to see Ike. He's won our first battle of the war. Thank you for your opinions, gentlemen."

They drove into the desert the day after his arrival, Kay driving the Cadillac with Roosevelt and secret service guards in the back. A convoy of military vehicles stretched a quarter of a mile behind.

A picnic area had been selected and surrounded with troops. Roosevelt chose otherwise and directed her to drive on.

"Child," he said tapping her on the shoulder, "There's a nice grove of palm trees over there. Let's stop and have lunch there."

Kay swung the Cadillac off the highway and drove over hot hard sand to an oasis of palm trees. The entire convoy followed, flashing headlights to protest against the change of plan.

Ike, the president and Kay, together with aides and security, watched as the secret service team transformed a small dusty corner of the desert into a suitable place for a presidential picnic.

That's what the president called it: a picnic.

He liked the word and repeated it, asking about its derivation and how and when it had entered the American vocabulary. Nobody knew. The consensus of opinion held that the word was French.

Whatever its origins, picnic was an absurdly understated name for the lunchtime arrangements that day. A huge tent was set up under the shade of the palm trees. A long table, covered in white linen and laid with silver and crystal glass, was placed beneath the tent. White House staff, not Arab waiters, served the food and drink.

Roosevelt was seated at the table in his customary wheelchair. A table flap had been raised to conceal the lower half of his body from view, conveying the impression he was sitting at the table like anyone else.

Roosevelt patted the table in front of an empty place next to him and looked down to where Kay was sitting at the far end.

"Come here, child, and sit by me," he said with a smile that turned all heads in Kay's direction. Kay froze. She was terrified. She had been introduced to him only briefly the previous day. They had spoken not a word in the car that morning until he had ordered her to break with the planned route.

Roosevelt patted the table more firmly.

"Won't you come back here, child, and have lunch with a dull old man?"

She looked questioningly at Eisenhower across the table, hoping he would step in and recommend a more senior and appropriate official as the president's lunchtime companion, but he merely nodded and grinned. She moved up the table and sat down.

Roosevelt was charming and very flirtatious, leaning over to draw her chair back, smiling, his head held slightly to one side, his grey eyes searching her out; she had heard so often about the president's charm, his ability to disarm even the most hostile critics with a smile and a breezy, folksy manner, that she had discounted the stories as the exaggeration of sycophants.

The food was served – cold chicken, ham, bread, fruit and cheese; the president ate with relish beside her while Kay toyed with her food, wondering how to make conversation.

Would she be revealing state secrets if she asked about the next stage of his overseas tour – the journey to Tehran where Roosevelt and Churchill would meet Stalin?

The president finished the first course, wiped his chin with a napkin, turned to her and began to talk. He asked about her Irish background, lowering his voice as if holding a purely private conversation. She told him about her childhood in County Cork, riding bareback, swimming in the freezing waters of the Atlantic, listening to stories from country folk of a long-ago famine that had blighted the land.

Roosevelt listened gravely and shook his head when she mentioned the tribulations of the Irish people at the time of great hunger and mass emigration across the Atlantic in the nineteenth century. He did not condemn, merely remarking: "The British loss was our gain."

Then he wanted to know about women in wartime England: what jobs did they do, did they work the same hours as men in the armaments factories, and exactly what was a woman "clippie" on a London bus?

Roosevelt had the political trick of listening carefully, making her feel as if he was really interested in what she said; but she didn't think this was a political game – he really did seem interested, especially when she told him how she had first met the then two-star general Eisenhower on a foggy morning in London.

"Yes, Ike told me how you two met up," he said. "He also told me you were the best driver he had ever had. So from now on, on this trip, I want you to keep driving me. Could you do that?"

She nodded, said yes, and looked down the table to where Eisenhower was watching the conversation. Everyone at the table was trying to listen. Roosevelt then put his hand on her arm and patted it.

"Thank you, child," he said. She realised that this great man, the president of the United States, was flirting with her.

"Tell me what plans you have, I mean your career, your future?" he asked.

"I just want to continue to serve the general," she said, "until the end of this war."

There was nothing else she could have said, but Roosevelt pondered the remark as if she had delivered a weighty opinion worthy of consideration.

"How would you like to join the Women's Army Corps?" he said quietly and suddenly, as if the thought had just occurred to him.

She sat back in surprise. The question felt carefully timed and well planned. Ike and he must have discussed it. These two great men had obviously found time to talk about her future, which was both gratifying and somewhat alarming.

"Nothing I would like better," she blurted out. "But that's an American unit and I'm not an American citizen."

Roosevelt laughed at that and again nodded down the table to an aide. The pencil and notebook had come out again.

"Well, who knows," he said. "Stranger things have happened."

The president had only once, and briefly, turned to the rather irritated official on his other side, and at the end of lunch Kay understood exactly what was meant by the famous Roosevelt charm. She felt that she had entered a magnetic force field.

Before leaving, the Roosevelt smile had faded as he leant towards her and said, almost in a whisper, "Mind you take good care of our commander."

She had assumed the offer of military rank in the American army was just one of the many half-promises a charming, flirtatious man, who led the greatest nation on earth, occasionally made; a throwaway line that would be forgotten and swept aside like confetti after a wedding. It was just another desert mirage.

North Africa that summer of 1943 threw up many such illusions. By night the desert froze under a clear sky scattered with countless stars that seemed close enough to touch. By day the sea of sand could have been the backdrop for a film set. Kay pulled back her tent flaps in the command camp every morning to look out at sand dunes rising and falling to the horizon in waves of molten copper.

Fantasy and reality merged in such surroundings. It did not take much imagination to place a distant horseman on the dunes waving a curved scimitar and urging his followers into battle.

The president's visit was swiftly followed by that of Winston Churchill, who was anxious to have his own desert picnic. Wearing a broad-brimmed panama hat, a linen suit and walking with a silver-topped cane, the prime minister strode across the desert to the chosen place for lunch, planted his cane in the sand and gave a customary two-fingered salute to the group of officers.

It was one of those occasions the prime minister loved: a long table shaded by an awning with his generals seated around him and white-robed Arab servants serving food and wine while he served up the conversation. Kay was grateful that this time she was seated at the far end of the table from the very important visitor.

Someone posed the question that Roosevelt had been unable to answer – the origins of the word picnic.

Churchill brushed the question aside. He wanted to hear every detail of the German retreat and defeat in North Africa and Rommel's recall to Berlin. He enjoyed the account of the

Allied victory as much as the food placed in front of him. He had not, however, forgotten the question.

"French used it first – *picque-nique* – a shared repast taken with friends in a country setting – seventeenth century – no one knows where it came from. Would you be so kind as to pass the wine?"

Seeing both leaders far removed from the trappings of power at home, watching them meet their generals and ordinary soldiers amid the heat and flies of the desert, Kay realised that both men were supremely happy. They were on the road to victory and Hitler was destined for defeat. They knew too that in Dwight Eisenhower they had found the general to bring the war to the conclusion. After his desert lunch Churchill had drawn her aside and said, building on his own words the previous year and echoing those of Roosevelt: "Thank you for taking good care of our commander."

The assumption behind those words was that Churchill thought she and Ike were lovers. Kay liked to think so too. The kiss had changed everything.

The touch of his lips on hers lingered long after they had broken apart. A simple hurried kiss in the dark hold of a transport plane had opened something in her heart and she hoped in his. She felt as ancient explorers must have done when they broke into the burial chamber of an Egyptian pharaoh. Secrets between two people had at last been revealed.

She had been sitting a few rows behind him on a night flight from Tunis to a camp in the desert. The cabin was dark and others on the plane were all asleep. She felt a hand on her shoulder.

"Have you got an aspirin? I have a hell of a head."

"Of course. Sit down."

She groped around in her bag and shook a pill from a bottle.

"You'll have to dry swallow it," she said.

He had sat beside her for a while. In the dark cave of the aircraft hold, deafened by the noise of the engines, surrounded by sleeping bodies, they felt alone and at peace. Nothing could have been less comfortable or more comforting.

He took her hand and squeezed it in the darkness. She had turned towards him, as he did to her, and they had held each other in an affectionate hug. It had felt a perfectly natural thing to do and it was just as natural when they began to kiss, not a snatched backseat cinema kiss, but a kiss that seemed to go right through her.

He had slipped his hands inside her jacket and cupped her breasts, still kissing her, when the plane hit turbulence. For a few moments they clung together tightly, his hands pressing into her as the plane shook and shuddered. People sleeping around them had begun to wake as the big aircraft rolled and bucked.

They quickly straightened up, guiltily adjusting clothing. Ike had gone back to his seat as people around began to wake up. They had landed in darkness and gone straight to their quarters. He took her hand outside his tent and held it for a few seconds. Then he turned away without saying a word. There was no offer of a nightcap. There didn't need to be.

She felt different the next day, not foolishly so, smiling at strangers and giggling at every passing remark. Women of her age did not indulge in the love-struck attitudes of the young. She just felt happily, confidently different. The kiss had told a story and she was beginning to see, or hope she saw, where that story would end.

Ike acted no differently towards her the next day nor gave any sign that he, the Allied commander, had found himself in the arms of his driver, personal secretary or whatever her title, the night before. She still had no official title beyond that of driver. She would talk to him about that the next time they were alone.

Meanwhile he spoke to her as he always did, army style: short clipped decisions to be acted on without argument or discussion. There was the occasional growl but more often a word of thanks delivered with a slight smile. Once or twice she tried to catch his eye but he did not notice, or if he did he ignored the obvious intent behind the way she looked at him.

It was very much business as usual, a fixed routine that unfolded throughout the day as if nothing had changed. Kay reminded herself of the kiss by recalling every move they made as they huddled between sleeping troops in the dark hold of the plane. She wondered if he had any idea what happens to the human heart when it is lifted, as he had lifted hers on that plane. Perhaps not. It was up to her to make him understand. Their embrace was not another fantasy of the Arabian night.

Tex and Mickey saw the difference in her. She was sure of it. They smirked and whispered behind her back. She didn't care.

She decided to do something for him that would surprise them all. The war in North Africa was over. The Allied commanders were meeting day and night to plan the next stage of the war, the attack on Sicily and beyond that the Italian Peninsula. There was talk of trips to Cairo to see the pyramids and to Jerusalem to see the holiest places in Christendom. Kay had other plans.

"I've got a surprise for you," she said to him one morning.

They had just finished the usual breakfast in the camp canteen, fresh rolls, honey, yogurt and gallons of steaming black coffee.

"I don't like surprises," said Ike, looking at his watch and wondering why the car had not been brought around.

"She's called Dawn. You'll like her."

"She?" said Ike looking up. Kay was smiling. "Look over there," she said.

The six-year-old bay mare stood with her right hoof tipped forward as if anxious to get going. Her freshly groomed coat was glistening in the sun. Alongside stood a handsome black horse.

A young Arab woman held both horses and looked shyly at Eisenhower as he walked over.

"Where did they come from?" he asked, patting the bay. The woman mumbled something inaudible. He looked at Kay who smiled and shrugged.

"All right, silly question," he said.

"I thought you might like a ride. We've got time."

"Nope. My car is due."

"Not for another half hour."

Ike raised his eyebrows, looked at her and then smiled.

"Okay, you win, let's go; which is mine?"

"You're on the bay," she said. "She's a Cleveland, a thoroughbred. You'll like her, she's calm and sensible."

"Just like me, you mean?" said Ike, patting the horse.

She was pleased and smiled. When he made fun of himself like that it meant she had taken the war off his shoulders, if briefly. They rode across hard sand towards a line of dunes and broke into a canter.

She turned and looked back. Two helmeted military escorts were following in a jeep. That had been the arrangement. She had worked it all out, including the route to an old dried-up marsh that filled up on winter rain and retained enough moisture to attract a variety of birdlife in the dry months.

"Great exercise," he shouted.

"I know. We all spend too long sitting on our backsides every day," she shouted back, twisting and turning in the saddle.

She rode well, leaning slightly forward with her seat raised slightly from the saddle, hands holding the reins gently but without slack, feet in stirrups gripping the belly of the horse. He followed as she guided them along a path through the dunes hardened by generations of herdsmen.

They pulled up at the summit and looked down at a swathe of desert darker than the rest, hinting at water below the surface.

"Where did you learn to ride?" he said.

"I was pretty much brought up on a horse," she said. "My father put me on a pony when I was just three, I think. I fell off of course but he caught me and put me back up. We weren't given saddles until we were ten. That's how we learnt."

"That's the only way to learn anything," said Ike. "This was in Ireland?"

"Yes. It was cold and wet in winter, warm and wet in summer. We had chilblains and runny noses all the time. It didn't matter. We thought everyone grew up like that. And where did you learn to ride, if I might ask, sir?"

"In the army," he said. "When I was commissioned in 1915. The military moved on horseback then. There were no jeeps in those days."

Ike didn't say there had been no ponies in his childhood either. He had grown up very much on the wrong side of the Union Pacific railroad tracks in Abilene, a frontier cattle town in Kansas. There was no piped water, the unpaved streets kicked up mud in the winter and dust in the summer, and there was little enough money for a family of six boys living in a two-storey wooden house with their parents. He hadn't mounted a horse until his second year in the army.

He followed her as she flicked the reins, took the horse into a trot and then into a full gallop down the path through the dunes.

They pulled up, breathless. Kay laughed. Eisenhower was breathing hard and feeling the sweat prickle against the back of his shirt.

"Oxygen clears the head and fires up the brain," she said.

"Maybe, but I think you're going to get me into trouble," he said.

He looked back. The jeep escort had just cleared the rim of the dunes and was coming down towards them with difficulty, the wheels slipping and sliding in the sand.

"Don't worry. I told everyone who needs to know that you wanted a ride today," she replied.

"Did you now?" he said with an edge in his voice that hinted at reproach.

She smiled nervously. Perhaps she had gone too far. It was the first time they had been alone since the plane ride.

"It's good for you," she said. "It's a breathtaking way to start the day."

"Time to go," he said and wheeled his horse into a canter up the dunes and towards camp.

8

January 1944

The old year had ended with a Christmas snowstorm that cast a white shroud over London and Paris. The roll-call of Allied victories that autumn and the slow-moving slaughterhouse of the Russian advance, which ground whole German armies into the mud and blood of the battlefield, had spiced the festivities in Britain and across the Channel in occupied Europe.

The national conversation in bars, in front of home fires and at Christmas tables was remarkably similar. If the Red Army could make progress against the Wehrmacht in the east, when would the Allies open a second front with an attack in the west?

Kay waited at an airport outside London on a bitterly cold morning in early January 1944 knowing that the answer to that question was about to arrive on an overnight flight from Washington. It seemed that she spent half her life waiting at stations and airports for a man who rose in rank every time he stepped onto English soil.

Now, this January morning in 1944, Eisenhower was coming down the steps of the aircraft as he always did –

slowly, looking around at the faces below – with four stars on his shoulder. His retinue, or family as he referred to them, followed with the baggage.

She watched him as he came down the steps. He looked tired after a long flight. The skin on his face was sallow and baggy and the eyes clouded. She could tell from his tight smile that he wanted to get through the formalities and on the road to London as soon as possible.

Ike had always been an impatient man, driving himself and others towards the next item on the agenda, the next thing to be done, the next objective. It was always the next with him.

She watched him looking around, his eyes resting briefly on the faces of the greeting party. She knew he was looking for her. His eyes opened and gave a quick smile when he saw her hanging back behind the main party. Then the smile vanished and he began shaking hands and returning salutes.

With the formalities completed he walked over to her. Tex followed with two large suitcases. She allowed herself a small smile and saluted him, quite unnecessarily because as a motor transport driver she had neither military rank nor its obligations.

"Good to see you," he said. "Have you been behaving yourself?"

She blushed. He had never been quite as familiar in public before. She wondered for a moment whether he had missed her, then dismissed the thought.

"What are you driving today?" he asked.

"Same old Packard, sir."

"Let's get moving. Tex, stow the bags and get in!"

She drove out of the airfield past lines of Nissen huts and turned onto the London road. She could see in the mirror that he had begun reading files passed to him by Tex.

He looked up, caught her eyes in the mirror, and said, "How was Christmas for you folks over here?"

"Just fine," she said, telling a lie to curtail the conversation. He was tired and needed to work and she needed to concentrate on the drive.

In fact she had hated Christmas that year. It was the fifth such celebration in wartime England and it had passed in a haze of cheap gin and Bing Crosby endlessly singing, "I'll be home for Christmas" on the radio. The bombing had become sporadic and the threat of invasion had long faded, but people were tired of the rationing, the blackout, the four inches of permitted bath water, the watered-down beer and the constant efforts by the Ministry of Food to persuade them that slabs of revolting dried fish from South Africa called snoek were edible.

Even the pervasive presence of Winston Churchill stomping the streets after a raid with cigar and homburg hat, talking on the radio of the coming dawn after the long hours of darkness, failed to lift the spirits.

Kay had spent Christmas with her mother in a small village in Surrey. There was a nanny goat in the back garden and a carefully tended vegetable patch in what had been a small rose garden in front of the house. Christmas lunch was a mushroom omelette followed by goat's cheese.

As they moved into the sitting room after washing up, they joked about the lack of a traditional festive meal, but then her mother's humour dried-up.

"People are fed up with this war. They don't see an end to it. There are Americans everywhere, but they don't seem to be doing anything. Invasion? What invasion? No one believes it's going to happen."

"Of course there's going to be an invasion, Mother – you can't move anywhere without bumping into troops. They say the Channel ports are all full of barges," said Kay.

Kay was wearily familiar with her mother's complaints. Mrs MacCarthy-Morrogh made much of the fact that she had lived through one war already but omitted to say that she had done so in the comfort of an estate on the coast of Ireland while her husband was away in the army.

Kay decided it was time for a drink. There had been no wine for lunch, only water. Now it was time for something stronger. She took a brown paper package from her handbag.

"Mummy, let's have a Christmas toast."

"Oh yes! What did you bring?"

"It's a surprise, but get some glasses and some mint from the garden."

Kay unwrapped a half-bottle of whisky. It was bourbon, not Scotch. There would be a complaint. There always was. Her mother returned with the mint and two heavy crystal tumblers. Kay poured what she reckoned was a treble measure into both and added water and the mint. She handed a glass to her mother who took an immediate gulp and said, with the conspiratorial air of someone about to divulge an important secret, "You know that some people in the village are saying that it might not have been a bad thing if the Germans had crossed the Channel in 1940. At least we would have had something to eat and water enough for a bath."

"Mother! How could you say such a thing? I'm shocked!" she replied, aghast.

Her mother took another gulp of her whisky, held up the glass and said, "It's all very well for you. You're in with the Americans. You can get this stuff and those nice nylons you're wearing. Most people haven't had sight of a pat of butter, a banana or a decent bit of meat since the war started, and that was five years ago. That's a long time to wait for a decent meal. A bloody long time."

Her mother never used bad language; she regarded herself as a refined middle-class lady. She had drunk far too much.

Kay yearned to tell her the news from America, announced on Christmas Eve, which for a day or two over the festive season had gone unnoticed in Britain, but she couldn't face the endless questions she knew would follow.

She had kissed her mother goodbye and walked to the car thinking of the announcement from the White House. There was so much news those days that a battle won, a ship lost or rationing rules changed all blurred into background noise broadcast by the BBC eighteen hours a day.

People shrugged, grumbled and got on with their lives, listening only to the news that really mattered, black market cigarettes below the counter of the local pub or real lamb's liver on sale at the butcher's.

So the announcement from Washington that Christmas was largely ignored across the Atlantic. President Roosevelt had surprised his government and the wider American public with the appointment of General Dwight Eisenhower as supreme commander, Allied Expeditionary Forces.

Eisenhower's mission had been laid out in a presidential statement of such forceful simplicity that it reminded those who knew their history of Lincoln's Gettysburg address. In two minutes President Lincoln had defined, in 1863, the national purpose in fighting for the principles of human equality in the American Civil War. He had told his countrymen from the far north to the deep south in stark simple language where their duty lay. Roosevelt's words were similarly resolute and of poetic brevity.

*You will enter the continent of Europe and
undertake operations aimed at the heart
of Germany and the destruction of her
armed forces.*

It took almost an hour to get to the four-storey town
house off Berkeley Square that had been requisitioned for
the new Allied Commander. In that time Eisenhower never
stopped talking. It was as if, once on British soil, he felt able
to give vent to the ideas, questions and plans that had been
piling up inside him since his appointment.

In a long monologue that invited no interruption,
Eisenhower talked calmly about the two greatest challenges
he faced: the Channel weather and the genius of Erwin
Rommel, the German general who had been ordered to
defend occupied Europe against Allied invasion.

She watched in her rear-view mirror as Tex handed his
boss a file and then prepared to take notes.

She wanted to catch his eye, tell him she had missed him.
Every miserable moment she had spent with her mother she
had thought of how he would be spending time with his
family, Mamie and the boys in Washington.

But he didn't look at her. The usual conspiracy of
quick half-smiles that were beamed into the rear-view
mirror had been set aside. Eisenhower was talking about
the need for an expert meteorologist, someone he could
trust to forecast the fast-changing weather in the English
Channel.

He wanted to know everything about the winds, waves,
currents and tides that made the sea between Britain and
France such a "disagreeable" stretch of water – the word
Churchill had used, apparently, when describing the role
the Channel had played in English history.

"Disagreeable for our enemies, but bloody helpful for us," the prime minister had said. Eisenhower wanted to know just how disagreeable or helpful the narrow seas would be as spring turned to summer.

"It's got to be a Brit," he kept saying. "Someone who understands the way the goddamn weather works in these foggy islands."

Then he opened the file on Rommel. Kay dropped her speed and drove carefully as they entered the North London suburbs. The car had become a war room and the man in the back needed to concentrate.

Eisenhower quickly flipped the pages of the file, clearly not satisfied with what he was reading.

"The Brits think too much of Rommel," he said, talking aloud to himself again. "They think he's some kind of military god and a decent gentleman with it. Even Winston has fallen for him. Anyway, there's nothing new here."

He closed the file and handed it back to Tex. It was well after dark by the time Eisenhower settled into his new quarters. A servant had taken his two large leather suitcases to the main bedroom and laid them on the bed unopened: Eisenhower had expressly forbidden anyone to open his luggage, let alone unpack it. Kay could see he was exhausted.

The housekeeper had lit fires and laid out plates of luxuries long unseen in London – ham, smoked salmon and fruit with real coffee and tea. The American ambassador and senior staff from the embassy had welcomed him in the richly furnished drawing room, but he had shooed them all away after a polite drink, allowed his staff to take what they wanted of the food, and sent them to their rooms.

He told Kay to stay. This had become a routine on their return to London after the North African campaign.

"Fix us drinks, would you," he said, unbuttoning his jacket and slinging it over the back of an armchair.

She wondered if he still remembered the kiss, but pushed the thought away. The boss needed a drink.

Kay went to the sideboard on which lay bottles of whisky, gin, vodka, vermouth and two soda siphons. She poured a large whisky into a tall glass, added ice and soda the way he liked it, and made a long gin and tonic for herself.

She handed him the drink, placed her own on a side-table by the sofa, kicked off her shoes and sat down.

She raised her glass. "Welcome back," she said.

He smiled, leant forward, raised his glass and said, "Mud in your eye" before drinking first a sip, then more deeply.

Kay sipped at hers and waited for him to speak. She sensed that the long monologue in the car had given way to more immediate concerns. He leant back in an armchair and said wearily, "Know what? I would rather be at the cottage than here."

So he wanted to go back. Eisenhower, the supreme commander in charge of one of the greatest and most secret operations in military history, referred to in whispers as Overlord, wanted to leave the lavishly appointed Queen Anne mansion only a heartbeat from his command headquarters in London's Grosvenor Square and return to a woodland cottage where he could close the door on the world and sit down with his "family" to relax for an hour or two with a hand of bridge or a game of golf.

It turned out that was not all. He wanted to take Grosvenor Square with him. The Luftwaffe knew full well that the elegant London square was a little bit of America in the heart of the capital. Apart from the embassy, every building around the square had been taken over for offices and apartments to house US diplomatic, military and intelligence personnel. Retaliation raids for the heavy bombing of German cities were still proving frighteningly effective. A stick of bombs on Grosvenor Square could seriously damage the invasion planning.

There was another advantage to Telegraph Cottage. It was far enough away from the resurgent night life of London to deny his immediate staff the temptations of the capital. Bushey Park, an anonymous collection of draughty, prefabricated buildings on the western outskirts of London, was chosen to be the new headquarters. There the entire Allied command would be only a few minutes' drive from Telegraph Cottage and everyone could be kept on the straight and narrow, safe from the distractions – and the bombs – of London.

"I want everyone to know that from now on we are getting in early, lunching at the desk, working late. No more club nights in London, no more weekends. Is that clear?"

"It's clear to me," said Kay, "and I'm pretty sure it is going to be clear to everyone else tomorrow."

"So get Mickey and Butch to fix it," he said.

He had finished his whisky, and she wondered whether to pour him another one. He smiled wearily, lifting his glass slightly. She realised it was a silly question. Of course her boss wanted another whisky. He had been back in the country for eight hours and he wanted to change every plan his staff and the British had made for him.

Just like that, she thought: he wants to move his personal staff and the entire command headquarters involving several hundred people out of central London. That was very Eisenhower. He thought it a very reasonable request of the people he employed. That's why he employed them: to make things he wanted done happen fast.

Kay poured him another well-watered whisky and said, "You can tell Number Ten of the move when you have lunch there tomorrow."

"Winston won't mind – he's got a lot on his plate right now."

Eisenhower knew very well what was worrying the British prime minister. Almost two million men were being assembled and trained in Britain for the greatest seaborne invasion in history. Everyone in London, Berlin, Moscow and Washington knew the invasion was coming, but they did not know where or when. It was the most closely guarded secret of the war.

It was midnight and Eisenhower still didn't want to go to bed. The time difference must be keeping him awake, she thought. She leant back and let her eyes close.

Suddenly he was gently shaking her shoulder. "Hey! Go to bed." He gave her a hand from the chair.

"I'm sorry, I nodded off."

She walked to the door.

"Just a minute," he said, frowning.

She turned, half expecting to be asked to fetch a pad and take notes, as was his way. He could never close the door on the day, at least not here in London. There was always another memorandum to be dictated, an appointment to be noted, a query to be pursued the following morning.

"Is Telek there? I mean at the cottage?"

"Yes," she said and couldn't help laughing, not at him, but at the absurdity of the newly arrived Commander of Allied forces worrying about a puppy.

She went to her room thinking of Telegraph Cottage and the black Scottish terrier that he seemed to miss more than anything. She wondered if he had told Mamie about the dog. If so what had she made of the name? Had he explained it to her?

He had answered Churchill's query on the subject by saying, "Tele for Telegraph Cottage and K for my driver, makes a great name, doesn't it?" The prime minister had raised an eyebrow at this. He wasn't the only one. She walked to her room feeling lightheaded after the gin. He was back and she was happy. She did a little skip dance on the thick corridor carpet and went into her room. She undressed and looked at herself in the full-length cheval mirror.

She looked good. Her skin was pale and unmarked, the stomach taut, and the breasts firm. There was no saggy skin under her arms or around her neck. The bushy triangle of hair needed a trim. She would do that in the bathroom tomorrow. She was not beautiful, she knew that. The nose was too bobbed, the forehead too high, her figure perhaps a little slender. But she had high cheekbones, a delicate mouth with full lips and deep brown eyes that men liked. Not beautiful, but attractive certainly.

She turned, looking back over her shoulder. All those hours sitting in the driver's seat had not done her any harm. Long slim legs, small firm bottom, or butt as the Americans would put it, and the gentle cleft of the lower back; she had the figure of a calendar girl.

Her reflection misted over for a moment and an older woman looked back at her, not smiling, but not frowning either, a tired face imprinted with the sorrows of age and experience. The stranger could see her, look through her as if she, like the mirror, was made of glass. There she was heart and body stripped bare, secrets unhidden, all mystery revealed. She was a woman falling, or fallen, in love.

She closed her eyes and shook her head. She must have drunk more gin than she thought. She turned from the mirror, opened her eyes slowly and turned to looked back. The stranger had gone. She was standing there, her own naked self in the mirror.

She put on a dressing-gown and walked down the corridor to a bathroom. She imagined the boss staring into his whisky, swirling it around while he weighed the tasks ahead. She took off her make-up, splashed water on her face and brushed her teeth. She knew he wouldn't go to bed until much later.

She thought briefly of going back, gently taking the glass of whisky from him and holding out her hand to him. He would take it, climb to his feet grumbling and head for the door.

But she couldn't do that, she in her dressing gown and he in his uniform. It would be an affectionate act of domesticity, revealing too much about what they wished to remain hidden from themselves.

She got into bed. The linen had not been aired. The sheets felt cold and clammy. It would be the same for Ike in his room somewhere down the corridor. He would hate that and growl at her in the morning. She got out of bed and walked back to the living room.

He looked up in surprise, noting the paisley patterned dressing gown and the face bare of make-up.

"What are you doing up?" he asked.

"You've got a long day tomorrow," she said. "You really should go to bed."

"I've been on a plane all day. I need to relax. Come and sit here," he said, patting a place on the sofa beside him. She pulled the cord of her dressing gown tighter and sat down. His hand reached out to hers. She took it and held it, squeezing gently. His eyes remained closed and she began to knead the back of his hand with her thumb.

"You know what?" she said. "You need a long, hot bath and a good back rub."

"No time for that," he said.

"You're like a coiled spring. You need to unwind that body of yours."

"What I need is another drink. I'll fix it, you go to bed, that's an order."

"OK, boss," she said. "But I am going to run you a hot bath. Don't be too long."

He got to his feet, patted her affectionately on the back and kissed her lightly on the cheek.

"I've missed you," he said.

She lay in bed, restless, cursing the house staff for the cold sheets and seeking sleep using the memory trick she had been taught by a doctor. Try to remember an important and happy event in your life and recall the time, the people and the places involved, he had advised.

Memory of past happiness will calm you. Truth of what you recall does not matter because memory is a distorting mirror which bends the truth and reshapes images, events and the very facts of a past life. Just remember what you want and let it sink into your mind. Then you will find sleep. That's what the doctor had said.

Kay turned her mind back to the first tours of duty with the general in the summer of 1942.

It wasn't the chocolates or the fruit he had given her, the curiosity he showed about her Irish upbringing or the way he insisted on her joining his staff for meals. Such was the generous but conventional behaviour of a decent man in high office.

It was the touch of her hand on his as she leant over to put his drink on the table, the soapy scent of her body as she placed the urgent overnight messages on his desk in the morning, and the way he looked at her on horseback as she rose and fell in the saddle.

They would ride together once or twice a week, just the two of them, when they were staying at Telegraph Cottage. When she turned to check he was following she could see that look on his face.

But that wasn't where it had started. It had begun in the Packard, that long snout-nosed car which looked like a young whale on wheels. Bunched up with his team beside him, Eisenhower seemed happiest when he was in that car listening and debating while documents were passed back and forth amid a stream of profanity.

That's what Ike liked about the Packard. It took him out of smoky offices with portraits of long-dead British grandees on the wall, to streets and roads of city and countryside where his impatience would be calmed by changing scenery and the knowledge that he could switch direction with a single command.

On those daily trips their eyes would meet in the rear-view mirror, usually after he had thrown up his hands in exasperation at the drafting of a document or the comment of an aide. He would flash a look at her eyes in the mirror as if to say: "Can you believe these guys?"

She would smile encouragement but he wouldn't see that. He only ever saw her eyes in the Packard. That's when it had begun, a conspiracy of eyes meeting in a rear-view mirror. You tell nothing from a face but see a world in the eyes. A long-ago poet had said that. It was true.

And that night on his first day back in the country he had taken her hand, touched her gently on the back as she left to go to bed and said he had missed her.

Such memories did not help her sleep that night. Whatever lay between her and the boss had aroused scurrilous gossip. There would be a price to pay one day; that's what the vicious backchat told her.

Either way, even if he was aware of it, the talk didn't bother Eisenhower. He never took her into top-level meetings, nor would he reveal the momentous decisions that were taking shape behind closed doors across London. She would wait patiently in the Packard, reading some of the western thrillers he liked so much.

Then, when he got back into the car, she would gauge the mood in the rear-view mirror; if he was alone, and the timing was right, she would drop a comment about the latest plotline or character she had come across from those wild days out west when good and evil faced each other on dusty main streets with guns in their hands.

He loved those stories and she made sure he always had a pile of the latest editions, sent over from New York. They were by his bedside every night with the Lucky Strikes, the lighter, and a carafe of water.

9

May 1944

Erwin Rommel stood on the cliffs overlooking the French port of Boulogne, surveying the defences along beaches and dunes for miles in either direction. This was Hitler's Atlantic Wall, which stretched from Belgium along the length of the Channel coast all the way to the Cherbourg peninsula. As the newly promoted commander of Army Group B, Rommel's orders were to strengthen the wall and defend occupied Europe against an invasion they all knew was coming – an invasion by one and a half million men and the might of the United States of America together with Britain and what was left of her Empire.

There were just twenty miles of open sea from this point on the coast to Dover on the English coast. This is where the Allies would try and force a landing. Rommel was certain of it. He knew that reports of invasion across the longer sea journey to Normandy were a carefully created deception. No general in his right mind would choose a sixty-mile crossing on a sea open to the Atlantic to a calm twenty-mile crossing farther up the Channel.

The key to the coming battle was to know the mind of the man who had just been promoted to supreme Allied commander charged with liberating Europe: General Dwight Eisenhower. Know your enemy was the first rule of Clausewitz's teachings on warfare.

He sat down to read the file on Eisenhower in the drawing room of his headquarters, a twelfth-century chateau forty miles north of Paris. He ordered a pot of coffee and told his staff not to disturb him.

The file raised more questions than it answered. Eisenhower was a country boy from Kansas who had not done brilliantly at college or at the West Point Military Academy. He had been a sportsman at the former and something of a star poker player at the latter. He came across as a steady, studious learner who displayed no evident ambition to command men in battle.

Rommel frowned. How had a man with a lacklustre academic record at college and an undistinguished time at America's most famous military academy climbed so far as to become supreme Allied commander of the British and American armies now gathered across the Channel? How had Eisenhower, who had graduated from West Point as a second lieutenant in 1915, coming sixty-first in a class of 164, risen so high?

He read on. The file had been first prepared by the German military attaché in Washington before Pearl Harbor had brought America into the war in December 1941. Events surrounding Pearl Harbor provided half the answer. When the American battleships of the Pacific fleet lay sunk or smouldering at their Hawaii base, General George Marshall, the army chief of staff, had summoned Eisenhower, then a lowly two-star general, to Washington from his base in Antonio, Texas and asked for a plan of action.

Eisenhower had shone at army manoeuvres the previous autumn, and Marshall wanted to see whether this unknown general could rise to the crisis facing the nation and deliver strategic thinking to match his tactical skills.

Eisenhower had returned the same day with a plan to set up a major base in Australia with secure lines of communication from which to launch forces to defend Hawaii, Fiji and New Zealand from the Japanese. There were not enough available forces to cover every Allied territory. This meant exposing the Philippines to attack and possibly sacrificing US forces there.

Marshall accepted the plan, with the result that General MacArthur, the commander in the Philippines, who was robustly demanding reinforcements, was denied them. Furious, Patton flew to Australia, leaving behind an army that was forced to surrender to the Japanese. But the Eisenhower plan had saved bases and sea lanes vital for an American counterattack. The unknown general from Abilene was on his way.

Rommel read further.

There had to be something else to explain the accelerated promotion of a man who possessed none of the intellect or the gravitas of the great George Marshall. Now there was a man Rommel could admire. The American chief of staff had proved himself to be a professional soldier with intellect, ambition and the ability to take difficult decisions at dangerous moments on the battlefield.

The Wehrmacht high command, and indeed Hitler himself, had expected the president to appoint Marshall to command the Allied invasion forces, not Marshall's protégé, Eisenhower. Perhaps there was the key to the enigma – that word, *protégé*. Marshall, the finest military mind in Washington, had seen something in Eisenhower that had eluded German intelligence.

There were no clues in the family history. The file merely noted that the Eisenhauers had emigrated from Germany in

1741 and anglicised their name to Eisenhower sometime
during the years of travel across America which finally took
the family to Abilene, then the wildest of the western cattle
towns.

Eisenhower's personal life seemed conventional enough:
married at the age of twenty-six to Mamie Doud, a young
woman from a well-off family which ran a meatpacking
business. Their first child, a boy, had died of scarlet fever at
the age of three. A second son had appeared shortly after.
The death of his first son had reportedly devastated
Eisenhower.

Eisenhower's family tragedy might explain a certain
emotional detachment that had been noted in the profile, but
it still did not explain his rise to such prominence.

Rommel found the answer he was seeking at the very end
of the file in a section headed "Postscript":

> *Eisenhower's outstanding quality apart
> from purely professional skills is his tact,
> an unusual asset in an ambitious American
> commander. He has a quick temper with
> subordinates but conceals it well when
> dealing with his superiors. He deals
> effectively with difficult colleagues, sooth-
> ing ruffled feathers after the inevitable
> rows and disagreements. He projects
> personal warmth which makes him well
> liked at all levels of the service. However,
> on a personal level he is said to find
> difficulty in expressing his feelings apart
> from occasional outbursts of anger
> especially when playing bridge or poker
> with his colleagues.*

So that was it. The man had a political side, a charm rarely found in a soldier of such high rank. But charm alone could not explain why Roosevelt had overlooked Marshall and appointed Eisenhower to the top job. Roosevelt must have seen something else in the little-known general from the Midwest. Well, Eisenhower would need all his charm when dealing with that vainglorious bastard Montgomery, not to speak of the warmongering drunk, Churchill.

Rommel was about to close the file when he noticed an addendum on the final page, to which grainy black-and-white photographs had been attached. He glanced at the photos. They showed an attractive uniformed woman, probably in her mid-thirties, standing beside and behind Eisenhower, almost always with a large Packard in the fame. Her uniform was not military but seemed to have been put together by an organisation trying to look military. Beneath every photo the name *Summersby* had been written in indelible ink.

An anonymous intelligence officer in some bureaucratic backwater in Berlin with too much time on his hands had created profiles of every member of Eisenhower's senior staff. Summersby's promotion from driver to personal assistant and "confidante" was noted.

Rommel was interested. Civilian drivers did not become "confidantes" of senior generals without a very good reason. He at first suspected misinformation, a propaganda plant by Allied intelligence, but could see no reason for that.

Rommel found that friendly Latin American diplomats in Washington had passed on to Berlin the endless gossip which enlivened the cocktail party circuit in Georgetown and played out in the US press: the magazine pictures of Summersby standing right behind the so-called supreme commander on almost all official occasions told their own story.

Eisenhower's personal life was not as conventional as Rommel had supposed. He was having an affair with his driver. He had promoted the Summersby woman from his car to his bedroom. There could be no other explanation. He looked more carefully at the photographs attached to the file. The woman was definitely pretty, but looked too conventional to have become a mistress. Rommel rebuked himself. It was a foolish judgement. How could he possibly know what moved a man like Eisenhower to take up with his driver?

The fact was that if the Allied commander couldn't keep his flighty girlfriend a secret from the Washington press, how was he going to fool the German high command with a double invasion feint on the scale suggested? The invasion was obviously going to come across the narrow neck of the Channel to the Calais-Boulogne region. Only the Führer thought otherwise.

Rommel had enjoyed the reports on Summersby because they had showed up that lunatic Goebbels and his mad ideas. The propaganda chief had wanted to make much of Eisenhower's "sluttish Irish mistress", as he called her. He had planned to beam English and Spanish language broadcasts across the Atlantic, hoping to entangle Eisenhower in damaging publicity.

The Führer had rebuked him, a rare but welcome occurrence as far as Rommel was concerned. Goebbels was told not to waste his time. All American commanders kept mistresses when on active service, Hitler had said; it was almost a tradition in the US Army. Rommel knew there was another reason for the Führer's reticence. Hitler's inner circle were well-aware that he kept his own mistress, Eva Braun, tucked away in the Berghof, his mountain retreat in Bavaria.

The German commander drew back the heavy brocade curtains of the drawing room and looked into the darkness.

The stars were disappearing behind cloud. A north wind would bring rain that night. The fast-changing weather along the Channel would be an ally in the battle to come, another line of defence.

IO

June 1944

For Kay Summersby and those who worked closely with her, the invasion of Europe began amid a rain-lashed tented encampment, generously described as a command head-quarters, and ended in the sunshine of a Normandy orchard.

The thread of time that connected these two settings unspooled at a pace so swift that those who found themselves camped among laden apple trees looked back in disbelief at what had happened since they had stepped out of their tents that rainy morning. Four weeks had passed. It seemed like a day.

It was just before four in the morning on the 5th of June when Kay brewed up coffee in a canvas kitchen tent alongside Eisenhower's camouflaged trailer in the woods near Portsmouth. She knocked briefly on the door and, hearing no reply, went in. Ike was sitting in semi-darkness on the edge of his bed rubbing his eyes.

"Boss, it's time to go," she said, handing him the steaming cup of coffee. Twenty minutes later, showered, shaved and wearing his battledress, Eisenhower was driven for a final conference with his generals, their senior staff and, crucially, the weather men.

Kay could hear every stitch of canvas in the tented camps around the headquarters straining in the wind and rain as they hurried, heads down, to the car for the drive to Portsmouth.

The night before, her boss had paced the carpeted floor in the trailer, chain-smoking, flicking ash into fag-end choked ashtrays, coughing occasionally and sometimes bending double with indigestion. All the while the wind and rain battered against the windows.

Well past midnight Kay had tried to leave, telling her boss to get some sleep. He refused.

"You're staying. I may need a driver any time."

"I'm not staying. You need sleep, not a driver."

She would not normally talk to him like that. But he didn't snap back. He just looked at his watch and lit another cigarette. It was just after one a.m. when she left the trailer, hoping for a few hours' sleep. As she closed her tent flap, Kay saw the light in the trailer go off.

It seemed only minutes later that she was opening the trailer door and handing him a cup of coffee. She next remembered opening the car door and watching Eisenhower walk through a gap in the camouflage netting that disguised the command headquarters of the Allied Expeditionary Force just outside Portsmouth. It was before dawn and still dark.

They were all there – Montgomery and British and American army, navy and air force commanders, all but Montgomery in battledress. Monty always liked to be different. He was wearing a fawn pullover with corduroys and a black beret.

They listened to the latest weather reports: a zone of high pressure was trailing a depression which was already passing through the Channel. Better weather could be expected to reach the Channel the following morning, June 6th. Critically the swell would have lessened, allowing landing craft onto the beaches.

The weather man brought the meeting to a conclusion. "Listen," he said. Outside the wind had dropped, the lashing rain had eased into a ghostly pattering on the windowpanes. The sky was lightening outside. Everyone turned to Eisenhower.

"OK, we'll go," he said, looking at every face in the room in turn, not seeking agreement but wishing to imprint the finality of his decision on those present. He was met with smiles of relief.

Outside Kay was waiting in the car. It was still raining. She wound the window down and threw out a glowing stub. It was against his orders, but if ever there was a day to break the rules it was this day.

Ike got back into the car, lit a cigarette, drew on it with one deep breath then threw it out of the window.

He looked in the rear mirror and nodded. "It's on," he said.

The greatest military adventure in history remained in Kay's mind as a series of jumbled images lacking sequence or meaning until placed in the context of the cryptic code name, "D-Day".

A child's drawing, a painted portrait of an ancestor, a blurred photo in a family album, an inky signature scrawled on an old love letter, a faded order of service for a funeral – such images open memories like flowers in the morning. So it was with Kay and D-Day:

The sun setting in a paint box of colours that evening, broad brush strokes of red, orange and purple.

Faces of the paratroops blackened with charcoal and cocoa.

The ghostly features of Eisenhower moving among these men in darkness, shaking hands, accepting whispered messages to loved ones. In his face the pride of a father with his sons, the love of a man for his true family, a brotherhood of men at arms.

The way his eyes clouded, the way he bent his head to hear a soldier's whispered remark, the way he took out a white handkerchief and blew his nose, the tears visible in his eyes, wiped away with the back of his hand.

Camouflaged troops, silky shadows in the darkness, their voices those of the night. In a few hours many would be dead. Everyone knew that.

Occasional torch flashes showing the easy familiarity with which the men carried their rifles and the way their battledress bulged with rations, spare ammunition and bandages.

Wingtips flashing white lights as the aircraft took off and climbed to join the armada above.

The sparkle of distant stars in a crowded sky.

Cigarettes glowing like fireflies as they watched from the roof of the control tower the first, and for many men the final, act of liberation.

She saw it all because he had ordered her to stay close as he moved among his men. She was to write down the names of those he talked to. She bent close to them with her notebook. Their breath smelt of chewing gum and whisky. He said nothing to her that night. He was not smoking. He seemed much calmer. Then came a story that would never be forgotten or retold.

It was well after midnight when they arrived at the final airbase that night. Unusually the men kept their distance. They didn't look their commander in the face nor did they crowd around him. Eisenhower quickly learnt the reason. A platoon commander, a young officer in his twenties, had retreated to the command hut and was refusing to come out. Kay heard the word "breakdown" whispered in Eisenhower's ear.

Ike looked at an aide and nodded towards the hut. The two men walked over, opened the door and went in. Eisenhower paused at the door, looked back at Kay and nodded. She slipped in behind him and stood against a wall.

The soldier was squatting on the floor, hunched forward, his back against a wall, visibly trembling. Kay noticed his hands immediately. They were twisting and turning into each other as if trying to break free. There were streaks of tears on his charcoal-blackened face. His rifle was lying some distance away, suggesting it had been thrown rather than placed on the ground.

Eisenhower leant his back against the wall, slid down and squatted beside him. The two men stared ahead, neither looking at the other; Eisenhower spoke slowly and softly.

"Soldier, I am your commanding officer, I want you to stand up. Right now."

The soldier sniffed, rubbed the back of his hand against his nose and remained where he was. He was still shaking, not violently but as if possessed of a high fever. His hands continued to writhe like tethered puppies. Eisenhower got to his feet. He did not look at the man. His voice hardened.

"Get to your feet, soldier. Now."

Slowly the man stood up and swayed slightly on his feet, looking down. Eisenhower faced him for the first time.

"Your name and rank, soldier?"

"McMichael, sir. Captain."

"Look at me, Captain."

The soldier remained looking down and spoke in a whisper.

"I can't do it, sir. I'm sorry."

Kay tried to gauge his age. He looked no more than a boy but was perhaps twenty-three, a young officer schooled in the art of war at West Point. There was no wedding ring on his finger but there would be a girl somewhere, a fiancée maybe. Behind the tears and the camouflage he was a good-looking young man.

Eisenhower unbuttoned his tunic and opened it.

"Put your hand on my heart, Captain."

The man shook his head and mumbled something inaudible.

"Do it."

Kay wanted to shout "Don't do it! Stay as you are!" The soldier wiped the back of his hand across his nose again, sniffed and, still looking down, placed his hand inside Eisenhower's tunic.

"Look at me, soldier."

The man looked up.

"What do you feel?"

"Your heart, sir."

"And?"

"It's beating, sir."

"If our hearts don't beat, what happens?"

"Sir?"

"We die, right?"

The man began to pull his hand back but Eisenhower took it gently and placed it back on his chest.

"Am I right – we die?"

"Yes, sir."

"If we die, we don't fight, do we, we don't win?"

"No, sir. I mean yes, sir – yes."

"We lose, right? All of us here on this island and back home in the States, we lose everything."

They looked at each other in silence. Kay wondered whether American officers were trained in this somewhat sinister way of dealing with reluctant soldiers. It was like watching a puppet being jerked around on a string or a child being coaxed from a hiding place.

"That's right, isn't it, Captain?"

The soldier nodded but said nothing.

"Say it, Captain."

"Yes, sir, that's right, sir."

The man was standing straight now. He was still trembling slightly but had stopped sniffing. Eisenhower took the man's hand away and buttoned up his uniform.

He had won, thought Kay. A broken man had been put back on his feet and patched up for the battle ahead. The honour of the unit had been saved. A cynical appeal to patriotism had denied a sick man the treatment he clearly needed.

For a moment the two men paused, looking at each other. Eisenhower spoke slowly and softly.

"Pick up your rifle, Captain."

The man hesitated for a moment and then walked across the room, bent down and picked up the weapon.

He straightened up, faced his commander and saluted.

Eisenhower returned the salute. Kay watched as he stood aside to let McMichael leave the room first. She did not know whether to feel admiration or repulsion for the scene she had just witnessed.

Long after midnight he sat in his command trailer, smoke rising from his cigarette, while she worked on his shoulders. They were as hard and tense as a ship's cable. Eisenhower had sent everyone else to bed.

McKeogh checked his watch. In a few hours it would be dawn. Ships and planes were on the move across the Channel. A million men were preparing to assault heavily defended beaches. He was shocked to see that once again that woman remained at Eisenhower's side. There had been no attempt to disguise the fact: he had said quite openly within hearing of those around, "Come and work my shoulders, Kay."

And that was what she did. He had stripped to the waist, and in the mirror on a side wall she watched his eyes close as she worked to unclench the fists of muscle around his neck and shoulders.

She knew it was the only way he would get a few hours' sleep. She knew too that in their tents pitched around Ike's trailer, his aides and security guards would exchange the same old vicious gossip. She almost exulted in the venom aroused by these late-night visits to the trailer. He had made her the queen in his circle. He needed her at his side, especially now.

That he needed his shoulders rubbed was all anyone needed to know tonight or any other. They did not need to know how, stripped to the waist, he enjoyed the warmth of her hands on his back and shoulders. In the early hours of D-Day, with Kay Summersby at his side in the command trailer, worries faded from his mind and became no more than the barking of dogs in the night. She put warmth and movement into what had been twisted into knots. After a few minutes he reached back, twisted round and took her hand.

"Thank you," he said. She kissed him quickly on the cheek, a touch of the lips, a whisper of a kiss.

I I

June 1944

A sudden vanishing. It was the old stage trick much loved in children's pantomimes. A bang, a puff of smoke, a *deus ex machina* rises to the stage from the bowels of the theatre, the scenery changes, new players come on.

After the sound and fury of D-Day the pastoral peace of a Normandy orchard, where Ike had made his forward base, felt just like that. The camp was a picture postcard of rural bliss, filmic fantasy, a Hollywood setting for a wartime epic.

The command headquarters had been set up amid fruit-laden trees that sloped gently down to a river. Next to an old stone barn, a large wooden-floored tent had been erected as an office. A communications room was attached under a camouflaged canvas wing of the main tent; a trailer served as the general's living quarters.

The staff all lived under canvas close to the river. Only Kay had a tent to herself. At night the only sound was the rhythmic murmur of the river, and the occasional sharp cry as a fox or a smaller predator made a kill. The rumble of distant artillery fire was the only reminder of the war that was being directed from this haven.

Kay fell asleep most nights thinking of Captain McMichael and remembering his tear-streaked face. She wondered what had happened to him.

Eisenhower had sent for his close aides, including Kay, when it became clear that the German lines were holding and there would be no early breakout from Normandy.

The reed-lined banks coiled around the orchard headquarters, providing a measure of security on which the Allied commander's special forces security unit had insisted.

The protection unit patrolled the surrounding woods and fields day and night, taking turns to sleep in camouflaged bivouacs. Eisenhower had personally supervised these arrangements. He had been told he was a target for assassination. At least that's what British intelligence said, but Eisenhower doubted it. The Brits were good at magnifying risks and dangers.

At night Kay and McKeogh produced rations from a makeshift kitchen in the barn. Ike had turned down offers from local farmers of food and suggestions that their wives might cook for him.

He was only ever alone with Kay late at night when the last planning session had finished and the rest of the team had returned to their tents. Then it was the usual last, long, weak whisky, a quick talk about Telek, who was said to be pining for his master in kennels in England, and perhaps questions about the progress of the vegetable patch at Telegraph Cottage. He would talk about anything but the war and the military stalemate that had followed the success of D-Day.

"What are you going to do when the war is over?" she asked one night.

"I hate that question," he said. "The simple answer is I don't know. I'll probably get some boring job in DC."

"Don't be silly," she said. "You're going to be a national hero. They'll put you in command of the whole army."

"I don't know who 'they' are, but a lot of silly things get said in Washington. And you, what are you going to do?"

She looked at him. He gave her the Eisenhower smile, quick and toothy.

"You know what I am going to do – I think."

"Sure I do."

"I suppose I might go back to London, wander around the bombsites and drink a lot of gin."

"Or you might obey orders?" he was still smiling.

"What orders? I'm not in the army."

Two could play this game, she thought.

"You're under my command, right?" he said.

"I know my duty, if that's what you mean."

"Touché!" he said and laughed.

Only the maddening behaviour of Montgomery and his failure to deliver repeated promises to break through German defence lines brought military problems bubbling into the evening conversations. Kay listened night after night as Ike vented his anger at the British field marshal. One night he went further than usual, kicking out at chairs as he paced the room.

"Montgomery could have finished Rommel off in the desert back in '42 but he didn't have the nerve. If he had had one tenth of Patton's guts or Bradley's imagination we wouldn't be stuck in this godforsaken orchard. He doesn't like spilling blood, that's his problem."

She calmed him, pointing out that if ever fate had decided to create two gifted but wholly incompatible military men it would be him and Montgomery.

He smiled at the remark and shook his head.

"You need to get some sleep," she said. She was always the one who decided it was time to leave, taking with her the brimming ashtrays and empty glasses.

She knew he was watching her as she left, and she knew too that his anger and frustration concealed desire. They both knew that. They had both chosen to ignore it. Tonight felt different.

"Kay, come here," he called.

She returned and he took her face gently between his hands. He looked at her, his face close to hers. Then he kissed her lightly on the lips. The kiss lit a flame. He moved his hands behind her head and covered her face and neck with little kisses. After a moment he dropped his hands and stepped away saying nothing. Their shared surprise had left them silent.

She wanted him to kiss her again, and knew he would, and that it would be very different from the chance encounter in the back of the big transport plane.

That quick kiss in the dark on the plane had brought them much closer. What had been clear on the plane was now even clearer in the apple orchard in Normandy.

He stepped back now, smiling, and turned and walked to the drinks trolley.

"How about a drink?" he said.

Still speechless with surprise, she nodded. He poured the drinks, put them on the low coffee table and sat down on the sofa.

"Come here," he said, patting the sofa beside him.

The bucolic setting did much to fill the family photograph albums that would be admired back home in years to come but did little to calm the nerves within the command tent.

Eisenhower left every morning to inspect units on the front line that now took in Normandy and much, but not all, of the Cherbourg peninsula.

In the last week of June the battle for Normandy was approaching a climax. The Allies had intercepted the German high command's instructions that German forces should be ordered to fight to the last man. Eisenhower noted with interest that Rommel had passed the order on but changed it to read "fight to the last bullet". The German general obviously had no appetite for Hitler's "death or glory" battle orders.

The German line was close to collapse. It was a matter of when and where the breakthrough would come. These questions wormed their way into every conversation in the headquarters camp, much as swarms of wasps fell on the fallen fruit around the tents.

Those under Eisenhower's command felt his frustration. Montgomery barked back in short sharp messages by cable and secure phone lines and occasionally apologised for his slow progress.

At the end of June Eisenhower left the apple orchard and returned to London to brief Winston Churchill and, rather more importantly, his own superior, George Marshall, the US chief of staff, on the military situation. He knew Marshall was sure to query the slow progress in breaking out of Normandy.

Kay was first off the plane at Portsmouth and slipped behind the wheel of his Packard, having made sure the car was flying both flags, the Stars and Stripes and the Union Jack, for the drive to the War Ministry in London. It was ten a.m. and she had promised to deliver him no later than noon. By now she knew every bump and bend in the road.

She remained, in theory, just his driver, although in the operational areas of Normandy he had forbidden her to take the wheel of his jeep. But she had still accompanied him every day as a secretary, diary keeper, coffee maker, always with a spare pack of Lucky Strikes in her pocket.

Everyone accepted that Ike rarely moved without her and did so only when he visited front line positions. Her presence alongside her boss was such a familiar sight that whenever they met General Bradley he would greet them with a salute for Eisenhower and then turn to her saying, "Oh, here's Ike's shadow." He didn't seem to mind a bit.

The day-long meeting at the ministry broke up shortly before five p.m.

Ike looked out of the window. Kay was standing beside the Packard, waiting to drive him to Telegraph Cottage, where Mickey McKeogh and Butch were preparing an evening meal. They did not have to be told what to cook – it was always the best Scotch steak. He could see she was anxious to get going. She would have to wait. Marshall had called him back to the conference room.

Eisenhower refused a cup of coffee and waited. The chief of staff had already made valuable tactical suggestions during the conference and drawn together the various strategic threads which criss-crossed the table as everyone spoke their minds, delivered their briefs and gave their opinions. He had woven these threads into a narrative that left everyone confident that they had just heard a plan that would bring the war to an end within months.

"You're looking tired," said Marshall.

"There's a lot on, General."

"Don't we know it. They're looking after you, are they?"

"Sure. I'm more worried about casualties – we're getting there but losing a lot of men. Same with Monty's people around Caen. He's flattened the place and the Germans are still fighting."

"Monty's a problem, I know that. But I'm more worried about you. Who's looking after you these days? You still got Lee, McKeogh, and that Brit on your staff?"

Eisenhower did not rise to the very obvious bait.

"Sure. I've got a great team. They take real good care of me."

"That driver you had in England, is she still with you?"

Eisenhower reached for the cigarette packet in his pocket and lit one, exhaling a long plume of smoke high into the air. So this was what the meeting was about. Marshall knew perfectly well that Summersby was still working for him.

"Sure. Kay Summersby is a member of my team. She does a great job."

There was a pause as Marshall in turn lit a cigarette.

"I'm sure she does. But there's a lot of talk in DC," he said.

"It wouldn't be DC if there wasn't."

"This is kinda personal talk, Ike, you and that driver."

He and Marshall were as close as two senior officers get in the military, but not Christian name close. Marshall wasn't like that.

"Really?"

"Yeah. She goes everywhere with you – lunch with Churchill, picnics in the desert with the president."

"That was a year back…"

"Then there's that cottage."

"Come on, George."

He wanted to see how Marshall would take the use of his first name: whether it would bring the meeting down to casual comradely talk between two brothers-in-arms.

Marshall stubbed his cigarette out, twisting the butt into the ashtray vigorously.

"It doesn't look great."

"Meaning?"

"Look, it's your choice, your command, your staff…"

"Thanks for reminding me."

"…but I wouldn't be doing my job if I didn't offer a little advice."

"Which is?"

"Drop her. Get another driver."

Eisenhower looked at Marshall, eyes narrowed.

"Are you telling me to fire a loyal and efficient member of my own staff at a time like this?"

"In a word, yes."

"Is that an order?"

"It's just good advice."

"Do you really think that's appropriate right now?"

"Some folks back home think it's not appropriate that you've got so close to her."

"Please tell some folks back home that we've got a war to win and that's rather more important than who drives my car."

Eisenhower stood up and looked out of the window. The engine of the Packard was running. He could see Kay in the front seat. She had lit a cigarette and was blowing smoke out of the window. That was against the rules. He would talk to her about that.

"OK, Ike. It was only advice."

"Thanks, General."

The two men shook hands. Marshall's grip was hard, and the metallic blue eyes that looked straight at Eisenhower were cold.

Damn you, thought Eisenhower. He was in the middle of a campaign that was costing heavy casualties. He was having difficulty dealing with a Brit field marshal who was not up to the job, and a prime minister who thought he could do Eisenhower's job. Patton was on his back night and day, and

Bradley was bitching about Monty. And he'd just got a piece of snide criticism from his chief of staff about a member of his team who happened to be an attractive woman.

Was that her fault? Was it her fault she was doing a great job for him? Was it his fault that he happened to like her company and enjoy a late-night drink and a chat with her? So what if people gossiped in DC or over here – damn the lot of them. And damn George Marshall. He loved him like a brother but he was well out of line on this.

So Marshall thought he was having an affair with her and couldn't bring himself to say so? Well, he wasn't. All right, he had kissed her. Plenty of times in fact. And he had held her close, feeling her body against his. Back in Kansas when he was young his parents would have called that making love.

But that was then. Now a kiss was just a kiss. It wasn't an affair. Did he want to have an affair with her? Hell, yes – who wouldn't? She was more than just an attractive woman. She meant a great deal to him. But he was a soldier. He knew his duty. And George Marshall should know his. Which was to leave him to get on with this war and stop worrying about what the gossips back home were saying.

Eisenhower told himself that was a sensible and logical reaction to an out of line intrusion into the way he ran the war. But there was another small voice which told him that Marshall might have had a point. He had feelings for Kay Summersby, he could hardly deny that.

They had kissed and would kiss again. The taste of her lips and the scent of her forbidden perfume lingered like a long sunset. Kay and her perfume were supposed to be against the rules, beyond reach. Maybe that was why he wanted her so much.

Or maybe it was the war. The casualty reports crossed his desk every morning. He dreaded those documents. The dead were not just numbers on paper. He had seen their bodies in the field, young men with bodies ripped open, their entrails spilling onto the earth, others gazing sightlessly at the sky without a mark on them but very dead.

He had seen men die in the forward nursing stations, some while they struggled to speak to him or shake his hand. No man could look on such sights without silent shame, rage and the fearful knowledge that there were many more deaths to come.

That is why he needed her, to help him escape, even for moments, from the battle orders and the death and destruction that followed.

Who was that Brit writer he had read about somewhere who had seen a woman being hanged, struggling in the noose, in London a century or so ago and who had sought "immediate release between a woman's legs".

Death does that to you. It makes you want to live, to erase forever the memory of that woman choking at the end of a rope. It is a fearful reminder that you are alive and have a life to live. There was no maybe about it; that is why he wanted her so much.

And Mamie? He wrote long loving letters to her, didn't he? And he loved her as any man would love a wife of some twenty-five years and the mother of his children. Of course he did. But Kay was different. She was here with him now.

He loved having her around. He still held the memory of cupping her breasts tightly in the darkness on the plane. He had held them in his hands, soft but firm, and felt her nipples harden. If it had been anywhere else he would have gone further. He couldn't do without her. That was the truth. And the men that really mattered, his senior commanders, Bradley, Clark and Patton, knew that and never raised an eyebrow.

Throughout the summer Eisenhower and his immediate staff flew regularly between his campaign headquarters at Versailles and the headquarters of the Allied war effort in England.

One night at Telegraph Cottage Kay cooked dinner, with Mickey's help in the kitchen – a roast chicken and vegetables from the patch that Ike had sown earlier that year. Averell Harriman, Roosevelt's ambassador to Britain, and his wife Marie had come for dinner, bringing with them a gift of malt whisky and London's latest gossip.

All the talk was of the damage done in and around the capital by Hitler's new rockets. Telegraph Cottage was only fifteen miles from the centre of London and several V1 rockets had already landed close by. Confidential reports that the V1s, which lacked any navigation system, had been replaced by a larger, more accurate rocket that would be immune to interception were even more worrying for those in on the secret.

Harriman said that Londoners would quickly realise that the Nazis' new and more deadly form of aerial bombardment was invulnerable to anti-aircraft fire. Civilian morale, which had risen to a crest after D-Day, would slump at the prospect of a new phase in the air war. *London can take it!* had been the civilian battle cry all through the Blitz three years previously, but that spirit had gone.

There was now a sullen and fearful awareness of sudden death from the skies. The incoming howl of the first V1 rockets cut out moments before impact, leaving those below wondering and waiting in dread and suspense for the explosion. There would be no sound at all from the V2s except a sudden *whoosh* as if the air had been sucked into the sky and then a shattering explosion. It would be hard to take.

Kay watched Eisenhower as he listened to the ambassador's account of the new dangers of life in a city that thought it had been freed from sudden death. There was a not-so-subtle subtext to the conversation, and she could see from the frown lines on her boss's face that he understood exactly what was being suggested: for God's sake break out of Normandy and nail those rocket sites.

After dinner the four played bridge. Kay partnered Ike, as usual, and they won the first rubber. As Harriman later said to his wife, the two played as if each knew the mind of the other.

"Hardly surprising," said a sleepy voice from the bed. "They play regularly together. It's his way of relaxing, they say."

"I could have sworn he squeezed her hand under the table. I think they were cheating," he said.

"Don't be so bloody naïve," she said and went to sleep.

12

July 1944

The truth which Rommel had dismissed as a ghostly apparition from the darkest depth of his mind had emerged to assume reality. He and his men were committing themselves to a losing battle on behalf of a bestial political order. His soldiers would die in their tens – no, hundreds – of thousands for a lost, satanic cause.

Eisenhower had done it. Rommel never thought the man had the imagination and the nerve to throw a million troops across the Channel at its widest point when the weather kept even the inshore fishermen in harbour. The main thrust and the obvious line of attack was to the beaches along Pas-de-Calais, but "obvious" had been a trap into which they had all fallen.

The Führer had reacted in characteristic and calamitous fashion. There was to be no tactical retreat. Every position must be held to the last man. Since telephone lines to coastal units had been destroyed and radio was not deemed to be secure, Rommel used motorcycle riders to convey the Führer's orders to the coast.

He could imagine what that would do to the morale of young soldiers shocked, deafened and terrified by the naval barrage. Thank God, he thought, that his son Manfred was not two years older.

That night in the chateau, Rommel briefly left his staff officers to grapple with the developing crisis while he retired to the study, where he reopened the file on Eisenhower. He turned to his days at West Point where the young lieutenant had proved so skilled in the weekly poker games. Poker was a game of deception and bluff.

Eisenhower had made money, if not friends, in those games. At the same time he had been trained in the art of camouflage and deception, an important part of the West Point curriculum; and deception was the crucial skill required for a winning poker player. Rommel hadn't thought this important when he'd first read the profile.

What was the Allied commander's next move? Where was George Patton really, the one general who could be relied on to make the big breakout from the beachheads the Allies would need? Could it still just possibly be true that Normandy was a poker bluff?

How could anyone read the mind of this man who faced him, not across the Channel now but on French soil?

And what of Hitler's secret weapons that were supposed to swing the balance of war back to Berlin? Rommel briefly thought of the rockets that were being launched at London from silos in the countryside near Calais.

They would not make any difference. Nothing would make any difference now. Rommel knew that. He also knew that the high command in Berlin and the Führer himself were in the grip of insanity.

Suspecting treachery after the initial success of the Allied Normandy landings, Hitler had sacked all his senior commanders in France except Rommel. The German general was left alone that month to face the Allied onslaught with orders from the Führer that forbade the obvious strategy of a fighting retreat. For the man hero-worshipped by his countrymen, it was further confirmation that the war was lost. He knew too that he had not long to live.

The pilot of the Spitfire saw the open Horch car driving at speed on a small country road in Normandy. The road was tree-lined but the vehicle was clearly visible when it left the cover of overhanging branches. From a height of eight hundred feet the pilot could see there was a pennant on the vehicle. He knew from briefings that this was the staff car of a senior German officer. He knew too that the car was driving on a small country road for a very good reason. The main roads were choked with burning, broken vehicles and with refugees fleeing the fighting further West.

Manoeuvring the aircraft into position and dropping to treetop height, he opened fire at a range of six hundred yards, pumping machine-gun and cannon fire into the vehicle. Bark and wood splintered off trees and fountains of earth rose from the roadside. As the plane flashed past he saw the car careen off the road, through the trees and down a steep slope.

Rommel recovered consciousness, though only barely, the next day in a military hospital. He had no memory of the attack nor any idea where he was.

He was told he was still in France. He had a fractured skull and was lucky to be alive. His driver and a third man in the vehicle were dead.

That same day, at his command headquarters near Portsmouth, Eisenhower paced the floor of his trailer like a caged tiger. The cinder track outside the trailer was gradually crunched into a smooth furrow as the restless commander walked back and forth, peering at the lowering clouds above.

Churchill arrived in time for lunch and didn't complain when presented with cold beef sandwiches accompanied by a bottle of red wine. Kay joined them at the table, officially as a note-taker, although the prime minister had long ago accepted that her role now was that of hostess. Eisenhower frowned, looked down at the table and seemed to sink into his own thoughts as Churchill launched into a long history of famous battles won by British generals.

The purpose of the sweeping summary of military triumphs became clear when he came to the Battle of El Alamein in 1942. Montgomery might be a difficult wartime colleague, Churchill said, but his victory in the North African desert that year had turned the tide of the war against Hitler.

Eisenhower raised himself from his reverie and said, "*Difficult*, did you say, prime minister?"

Churchill, ever the conversational tactician, changed the subject and looked out of the window at the grey murk outside.

"You won't be flying today, general," he said.

"I'll cross that damned Channel tomorrow even if I have to swim," came the reply.

Churchill raised his glass and proposed a toast to a safe journey.

The trouble, as usual, was the weather. Fog had descended on the south coast, and the commander's B-25 plane was grounded. Kay had never seen him so frustrated and depressed; he was a man wrapped in a mood of pure blue indigo, as Tex put it, a remark so memorable that Kay made a mental note to put it in her diary later; she thought she might try to turn it into a song she would sing for him that night at drinks before dinner.

It was a silly idea, but she and the rest of the staff were prepared to try anything to take the boss's mind off the frustrations of the weather. Ike badly wanted to take a hard look on the ground at Montgomery's bungled campaign since D-Day.

The time had come for a face-to-face talk with a man who was causing division and dissent within the Allied command. Senior people around Eisenhower, and not just American generals such as Omar Bradley, who had never disguised his loathing of Monty, but also his British deputy, Air Marshal Tedder, were urging Ike to sack him.

Monty had failed to deliver his long-promised break-through on the Allies' northern flank. He issued communiqués, without reference to Allied headquarters, in which every setback was somehow hailed as a victory. Ike had had enough. The mere mention of Montgomery's name was enough to send his blood pressure soaring.

"Fact is that if Rommel had been British and Monty German, the war would have been over long before now."

Having blazed with praise for the supreme commander after D-Day, American radio and newspaper journalists were now criticising Eisenhower for being little more than a figurehead in a war in which the British were taking all the credit and doing far too little of the fighting and dying.

Montgomery wasn't the only problem; Churchill was another. The prime minister prowled around Allied headquarters, criticising plans for an invasion of southern France, demanding to be allowed to visit the battlefront, and above all thundering on about the damage done by the German rockets. He was always meddling, and had even visited Ike and the family at Telegraph Cottage, there to marvel at the general's interest in his vegetable garden.

Kay smiled as she watched Ike walk Churchill around his small kitchen garden, pointing out rows of vegetables, some already climbing neatly placed bamboo canes, and explaining when he had personally seeded the beds. He was especially proud of the large-sized marrows but admitted that American corn had failed miserably in the English climate.

Churchill pretended to take an interest. It was a mark of his humanity, Kay told her mother in a letter, that he completely understood Eisenhower's need to find a sanctuary at Telegraph Cottage.

"You wouldn't believe how two men could be so different," she wrote. "Ike handed the PM a marrow and Churchill looked at it as if someone had thrust a dribbling baby into his arms. He was smoking his usual cigar and the ash fell all over the marrow. Ike took it back looking offended. I don't think Churchill had ever seen a raw vegetable, let alone a marrow, in his life."

Drawing Kay aside before he left, Churchill said, as he had said in North Africa the year before, "I am so glad you're continuing to look after our general, giving him all he needs."

Looking into his face, Kay found not a hint of hidden meaning in that remark. Whatever he was inferring Churchill knew exactly how important she was.

Eisenhower was at his desk at the Portsmouth headquarters with a gusting wind threatening rain outside. She was still wearing the light cotton uniform he had ordered for her in North Africa. He looked up, took off his reading glasses and said, "Take a seat."

She sat down on one the chairs in front of his desk.

"I think you need a new uniform."

"Oh, no thank you, sir, this will do fine."

"Nonsense. It looks worn."

He was right of course. Her skirt was not only baggy but had a shiny seat from sliding in and out of the staff car. And the thin cotton offered little comfort against the chill of an English summer. She had been forced to buy thick woollen underwear to wear against the cold.

"But you've already given me two new uniforms, sir. I don't need another one."

"Those were desert uniforms. You'll need two new ones. I'll have them made up for you."

There was no point arguing with Ike. When he wanted something done he issued an order and that was it. Life in the army was so simple, she thought. You gave orders and obeyed them. There were no arguments, no appeals to common sense, no shades of meaning, none of the misunderstandings that tangled the lives of ordinary people.

The military admitted none of the complexities and mysteries of civilian life where ordinary people sought guidance from custom, conscience, religion or maybe even the stars above. It was easy to get lost in the real world. In the army you might get killed but you never got lost.

Kay wondered what the rigid certainties of the military mind would make of the greatest mystery of all: in some far stratum of the sky beyond sight but within the girdle of the planet there must be someone or something who understood the mysterious attraction one earthbound mortal feels for another. Poets called it love, but that was too easy. Kay knew that no one who had spent a lifetime in the army would ever understand that.

"Thank you, sir," she said.

"They should be ready in a couple of weeks. They don't work as fast here as in Tangiers."

"Sir," she said.

"Yes?"

Ike looked at her sharply. She took a deep breath.

"Everyone else has to make do with what they've got. I don't want any special favours, thank you."

He said nothing but came round the desk and sat next to her as she lowered her eyes.

"You do a lot for me and I just want to say thank you. That's all. If people want to talk let them."

"You don't have to thank me. I'm just doing my job, sir," she said. She was whispering and didn't know why.

"And I'm doing mine. Part of that job is to look after my staff who are very special to me – all of them."

"I know, sir," she said, wanting to fling herself into his arms and say, "You're very special to me too."

But she didn't. He briefly took her hand and squeezed it, then suddenly stood up, returned to the desk and said in a clenched voice, "That will be all for now."

Afterwards she put his words together as one might a jigsaw puzzle. She wanted to understand what this man really felt for her.

He had told her after the *Strathallen* sinking that she meant something special to him, that he had missed her, that he had cursed himself for putting her at risk on a convoy vessel.

Those words and the way he touched her, leaning on her shoulders while looking over her head at a document, holding her hand after a long shoulder massage, would be a declaration of love in any other man. But her boss fought such emotions. He recoiled from anything he said or did that might reveal inner feelings.

The next two days were the worst any of the staff could recall in Eisenhower's service. His temper flamed at odd moments over minor matters. He snapped at innocent remarks and snarled answers to questions raised even by senior colleagues.

"What the hell has got into him?" said Tex to no one in particular.

None of the staff could find logic in the sullen temper of the man they served. Montgomery had not crossed the general's path for several days, and that other irritant, General de Gaulle, was sulking as usual over some perceived slight.

Stranger still, the Allies had finally broken out of Normandy and the war was going well with General Patton on the rampage towards Paris.

"Beats the hell out of me," said Tex. "What's up, Kay, any idea?"

Kay shook her head. Whatever the problem was, and she had a shrewd idea, she felt it was time someone talked to the general about his behaviour.

She went to his office, knocked on the door and entered on a barked command from within.

"Yes?" he said without looking up.

"I've decided that I do not need new uniforms, sir. They are a wartime extravagance, but thank you for the offer."

He looked up, frowning.

"You're going to get measured for those uniforms and you will do so tomorrow. The tailor will be here at nine a.m."

"I would rather not, sir."

"That's an order, Miss Summersby."

He stood up, red-faced, leaning forward on the desk on clenched fists.

"And I am not allowed to refuse an order from my commander-in-chief?"

"Damn right you're not."

He came round the desk and stood in front of her. They glared at each other.

"Have you got anything to say?" His voice was softer this time.

"No, sir."

"You walk into my office and tell me you don't want new uniforms when only a few days ago you told me you needed them!"

She hadn't said anything of the sort, but there was no point arguing.

"I explained why, sir."

"No, you didn't. What's going on?"

"I was going to ask you the same question, sir."

He looked down, shook his head, stepped back and threw his arms up in the air.

"Sir, I..."

"Listen. When the signal came through that night the *Strathallen* went down I felt as if the ground had been cut from under my feet. I went through hell that night. I cursed myself for not having had you fly out."

"Sir..."

"Don't say anything. I was never going to tell you how I felt, and sweet Jesus I don't know how I've found the guts to do so now."

"Ike, I just want to say..."

"Goddammit!"

He had his hands on her shoulders and shook her lightly. Suddenly they were in each other's arms, kissing with the passion of a lovers' farewell.

It was Kay who broke away. What if Tex walked in as he had a habit of doing without knocking? There were lipstick smudges all over Ike's neck and cheeks. She licked the corner of a handkerchief and began wiping his face. She tried to keep hold of her thoughts, which were tumbling over each other like flotsam in floodwater. He loved her. That was all that mattered.

Ike looked serious and said, "I don't want you to be hurt. I don't want people to talk about you."

"It's too late for that, sir," she said. They were both taking risks, her boss far more than her. Eisenhower had a reputation, a career and a marriage to lose. She was just a junior who would survive the limelight of any scandal. But Ike was always hopelessly naïve about the gossip that had trailed them since they first met.

"Maybe we should be more careful," she said.

"What?" he said.

"Maybe we should stop…"

"Stop what?"

"…being so close."

"I don't understand."

"Yes you do."

"What are you talking about?"

She waited. The question twisted slowly in the air between them like a spider hanging on the single filament of an unwoven web.

"It's called an affair, sir."

13

July-August 1944

On 27 August, two days after the liberation of Paris, Kay drove her boss into the city in an armour-plated limousine. Four years of German occupation had ended and Paris had gone wild. General Patton's fast-moving armoured columns had rolled up the German flank, driven the occupying forces beyond the Seine and delivered the prize of the French capital to Eisenhower.

She drove slowly through the cheering crowds surging up and down the Champs Élysées, taking Eisenhower to the Arc de Triomphe to pay their respects at the Tomb of the Unknown Soldier.

She saw him smile for the first time in all the weeks since D-Day, weeks that had flickered past like a newsreel film. Then he laughed right out loud. She knew the grin well enough, he was famous for it, but very few people had seen Eisenhower laugh; and now here he was, leaning back on his jeep and laughing at the sight of General Omar Bradley emerging from a mob of French women well-wishers with his hat askew, buttons torn off his uniform and lipstick smeared all over his face.

The military police had formed a tight ring around Eisenhower as a huge crowd tried to get their first sight of the man whose troops had liberated Paris two days earlier. General Bradley, recently promoted to take charge of the 12th American Army Group with almost a million men under his command, had decided to leave the cordon and talk to the crowd. Back at the jeep, bruised, breathless and not a little shaken, he said, "I didn't think I would get out of that alive." Eisenhower laughed all over again.

The fall of Paris in August threw up problems for Eisenhower that no American general had ever had to face, nor had they ever made their way into a military manual. After four years of German occupation during which the swastika flew over every public building, the city lost its collective sanity at the sight of the Stars and Stripes, Union Jacks and occasionally the Canadian Red Ensign of the Allied forces.

The brothels, bars and restaurants did no greater business than the back-street Parisian entrepreneurs turning out national flags of all the triumphant Allied nations in every shape and size: to be waved in streets, flown from every flagpole in the city, hung from buildings, laid across the tables of pavement cafés, and attached to every vehicle that managed to move through the throng of people on all major streets and avenues.

In the first days of celebration it was as if time had retreated with the defeated Germans. The city's clocks stopped, no one bothered to look at their watch, night became day and day night.

The weather was hot. A heat haze hung over the city in a misty cupola that beamed a translucent light on the streets below. Nothing looked or felt real. People acted as if they had stumbled into a new play without learning their lines.

There was no shortage of cheap wine or beer, the only comfort lacking was accommodation. Americans had taken over every single hotel and guest room in the liberated city and they seemed to have done so on the basis that the Parisians would be happy to provide such service free to the liberating army.

Eisenhower told his own staff to find him a headquarters decently removed from the city. He pointed a finger on the map.

"Versailles," he said. "That will do." And that is where Kay and the rest of his family moved to, leaving with some sadness the apple orchard calm of rural France for the splendour of the Trianon Hotel, which had until only days earlier been occupied by the German military headquarters in France.

The Trianon had once been the stables for the nearby Palace of Versailles where the Sun King, the great Louis XIV, lived during his reign of seventy-two years. The whirligig of history now placed Eisenhower's staff in the former stables while he was quartered rather more comfortably in the palace itself.

Eisenhower's staff found evidence everywhere of the speed and surprise of the German departure. Confidential papers were lying half-burnt in fireplaces, clothes were still hanging in the wardrobes, and shaving equipment and toiletries were scattered about in the bathrooms.

While the protection unit set up a security perimeter in the woodland around the Trianon, Kay and the rest of the staff cleaned up their new quarters.

For a man who read nothing but pulp cowboy fiction outside his official reading, Eisenhower often showed a surprising interest in history, or rather, as Kay noted, he became interested when he was face-to-face with it. The first orders of the day issued from the Trianon ended with a final addendum to his staff.

"I want a detailed brief on this whole shebang," he said, waving his hand vaguely towards the windows of the opulent room in which they were meeting. He either did not notice, or paid no attention to the fact that everyone in the room was staring at Kay. She enjoyed the attention. Eisenhower would explain soon enough.

"Shebang, sir?"

It was Walter Bedell Smith, the chief of staff, teasing the supreme commander.

"Yeah, Versailles. I told you all to learn your European history. We're going to have a lot of visitors here, and we might as well know something about the past of this place."

Bedell Smith had anticipated the question.

"Apparently, when Hitler paid a flying visit to Paris in 1940, his staff wanted to take him to Versailles but he said he had no interest in old royal palaces. He preferred the Eiffel Tower. He thought that was wonderful."

"Is that true?" asked Eisenhower.

"It falls in the category of good historical gossip which is probably true because it is likely to be so, but which can be neither proved nor disproved," said Bedell Smith.

"You should have been a lawyer," said Eisenhower.

"If I'd had any sense, I would have been."

"Well, that's history for you," said Eisenhower. "Now, let's get some facts – Kay?"

She stepped forward and began reading from a piece of paper on which she had hurriedly scrawled some notes.

"Versailles was once an old hunting lodge which Louis the Fourteenth, the Sun King of France, had turned into the most famous palace in the world. It was from here that he ruled for seventy-two years, much of it spent fighting wars to ensure that France became the greatest power in Europe.

Louis is famous for centralising the power of the French and for many well-known quotations…"

Eisenhower interrupted.

"*Après moi le deluge* – right?"

"I think that was another French king," said Kay, looking at Bedell Smith.

"Louis the Fifteenth," he said.

"So what did the great Sun King say that was so memorable?" asked Eisenhower.

Kay looked at her notes again, wondering briefly whether anyone would believe that in the middle of a world war General Eisenhower was asking for a history lesson about a long-dead French monarch.

"As the Sun King was dying – I found this in a guide book – he gave this advice to his successor: 'I have often undertaken war too lightly and sustained it for vanity. Do not imitate me but be a peaceful prince and apply yourself to the alleviation of the burden of your subjects.'"

"No wonder Hitler didn't want to come here," said Eisenhower.

He glanced around the room. No one could help looking at Kay. He smiled.

"I guess I should have made an announcement a little earlier. If you wonder why Miss Summersby is wearing an American army uniform it's because that's where she is now – in the American army. Let's give her a hand."

Kay acknowledged the applause with a small blushing bow. She was wearing the freshly pressed olive-green uniform of the Women's Army Corps with the shoulder insignia of a second lieutenant.

Kay could no more grasp her new status as a military aide to the supreme commander, Allied Forces, than she could believe that Paris had fallen without a fight.

She, Kay Summersby, formerly a pool driver in the Motor Transport Corps in London, now had rank in a new American army unit. What's more, her recruitment had been officially agreed and arranged by the president of the United States, Franklin Delano Roosevelt.

She kept telling herself that, because it was very difficult to believe. But it was true. When she had written to tell her mother, she had written the word in capitals: TRUE. And it was true.

Eisenhower told her the news himself and had done so with a big grin one afternoon back at the Portsmouth headquarters.

"You've always said you were interested in joining the WACs and I decided to do something about it."

"The president mentioned it way back, but I thought that was just talk."

"Kay, the president doesn't do 'just talk'. He wants it done and it will be done."

She looked at him, robbed of words, her mouth open.

"You're going to swallow a fly if you keep looking like that," he said, still smiling.

"Me? A WAC? But... I'm not a..."

"You're not a citizen. I know. It doesn't matter. The president ordered it done."

"But I thought Roosevelt was... well, I thought it was some sort of joke."

He laughed and said, "The president doesn't joke about such matters. He liked you and he meant it."

All she could say was, "Oh my goodness."

Then his smile faded and he talked in that brisk way she had heard in meetings.

"I'm planning ahead. The war is far from won, but we are going to win it, and I will not be in Europe forever."

"So you'll go back to Washington?"

"Yes. I've told you. And you are coming with me. We work very well together. Once you're a WAC, I can keep you on my staff."

Disguised in the clipped manner of an officer outlining routine orders for the day at a staff meeting, he told her she was to join the American armed forces. Her formal induction would not take place for a few months because there was simply too much going on to complete the necessary paperwork.

But she could wear the uniform of a second lieutenant immediately. Until she officially became a member of the American armed forces she would remain his driver. And she could continue to carry the Beretta pistol that fitted so snugly into her handbag.

Most important of all, once she had joined the US Army with the promise of citizenship she could join him in Washington.

Whenever she examined the logic of this conversation – and she did so frequently – she reached the one inescapable conclusion. Eisenhower, Ike, the boss, was planning a life with her after the war. She always rebuked herself after these flights of fantasy because that is surely what they were – the febrile imaginings of a woman trying to turn dreams into reality. Then she would take the Beretta out of her bag, grip it tightly and point it at herself in the mirror. The gun made her feel good. But it wasn't who she was. It was a useful reminder that life is not always what you see in a mirror.

She kept the Beretta with her at all times and even slept with it on her bedside table. Ike insisted that she practise regularly on a range wherever they were and she had become a very good shot.

He joked about the gun to his staff. "I wouldn't argue with Kay," he would say when an argument arose over some minor dispute. "She's armed and dangerous."

The phone rang on his desk and Eisenhower turned to answer it. "Does that all make sense?" he said to her with one hand over the mouthpiece.

"Yes," she said, slightly dazed at the way in which such startling information had been delivered, as if he had been telling her the destination for the next day's drive.

Professionally speaking it made a great deal of sense. They worked well together. He had said that. She helped him do the most important and difficult job in the world. Promotion to a military role in the Women's Army Corps would enable her to do that job more efficiently. As his driver she had never had difficulty dealing with the big men around Eisenhower: Churchill, Bradley and Patton.

They accepted that the Allied Commander drew emotional strength from a loyal and fiercely protective team of aides who created a tightly controlled world which revolved entirely around him. Kay Summersby was an important part of that world.

Men such as Bradley and Patton also accepted without comment or criticism that Kay provided her commander with "physical comforts". It was a coy and very English way of saying that she was sleeping with Eisenhower, an assumption widely held in the Allied command.

Kay had heard that Churchill himself had squashed all criticism of her affair – and there was no other word for it – by responding to a suggestion that she be transferred to a new post, "Leave Kay alone, she's helping Ike win the war."

Those who sought to criticise were simply told to shut up and mind their own business. The fact that Winston Churchill accepted the arrangement without murmur gave Kay the perfect answer to her critics.

So yes, at one level, she told herself, it all made perfect sense. Her promotion and his commitment to her future met his professional requirements, those of an ambitious soldier in high command.

But at another level, it made no sense at all. He'd said he was never going to let her go. Those were his words, even if they were uttered as if they were no different in tone or meaning from the rest of his surprising statement about her newfound status.

So perhaps it was wishful thinking on her part that the man she had served for two years, the man who insisted that she remain at his side even when meeting leaders of the free world, the man with whom she had chastely shared the comforts of Telegraph Cottage, wherein she had partnered him at bridge, poured his drinks, lit his cigarettes, made his breakfast, spoiled the dog they both adored, was in love with her.

14

August-September 1944

The slaughter in the climactic battle for Normandy which had opened the gates of Paris to the Allies cast a long shadow over the grandeur and gaiety of the city. Kay and others on Eisenhower's staff visited the battlefield in the immediate aftermath of the fighting.

Kay had seen plenty of dead bodies before, but nothing prepared her for the sight of corpses of men and horses piled on top of one another along the roads of France. The dead were almost all young Germans. They had fought harder and resisted longer than the Allies had believed possible without the presence of their commander-in-chief, Erwin Rommel. Now their broken bodies lay in hedgerows, ditches, fields, in wrecked vehicles and tanks, faces frozen in expressions of pain and shock.

Eisenhower was silent as Kay drove his armoured vehicle through the carnage with escort vehicles front and rear. The spectacle was made worse by the birds that flocked to the carrion. Crows and occasionally larger kites would lift their bloated bodies from the corpses and flap slowly away to seek a nearby tree or ruined building from which to look down on the intruders who had so carelessly disturbed their feast; as the convoy passed they would return, their blood-red beaks stabbing into flesh, always the horses' carcasses first, then the human flesh.

It was possible to walk for hundreds of yards over dead and decaying bodies, and in many cases, along the roadside and in small villages, it was impossible not to.

"These are scenes that could only be described by Dante," Eisenhower said quietly. He wasn't speaking to anyone in particular but giving vent to feelings shared by them all. In her mirror Kay saw him staring intently at the birds as they lifted lazily in flocks.

"I've seen plenty of dead before, especially in London during the Blitz, but never like this," she said. "So many young men, lying there like broken dolls – and what for? Nothing."

She put the back of her hand to her eyes. Ike fished out a handkerchief, leant forward and handed it to her. She dabbed at her eyes and handed it back to him.

"Keep it," he said. "You're going to need it."

"Can't we bury them at least?" she said.

"We haven't got the time or the men," he said.

Kay heard harsh words of recrimination hurled back and forth in the car as she drove away. The inquest continued in closed meetings in which she could imagine Ike thumping the table, veins throbbing in frustration. No imagination was needed to understand his fury, written in the cold black ink of the teleprinter messages that clattered day and night into the command headquarters.

More than once Kay was summoned into a meeting to take notes as Eisenhower upbraided his commanders for letting the Germans escape in such large numbers to regroup and fight again.

During August and September Eisenhower moved between two different worlds: those of the Allied Commander and military mayor of Paris. The joy of liberation could not mask the violence of revenge wreaked on those who had collaborated.

Most days Kay would be forced to cross the road to avoid bodies sprawled on pavements or in the gutters, not in the back streets but on major roads where they could be seen. She and other passers-by would step over them without a downward glance, except perhaps a flick of the eyes to take in the blood-smeared notices pinned to the corpses bearing words such as *traitre* or *collaborateur*.

The Seine reaped its harvest of this murderous revenge; every week boatmen brought bodies of men young and old to the banks to be laid out, waiting for relatives to identify them, which they did quietly at night to avoid the taint of treachery.

It was far worse, thought Kay, to find the body of a young man with his hands tied behind his back, his throat cut or half his head missing in the shadow of Notre Dame or with the Eiffel Tower in the background than to view the dead on the battlefield of Falaise.

Ike had told her to keep her Beretta with her and loaded at all times. He need not have bothered. The gun was always in her handbag or concealed in a pocket.

At night, after a day of driving him from meeting to meeting in Paris, it was a relief to get back to Versailles where she would wash away the sweat of the city, the stench of blood, and then sit down at the desk to go through the correspondence that followed the boss around like a faithful dog.

Eisenhower had taken the largest room in the house for his office, and a partition had been built for Kay. Since the partition did not reach the high ceiling, she heard everything that took place in his office and knew exactly when he began clearing papers from his desk to leave.

A small hatch had been cut into the partition so that mail and documents could be passed through. She watched him working at his papers, bent over his desk, meeting his smile with a smile when he looked up, then quickly breaking her gaze.

She knew this was not where he wanted to be. She saw deep frowns crease the smooth skin of his forehead and nicotine-stained fingers lift cigarette after cigarette to his lips. He wanted to be on the front line with his troops pushing into Germany.

The images of a man pushed to the limit of endurance crowded through the partition hatch: frowning, muttering expletives, chain-smoking, sipping coffee, drumming bitten fingernails on the shiny desktop, tilting back on his chair until it seemed he must fall to the floor – this was Eisenhower under pressure as Kay had never seen him before.

One night he poked his head through the hatch to her office and said, "It's late – time to knock off."

Kay looked at her watch. It was nine p.m. and just getting dark outside. She shook her head and pointed to the teleprinter, which was adding to the coils of paper gathered in a wire mesh basket, and to the pile of correspondence on her desk.

"Oh, come on – I've hardly seen you since we got here," he said.

"Boss, I've driven you every day since we set up base in Normandy – everywhere."

"I know, I know, but that's not what I mean. Come on, let's have a drink."

Kay hesitated, looking at the paperwork on her desk.

"That's an executive order," said Eisenhower and vanished with the dog. She could guess what he was going to do.

She went to her room. She would surprise him and change from her drab military uniform into... well, what? She looked at her only two dresses hanging in the closet. One was dark red, made of clingy satin and fell well below the knee. The other, a classic little black dress and a little low-cut, was a more obvious choice.

She wore them only occasionally, for official cocktail parties, although Ike didn't really approve. He liked her to remain in uniform. He had conceded, however, that when they were entertaining French guests she made a better impression in a cocktail dress, especially the black one.

She changed into it and went to the bathroom to apply a little make-up. She didn't use too much or put on perfume. Ike didn't say anything but she knew he didn't really approve of that either. Charlotte had advised her to ignore the edict. "He fancies you whatever you look like, doll," she'd said, "so don't let him boss you about. Put as much slap on as you like."

She had done so, and Ike had never complained. She was going to make sure she looked her best for him tonight. She flipped open her compact, adjusted her lipstick, and grimaced at the pale face careworn from the endless sixteen-hour days. She needed a large gin. She went downstairs.

Ike had summoned the night staff, a chef and two orderlies, and was talking to them in the marble-tiled hall. As Kay went down the stairs she heard him telling them to take the night off.

"Go and enjoy yourselves," he said, "but first fix us something to eat, something light – what have you got?"

"How about thinly sliced ham laid in fresh baguettes on thick Normandy butter with mustard and a tomato salad on the side?" said the chef.

Ike smiled. "Just great," he said, "Leave it in the kitchen."

"You've certainly got them well trained," she said as they walked into a big drawing room which was made to feel larger by a gilt-framed mirror hanging over a marble fireplace. A dark brown leather sofa faced the fireplace with two matching armchairs on either side. She glanced in the mirror. Yes, she looked tired.

Ike went to a side-table, poured a large whisky into a tall glass and added ice and soda. He turned and raised a gin bottle enquiringly.

"Yes please," she said, "army size."

She sat down and watched him mix the drink. She preferred the bitter-sweet taste of gin and the fizzy kick of the tonic. It was so much sweeter than the peat and smoke of whisky.

He handed her the drink, sat back on the sofa, unbuttoned his tunic and raised his glass. "Mud in your eye," he said.

She raised her glass to his. "May you get to heaven ten minutes before the devil hears you're dead."

He laughed. "I never heard that one before. Irish?"

"It is so," she said with a suitable accent.

It was the first time they had been alone together for weeks. She knew he had planned this moment. He wanted to talk with her alone, even if only for the brief time it took before the phone rang or a despatch rider arrived with an urgent message.

"Come and sit here," he said, patting the sofa beside him.

She got up and sat on the sofa. He stared at the empty fireplace. It was a warm August evening but even so she thought it would have been nice to see the glow of even a small coal fire. He began to talk, not looking at her.

"It has got to stop," he said. "It's going to stop right here and now."

There was anger in his voice. She knew he had been fretting for days over the rising number of complaints about the indiscipline of Allied forces.

"I'm going to order a firing squad when we get an open-and-shut case of rape. That should stop it," he said.

Kay said nothing. She had seen all the correspondence already, although the notion of a firing squad was new. He would never do it, though – never shoot one of those men he had bidden farewell to on the eve of D-Day. Too many had died already. She changed the subject.

"That officer you helped, the one you talked to…" she said.

He looked at her with eyebrows arched.

"McMichael?"

"Yes. Did we ever hear…?"

"He didn't make it."

The words were spoken without regret. An officer must never show any emotion about the death of those under his command. Those who do quickly lose control of themselves and their men. Ike had told her that.

"He was only a boy," she said. "What a shame."

Eisenhower ignored the implied rebuke. He got up, poured himself another drink and raised the bottle of gin, looking at her enquiringly. She shook her head. One large gin after a day in which she had eaten little was already making her dizzy.

She watched him sit down again at the far end of the sofa, careful not to spill the drink in his hand. He wasn't with her yet, she could tell that. He was somewhere else, lost in the tumble of thoughts in his head.

"These V-bombs are going take a lot of lives," he said suddenly. "The Brits are getting good at knocking them down, but we think the Krauts have a stockpile of ten thousand. They're shooting them off like fireworks."

Kay knew there was no point trying to change the conversation.

She let him talk the worries out of his head. That and the whisky usually did the trick. His main concern was not German rockets but the battle that had broken out between his main generals, Patton and Montgomery.

"The trouble with those two is that they believe their own publicity. They don't understand the Germans are going to fight all the way to Berlin – and if the Russians get there first, frankly, so what," said Eisenhower.

"Is that going to matter?"

"What?"

"Berlin?"

"It certainly will for the Germans."

"Hitler?"

"Oh, he'll kill himself; we'll never take him alive."

"And the rest? Rommel?"

"Rommel's damn nearly dead. We'll hang him when we get him. Unless the Russians nail him first."

He sipped the whisky. She could see the veins beginning to throb in his temple. It was time for a change in the conversation.

"I hear interesting news that Congress is going to pass a bill authorising the creation of five-star generals."

He laughed. "You hear too much."

"It's difficult not to in that office."

"I know. Well, it's true."

She moved along the sofa and put her hand on the stars across the shoulder of his jacket.

"There's room for another star."

He took her hand and squeezed it gently.

"They won't give it to me until after the war," he said.

She put her finger to her lips, kissed it, and touched it to his mouth. He blinked at the gesture, then grinned.

"You tell people not to talk like that," she said. "There's a lot of fighting still to be done, remember?"

He wasn't listening. "You're going to be a WAC in the fall. I mean, officially."

"I know, you told me. I'm just thrilled."

"You know what I said."

"Yes."

"I meant it."

She nodded. He had said he was never going to let her go. She leant forward, allowing her head to rest on his shoulder. He put his arm round her and pulled her into him. There they remained for what seemed to Kay like hours. The burdens of command and the worries of war seeped out of the room. She could feel him relax, his whole body soften.

Then without warning he turned and kissed her, twisting his body with such speed and surprise that she panicked and tried to push him away, but he resisted and pulled her into him, almost lifting her from the sofa, and then fell backwards with her on top.

He was smiling, a big lipstick-smeared smile now, his hands sliding beneath her jacket and up her back. She knelt over him, her hair falling into his face, and she kissed him back with a passion that she had long felt but never expressed.

They kissed again, hesitantly at first, two dim figures in a fog moving slowly towards each other, and then she unleashed an explosion of little kisses on his face and neck until he stopped her, breathing hard, and held her close, her head on his chest.

She hugged him as hard as she could, her head pressed against the rough serge of his uniform. His body was taut, a muscular rider's body. It was like hugging a tree: the bark was rough, the trunk was hard, and only a brilliant canopy of leaves above said that somewhere inside there was life, the sap was rising.

She unbuttoned his shirt and they began to undress, clumsily and without speaking. She pushed him gently back onto the sofa and began to massage the twisted muscles in his back. She could feel the muscles unclench.

He closed his eyes and sighed as her hands and mouth moved slowly over his body. She was making love to a man exhausted by high command and the endless slaughter that flowed from his battle orders. She wondered if there had been many women before. Perhaps life in the army precluded such pleasures outside marriage.

She did not count herself promiscuous but she could not remember how many lovers she had had. Married men had certainly been among them. Most had been surprised that a lady so elegant when dressed for the drawing room could become so uninhibited when undressed in the bedroom.

Charlotte of course never stopped talking about sex and treated Kay as a novice recently released from monastic orders.

"Kiss them where they've never been kissed before and you'll put a smile as wide as a mile on their dear little faces" was Charlotte's view on lovemaking. "The trick is the timing, doll, you don't want them coming too quick. Keep them on the boil until you get up there too."

They made love quietly and with passion. They paused while she broke away and walked to the drinks table. He watched as she lifted a bottle of Scotch, tilted it into her mouth and skipped back across the room. She kissed him, the whisky flowing from mouth to mouth, dribbling down his chest. She licked it off very slowly.

"I thought you didn't like whisky," he said.

"I don't, but I do like kissing you."

Hours later, or maybe it was minutes – she had lost touch with time – she lit a cigarette as they lay there and handed it to him.

He blew a smoke ring and watched it rise to the ceiling. It was perfect, a circle of vapour fading away as it drifted upwards. Some things were easier than others. He had never seen her naked before, never imagined her that way. He would remember the sight, the fragrance and the feel of every soft curve and cleft.

He was breathing deeply. "Sorry," he said. "I don't know why this is happening. It's not that I don't want you."

She laughed, a real laugh.

"It's not what's happening, Ike, it's what's not happening. And you know something? It doesn't matter one tiny little bit. Put that cigarette down and kiss me."

He laughed too and kissed her again quickly before breaking away.

"What's that over there?" he said, looking across at the side-table.

"That's the sandwich you ordered for dinner."

"A ham sandwich? This is Paris, Kay. Get dressed and get the car. We're going out."

"But you said…"

"Never mind what I said."

"But you can't just…"

"Yes I can," he said, holding out his hand. "Come on."

They drove back into the city, Ike sitting beside her. They were quite alone. The security detail had been told not to follow them.

"Any idea where we're going?" she asked.

"Nope," he said. "When we see a restaurant we like the look of we'll go in."

"But they'll recognise you."

"So what? We might get a free dinner."

If this is what making love did to her boss Kay was determined to repeat the performance soon. He was like a schoolboy skipping class, knowing he had broken the rules but enjoying the sudden sense of freedom.

It was almost ten at night and many of the restaurants in the western suburbs were closing. As they drove into the city itself he suddenly pointed to a well-lit brasserie with a crowd inside, dimly seen through misted windows. It was called Le Chat Noir.

"There!" he said.

Curious glances followed them to a table at the back of the restaurant. A waiter briefly handed them large menus and left to return a minute later and lower his head as if to impart a secret.

"Le patron vous offre une boisson," he said.

Ike looked at Kay. "Champagne," she said.

They clinked fluted glasses, tore open brown rolls and dipped them into small bowls of olive oil spotted with vinegar.

The waiter came to take the order.

"Steak medium rare with a side salad and potatoes," said Ike.

Kay rolled her eyes, shaking her head slightly. The waiter began to write the order down. Ike looked at Kay for a moment, then back at the waiter.

"What else have you got?" he said.

The waiter let his pen drift down the long menu.

"While you're making your mind up, I will have the asparagus to start followed by fillets of bream meunière with new potatoes and an endive salad on the side," said Kay.

Eisenhower looked at the menu for a moment more, then returned it to the waiter.

"That'll do me."

The waiter vanished into the kitchen. Ike leant forward.

"How come the French are so good at cooking?" he asked.

"Same way you're a good soldier – training and tradition."

"They laugh at our food. They think of us as the nation that polluted the world with chewing gum, hamburgers and Coca-Cola."

"They're not laughing now," she said.

"No, but it's against Gallic pride to recognise what we have done for them. Anyway no war talk please. Let's talk about something else – anything."

They paused, sipped the champagne, then Kay said, "OK. What would you do if you looked in the mirror one morning and saw a stranger looking back at you?"

He laughed. "Oh, you Irish and your fairy tales."

"Go on," she said.

"I'd shoot him."

"And get seven years bad luck!"

"Better than have a madman stepping out of a mirror."

"Have you ever…?"

"What?"

"Shot someone?"

"No. I've been lucky. I have always had others to do it."

"That can't have been easy."

Ike finished his champagne and allowed the waiter to pour another glass. People in the restaurant were looking at them. No one seemed sure who the uniformed stranger was.

"It's worse when others do the dying for you," he said.

He reached out, took her hand and squeezed it.

"I know," she said, "I've seen it in you."

The asparagus arrived dressed in melted butter and flaked with parmesan. They ate in silence, gratefully accepting a bottle of fine white wine from the patron, and went on to the fish course. Kay ate slowly, chewing carefully as she had been taught as a child.

Eisenhower finished quickly, leant over his empty plate, tapped his forehead. "Know something? I sometimes think you're the only one who knows what's happening up here."

It was almost midnight when they left, leaning into each other as they walked to the car. Kay giggled. "I've drunk too much, I shouldn't be driving."

"You're fine," he said. "Get in."

They got in the car. Kay looked back at the restaurant. The patron was framed in the doorway, a silhouette against the bright interior, holding a salute. Ike got out and stepped away from the car. He faced the patron and returned the salute. The two men remained motionless, facing each other across the car park for a moment, then broke away. Kay didn't know whether to laugh or cry.

15

October-December 1944

Eisenhower drew a grim conclusion from the announcement of Rommel's death on German state radio. The German general was said to have died from war wounds and was to be honoured with a full state funeral. The assumption in the Allied command was that he had been either murdered or forced into suicide, which amounted to the same thing.

Eisenhower did not care what lay behind the death of the man who might well have cost him the D-Day victory; the one leader who could have united the German people behind a new government that would negotiate a surrender had gone.

More than ever before Hitler's hold on power was absolute, as was his determination to fight to the bitter end. There were still three and a half million men under arms in Germany despite appalling losses on both the Eastern and Western Fronts.

Men aged sixty-five and over and schoolboys as young as fourteen were being conscripted into new units. Despite saturation bombing, many factories had moved underground and were still producing weapons, ammunition and spare parts – and the V2s were still falling on London.

As an unseasonably warm autumn turned into a bitter winter, more pressing matters gripped the Allied commander and his staff. The over-extended supply lines from Normandy ports were hindering the advance into Germany itself. Every bullet, every tin of spam, every consignment of blood packs for transfusions for front-line troops had to make a three-hundred-mile journey across France. Eisenhower fumed at the delays and raged at Montgomery's refusal to accept orders without arguing about everything asked of him.

And then there was Kay Summersby. Since that evening in front of an unlit fire she had become two people, both powerful presences in his life; his driver, secretary and problem-solver, and then there was the woman who indubitably had become his lover. It was difficult to reconcile the two. He could see she felt the same way.

She came into his office as usual, knocking first and opening the door when he gave the gruff command to do so.

"Is this a good time?" she asked.

"For what?" he asked.

"I need to explain something."

She looked pale, with dark rings under her eyes showing through make-up. She was nervous. Ike had not seen her like this before. Normally she walked in confident, smiling, a file under her arm, ready to plan the day ahead.

"What's up?" he said.

Kay took a deep breath sighed and looked down at her feet.

"What is it?" he said.

"I want a transfer to another post."

Ike rose from his chair: "What?"

"It's time for a change, sir. I have been with you for two years now."

"So?"

"I don't want this to go on between us."

He looked at her blankly, trying to find the words for a reply.

He had worked so closely with this woman. He had trusted her, as much as any of his staff, with many of the secrets of the campaign; it didn't seem possible that she who meant so much in every way, who had given herself joyously to him in front of a cheerless fire, that this woman should want to leave him now.

He put such personal thoughts aside. She helped him handle the clashing egos within the Allied command. She was always there when he needed her. She made his life possible. What had he told her in that restaurant – "You make me happy because you understand me" – that was the truth. Why on earth would she choose to leave now? She had told him she loved him, hadn't she? And he had said what? "I'll never let you go."

Kay broke the silence that had descended on the room.

"I know this is a difficult time but I just think it's better this way," she added.

"What way?" It was all he could say.

"It's got to stop. It's dangerous. It isn't right. You are married for one thing. There is a lot of talk about us among your staff and it's much wider than that. The English papers are sitting on the story that we're having an affair and for all I know the American papers are too."

"For Christ's sake – so what?"

"You can't keep saying so what. So it's going to be very damaging to you. Think of the headlines: supreme Allied commander having affair with his English mistress at the height of the war."

Eisenhower knew the truth of the old cliché: he was lost for words. He grew angry.

"The hell with that, Kay. You can't do this. It's that simple."

"I can. You can. We must."

Eisenhower slammed his fist onto the table.

"No we mustn't. It doesn't make sense."

"It makes very good sense. Think about it. The war is going to end soon. In months, even before Christmas maybe. Then what?"

"Then I go back to Washington."

"Exactly. And what do I do?"

"You come with me."

"As what exactly?"

"I'll get you a job – in the Pentagon maybe."

"I'm not a US citizen. You know that's not possible."

"You will be soon."

"What do you mean by that?"

Eisenhower sat down, reached for a pack of Lucky Strikes and flipped one out. She stepped forward and flicked open a lighter. He waved it away and struck a match. She desperately wanted one too.

"Mind if I smoke?" she said.

He waved an arm to indicate agreement and fiddled with the file she had placed on the desk. She had seen him so many times like this, frowning, smoking, trying out answers to a problem and closing in on the answer. She lit her cigarette.

"Don't push me, Kay," he said. "You'll be coming back with me after the war. That's a fact."

"What about your wife – Mamie?"

He paused. He had not got that far. There were far too many other things on his mind. A war to be fought. Victory to be won. Why bring Mamie into it now? What was she trying to do to him?

"That's for later. Right now your duty is to be here with me."

"My duty is to serve you as best I can. That means ending this."

"This what?"

"Don't make this difficult, Ike. You know what's between us."

"And what would you say that was?"

"You know perfectly well what that is. We never mention it. Love is a four-letter word, isn't it?"

"I need you, that's all I know. You make me happy. Now the hell with this nonsense. There's work to do."

"Ike, I can't, I'm sorry."

"Sorry? I thought you said you loved me."

"Yes, of course I do."

"Then don't do this."

She turned away from him and looked out of the window. Two gardeners were tending the elaborate lawns and flower beds that had been laid out when Louis the Sun King was on the throne and France was a world power. They were using hoses from large canisters strapped to their backs to water grass, flowers and plants wilting in the summer heat.

They were French and had performed the same task when the German command in France had been based here at Versailles. The water canisters were heavy. The men were old and weary. They had seen history move with the speed of a camera shutter. Yet the Allied victory and the German occupation before made no difference to the work they did here.

Men had been tending these gardens for two hundred years, Kay thought. There was a truth to be found in such a timeless scene – the stoic virtue of facing and accepting the inevitable fate that is stamped upon us from birth. Well, to hell with fate. Charlotte was right.

"I've told you before and I'll say it again," Charlotte had said, "He's using you. He doesn't know it because he's a decent man and he doesn't think like that. But they all do it. Get out of there before it's too late. Make your own luck, no one is going to do it for you."

A small voice, the still small voice of reason, told Kay that Charlotte was probably right.

She turned back to face Ike.

"Think about it, Ike. What do I do for you? I manage the diary, light your cigarettes, make coffee the way you like it, mix your drinks in the evening and look after the dog back in England. Anyone can do that."

"There's more to it than that and you know it."

"Of course there is. That's why I'm leaving."

She stepped back as he walked briskly around the desk. He placed his hands on her shoulders.

"Look at me," he said.

"I've made my mind up, sir. Don't make this difficult."

"You've said that already. You're the one making this difficult."

"This will be better for both of us. You have a meeting now, by the way."

"Kay, you don't want to do this and nor do I. Is that right?"

"That's not the point."

"Of course it is." He was almost shouting. He stopped. He was not going to lose his temper. He looked at his watch. He did indeed have a meeting scheduled.

"I'm doing this because I want the best for you."

"That's romantic bullshit, Kay. Get the hell out of here and don't talk this nonsense again."

Kay saluted, put the file on his desk and turned towards the door.

"Kay!"

"Yes, sir?"

"Your request for a transfer is refused. And this stays between us. Not a word outside this office. That's an order."

She left, closing the door quietly. General Bradley and other senior officers were outside waiting for their meeting. She wondered if they had heard anything. She heard Ike yell "Come in!" as she walked down the corridor. They were in for a difficult meeting. She walked outside and took several deep breaths. She felt bruised and winded just like when she had fallen badly from a horse back in Ireland.

She leant against the wall and took a handkerchief from her bag. Her hands were shaking. She wasn't going to cry. She shook a cigarette from a pack of Marlboros and lit it. She inhaled, drawing the smoke deep into her lungs then expelling it in a long plume. She felt calmer and tried to think. It was hopeless. She couldn't get a transfer unless he agreed.

She could resign from her position, no one could stop her doing that. She had not formally been inducted into the US Army despite her uniform – but then what? The MTC wouldn't have her back. She'd be a single woman in London without a job or means of support. Charlotte would be in full "I told you so" mode and would introduce her to the kind of man who would try and put his hand up her skirt after the first large gin and tonic and forget her name after the second. She threw the butt of the cigarette away and lit another one.

None of that was the point. She'd been a bloody fool. That was the point. He didn't want her to leave and she didn't want to leave him. Her boss was right. He needed her now. As for their affair, Ike was probably right about that too. The hell with what people think. So maybe, like the gardeners, she should just water the flowers and let life take its course.

She threw the cigarette away and went back inside. She sat on a chair outside the door. The voices inside were loud and bad-tempered. She waited, chain-smoking, for twenty minutes or half an hour. She lost track of time. The door opened. Bradley's party left unsmiling and unhappy. She stood up, smoothed her skirt and opened the door without knocking.

Ike looked up frowning. She said, "You've got a lunch across town. I'll wait for you in the car."

Kay had never forgotten the string of oaths in the back of the Packard as she drove Eisenhower away from his first meeting with Monty. That had been two years ago, and every message that had crossed her desk between the two men since told her that the relationship was becoming more venomous.

Montgomery was the only commander who refused to allow her into his meetings with Eisenhower; all the others, including Omar Bradley and George Patton, welcomed her as someone who could take a good note and keep the supreme commander well-supplied with coffee and cigarettes. Only the very secret meetings were off-limits, and even then Ike made her wait in the corridor outside the door in case he needed her.

With Montgomery it was different. He made his disapproval of her presence obvious. He never bothered to greet her with even normal civility when she accompanied Eisenhower to a meeting. He simply ignored her. He didn't even arrange for tea or so much as a glass of water to be offered to her. On the one occasion he had talked to her it had been with open hostility.

She had been waiting in a conference room. The British field marshal bustled into the room with an aide. He looked at Kay sharply and said, "Who are you?"

"Summersby, sir. I'm with General Eisenhower."

"You're his driver, aren't you?"

"I'm his assistant, sir."

"What are you doing here?"

"I've told you, sir. I'm with General Eisenhower."

"You're his driver. You have no security clearance to be here."

"I am security cleared by the supreme commander, Allied Forces, sir."

She felt her face colouring and her Irish temper rising. She was damned if she was going to be pushed around by this pompous little man. She could see Montgomery's aide raising his eyes to the ceiling.

"I shall have to ask you to leave," snapped Montgomery.

"I can't do that, sir. I am under General Eisenhower's orders to remain here."

"Well where is he, for God's sake?"

"Taking a leak, sir."

Montgomery looked at her as if she had slapped him.

"What did you say?"

Before Kay could reply the aide stepped forward and whispered into Montgomery's ear.

"Well why didn't you say so?" he barked at Kay.

"I just did, sir."

"Inform me when he arrives," Montgomery said and left the room.

Kay thought the scene was funny, but Eisenhower did not laugh when she told him about it later.

"Montgomery is a royal pain in the ass and always has been," he said.

By strange circumstance it was Montgomery's refusal to meet his commander in chief at the Versailles headquarters that brought about Kay's last drive as General Eisenhower's chauffeur. Pleading pressure of work, Monty insisted on meeting Eisenhower at his own headquarters in Brussels.

The two men decided to end an argument that had divided the American and British Allies for weeks. The scene was set for another grim showdown. The Allied commander and his immediate staff set off in a convoy of cars in heavy rain that had prevented a journey by air.

Kay drove the lead car behind the military escort. The mood in the car at the prospect of the meeting ahead was not improved by the weather. The downpour continued throughout the journey. The motorcycle outriders were quickly soaked to the skin, while those in the car peered through a waterfall of water on the windscreen.

In Brussels Eisenhower went straight into the meeting at Montgomery's headquarters. The debate was lengthy and acrimonious. Waiting outside, Kay heard the soft growl of her boss turn to harsh-edged anger. It was like listening to a chainsaw on wood. Montgomery had a voice like an old crow cawing at dusk. He spoke in clipped sentences peppered with "With respect" and "You must surely see".

Eisenhower hated the effortlessly patronising tones of the British commander. In fact he hated Montgomery. Kay sat outside, trying to look disinterested, as the conversation raged within. The clash of voices and the thud of document folders being slapped onto the table were clearly audible in the corridor.

Various aides walked past and looked at her strangely. From fragments of conversation she gathered that Montgomery wanted a single thrust in overwhelming strength to bring the war to an end while Ike preferred a broad-front strategy. The argument ended when the British field marshal was ordered to accept the American strategy. Eisenhower rolled his eyes at her as he left with a look that said "*Get me out of here*".

Montgomery took swift revenge. Stories began to appear in the British press that the war was being unnecessarily prolonged by the supreme commander's tactics.

The criticism spread. The press began to suggest that the American general was "detached" and was spending too much time "with his lady chauffeur on the golf links at Reims".

The Allied commander had set up a new forward base that autumn at Reims, famous as the champagne capital of France. The snide newspaper comments thus cleverly projected the notion of Eisenhower's champagne lifestyle spent at ease on the golf course with his lady driver, companion, bridge partner and perhaps mistress. The gossip brought into the open the question that was increasingly being asked within the Allied command and by the accompanying press corps: just what was Kay Summersby's role?

No one knew, but everyone liked to speculate. For the first time, the British press began to publish the same photographs of the commander-in-chief and his driver as those circulating in the US media.

Until then, whether by a quiet word from Winston Churchill to his old friend, the newspaper baron Lord Beaverbrook, or simply prurience on the part of the press, Summersby's name and photo had never appeared anywhere in Britain.

"You know what they're saying about you, don't you, doll?" said Charlotte.

Kay had flown in from the Allied headquarters at Versailles that morning with secret papers for delivery to the American embassy. She and Charlotte were having coffee in the same small café near Grosvenor Square where Kay had breakfasted on the morning she'd first met Eisenhower. It was exactly as she remembered it. Greasy Formica table tops, a waft of frying in the air and the same limited menu: weak tea with powdered milk, porridge and braised liver with onions or fried spam. The Allies might be winning the war, but the food in London had not improved.

"No, but I have a feeling you're going to tell me," she replied.

She was pleased to see Charlotte again. They had last met in London a month before D-Day for a quick drink in a dubious Soho club. Entry was gained by ringing three times on the doorbell and waiting for a key wrapped in a sock to be thrown into the street from an upper window.

Charlotte had friends everywhere, and she was greeted warmly that night by a colourfully dressed woman of indeterminate age called Margot. They had climbed two floors up a rickety staircase to find themselves in a large room full of people drinking and talking very loudly. They had drunk gin and talked of Charlotte's new boyfriend, a thirty-year-old American with a mysterious job at the embassy.

"He's very big, you know," Charlotte had said, and laughed.

"What on earth do you mean?" Kay had replied.

Charlotte had laughed even more, spilling her drink. "Don't come the choirgirl with me, doll."

Now Kay was hearing about a new boyfriend, this time a married man who worked in a government department supervising the nation's water supplies. Judging from Charlotte's deprecating remarks about his personal hygiene ("when he takes his socks off the pong is awful"), he would soon be replaced.

"There's plenty of fish in the sea for a single girl in London," Charlotte said. "I don't go out with men in uniform because they just vanish off to the war and get killed, but I do like a married man. They get the train home at night to some dreary wife in the suburbs, so you don't have to wake up with them in the morning."

Kay laughed. Charlotte's outrageous descriptions of her love life were a tonic after a four a.m. start and a bumpy flight through low cloud over the Channel.

"So what are they saying, whoever they are?"

"They're saying you've become Ike's mistress and that you put a smile on that grumpy face of his."

Kay frowned and put her mug on the table with a thump.

"Firstly, he's got every right to be grumpy – have you any idea what's happening over there?"

"Come on, doll, I'm not being serious. But you can hardly blame people for talking. You pop up in the background of every photo taken of him."

"So?"

"So – what about it?"

"For God's sake, Charlotte, I am not his mistress. We're not having an affair – that's just nonsense. You mustn't repeat things like that."

Charlotte looked at her and raised her mug. "This is the best coffee in London. You know why? This place is right next to the embassy and they provide it. You can get anything out of the Americans if you try."

"Don't change the subject."

"All right, I won't say another word."

"Promise me."

There was silence. Charlotte leant forward, looked with theatrical exaggeration to her left and right, and whispered: "What's he like?"

"What do you mean?"

"When the lights go down. You know. Do tell."

"You've got a disgusting one-track mind."

"I'm a disgusting one-track kind of girl. Why not? Anyone could die at any time in this town. It's all very well for you – you're safe over there in France. Here we get these rockets coming out of nowhere without a sound, just a whoosh, a big bang and then bodies everywhere."

Kay sipped her coffee. Charlotte was right. It was very good, shipped in from America probably. And it was true. She was safe in France. She knew nothing of the horrors of life under the V2s in London. Her mother made much of the danger despite living miles away in Surrey.

"So come on," said Charlotte, "what's he like in the sack? Those army men can come three times a night, they say. It's all that steak. I've never had such luck. I won't tell a soul. Cross my heart and hope to die."

Kay laughed. Outrageous, funny and obsessed with sex, Charlotte was just what she needed right now.

"There's nothing to tell," she said.

"You mean there's nothing to tell me."

"Precisely. And no man I've ever met has or could come three times a night, by the way."

Charlotte laughed. "You haven't lived, doll," she said.

They smoked their cigarettes in silence, eyes wandering over the crowded café where the smell of unwashed bodies, smoke and rancid fat congealed into a malodorous fug.

"I am never, ever going to get married," said Charlotte suddenly.

"Don't be silly – you're young. The war won't last forever."

"No, doll, it's not that. It's just that, well, I know a lot of people who've died, most of them very young. I just want to have fun. Anyway, can you imagine waking up next to the same man for the rest of your life?"

"Yes I can, actually."

"Well, bully for you. But it won't be your General Eisenhower, I'll tell you that."

"Oh, do shut up, Charlotte."

"Anything you say, doll. But remember what they say."

"Which is?"

"A woman in love will believe anything."

Kay was suddenly irritated. She looked around for something to throw at her friend, a bread roll perhaps. Charlotte just didn't understand. Or perhaps she understood too much, which was even more aggravating.

"He's winning the war for us," she said with the emphasis of a teacher talking to a sleepy classroom. "He's doing a great job and he's under a lot of pressure. I'm just one of the team. It's my job – right?"

"Don't be a crosspatch," said Charlotte.

"I'm not cross. It's just that you talk as if I was having a raging affair with my boss."

"Well aren't you? You certainly seem to spend an awful lot of time together."

"That's hardly surprising, is it?" Kay snapped. She stood up looking for the door.

Charlotte got up from her chair, gave Kay a quick kiss on the cheek and whispered, "You know the mark of a true gentleman?"

"Go on."

"A man who takes his watch off before he gets into bed."

"Do you think of anything else, Charlotte?"

"What else is there to think about – the bloody war?"

She gave Kay another kiss on the cheek and said, "Don't forget what I said."

"*Carpe diem*?"

"No. A woman in love will…"

Kay turned and left.

The discomfort of a packed military aircraft on the way back to Paris that evening was made worse by bad weather which threw the plane around the sky as if it were a toy in the hands of an angry child.

Kay fought to keep down her nausea as people around her began vomiting into brown paper bags. She pretended that she was on a scary carnival ride in one of the travelling circuses that occasionally toured Ireland when she was young.

That didn't help. She played the numbers game instead. It was two years since she had met Dwight Eisenhower, well two years and two months to be exact since this was August 1944. It was just over three years since she had become a Motor Transport Corps driver and four years since she had begun driving an ambulance in London.

She had joined the ambulance service when the streets of London were peaceful and the only sign of war was the signature of the Battle of Britain written in vapour trails in the sky. Her mother had told her it was a safe and sensible way of doing her bit for the war effort. A month later, in September 1940, the Blitz began and she found herself in the middle of a war zone.

The numbers would take her back through marriage, divorce and the long dreamlike years of childhood in Ireland. And now she was thirty-five years old. She felt as if she had lived several lifetimes in the last four years.

The war had gone on too long. It had stripped people of their old lives and flung them into a new and violent world. Too much had happened too quickly. No wonder a woman like Charlotte had thrown herself into casual sexual encounters as a means of coping with a world in ruins.

Charlotte told her that one night in the blackout during the bombing she had clung to a passing stranger against the railings of Eaton Square in London's fashionable Belgravia. They had been terrified as shrapnel and masonry flew around them. Fear turned to lust. He had unbuttoned his trousers and she had raised her skirt. Kay always felt amused and slightly jealous when she heard such stories.

Her own life had hardly been virtuous. Bedded by all the wrong men, then married, divorced, engaged again and now, finally perhaps, just maybe, she was in love.

The plane found calmer weather as it left the clouds on the approach to Paris. The cabin reeked of vomit and the pale-faced passengers scrambled down the ladder in relief. All Kay wanted was a hot bath and a long sleep. After that she would suggest to the boss that he arrange a small drinks party for his staff and chosen members of the press corps. It was time everyone cheered up. The Allies were winning the war after all.

A week later a small ceremony took place in Eisenhower's office to which the press were not invited. The row of champagne bottles in ice buckets on a side-table was an unusual extravagance. Kay looked around the room.

The Falstaffian figure of Colonel T.J. Davis, an old friend of Ike's but officially his adjutant general, was opening bottle after bottle, sending corks flying to the ceiling with loud pops. Kay knew that Ike and Davis had served together under the leadership of General MacArthur in the Philippines, a searing experience under an egotistical boss which had created a warm friendship between the two men.

If the colonel was opening champagne, clearly this was no ordinary briefing. Kay looked around to see the usual crew of staff and aides, all of whom were looking at her rather oddly, she thought. She wondered if she had missed a briefing note.

Ike was in one corner peering at speech notes.

Something special was about to happen, probably a surprise visit by one of the political grandees, Churchill or de Gaulle. Her uniform was a crumpled mess and her hair needed a good brush – she wished someone had told her this was happening. Her smarter second uniform was hanging pressed and freshly laundered in her room. She just about had time to change, and began to edge towards the door.

A hand took her arm and she turned.

"Where are you going, just when we need you," said Colonel Davis.

"I'll be back in a minute," she said.

Davies smiled and pointed to Eisenhower. "Sure thing, but first could I ask you to stand over there by the boss."

Kay looked across the room. Eisenhower was smiling and beckoning her over. She walked towards him, conscious that everyone was staring at her. She had not an idea in her head except the consoling thought that Ike never bawled his staff out in public.

He motioned her to turn and face the room, looked down at his notes and said, "Most of you will know that the army way at times like this is to get to the point – and then get to the champagne. So let me ask Miss Kay Summersby a question: will you accept a commission as Second Lieutenant in the Women's Army Corps of the United States Army?"

The surprise was total. She swayed on her feet and felt her legs buckle. Then Colonel Davis was speaking loudly and solemnly, swearing her in as a member of the American Armed Forces. She managed to mumble her assent. Eisenhower stepped forward, took her arm and steadied her. Grinning, he pinned two gold bars onto her shoulder epaulettes. Champagne was handed round in fluted glasses.

After driving him many tens of thousands of miles, she was no longer his driver. From now on she would ride in the back of the car as his secretary, diary keeper, bridge partner and co-owner of the dog they both loved.

This was Eisenhower's answer to the innuendo and the gossip of journalists, and to anyone who questioned the presence of Kay Summersby at his side.

"How do you feel?" he asked.

"I feel like someone has sent in a rocket to the moon and I'm slowly floating back to earth. I'm amazed. But how? I'm a Brit."

He leant forward and whispered in her ear. "Citizenship comes next. Don't worry, I'm fixing it. The president has agreed. You'll be a Yank soon."

That was what she wanted above all else. With citizenship she could return to America at the end of the war and work with him in Washington. He had promised her a commission in the Women's Army Corps and he had done that; he had promised her citizenship and she knew that too would come.

This was, she told herself, truly an affair of the heart; she could trace it back to the moment he gave her that box of chocolates after his first trip to London. She had only worked for him for ten days then, but in that time she already felt that she meant much more to him than just a Motor Transport Corps driver.

When he came back that first time he had remembered how she'd said she missed fruit more than anything else in wartime London. There had been fruit on her desk, exotic fruit, bananas, mangoes and pineapples, the next day.

Then there was Telek, the Scottish terrier he had named after her, the bridge nights when he would softly squeeze her leg under the table, lunches with Churchill and Roosevelt when he would make sure she was well seated. He had congratulated her after those lunches and said he was proud of her.

She had held her own with two of the most powerful men in the world. They liked her and they had both told her to look after their commander. They had praised her to Ike, and that had pleased him even more – it had placed an official seal of approval on a relationship that everyone talked about but no one understood.

They knew what was happening to them. For a few brief moments every now and then they could leave the world at war – that kiss on the darkened plane flying back from Tunis and their lovemaking in front of a cold fire at Versailles, that was their world now, which they reached for when they could.

The first time they had seen each other naked in front of the fire that night, there had been no shyness but a hunger between them that had surprised her. It was as if he'd been waiting for that moment since they'd met.

And what did it all add up to? Just a minor fling with a man who wished to relieve the pressures of high command with a little wayward behaviour, a quick foray off the marriage reservation?

No, it was so much more than that. Dwight Eisenhower was in love with her, and increasingly, it seemed, he did not care who saw or heard how happy she made him.

And she had seen a confidential cable from Washington that would make him happier still.

In early December, Eisenhower received a promotion that made him the first five-star general in American history. He was now formally general of the army. Since there was no room for the extra star on his epaulettes, a special badge consisting of five stars sown with gold braid had to be made and stitched into the shoulder of his uniform. He had achieved the same rank as Montgomery. He insisted that Kay also had insignia on her uniform that showed she worked for a five-star general, a smaller version of his, stitched like his, into the shoulder of her uniform.

Kay watched as her boss tried hard to shrug off his promotion as just a smart piece of public relations by the Pentagon; but the back-slapping, the letters and wires of congratulation, the festive drinks at headquarters and to cap it all the new insignia on his uniform made him a happy man. Eisenhower knew that the man he admired more than any other in the military, George Marshall, would have arranged the promotion.

Amid celebrations in the days before Christmas and the lengthy meetings to plan the next stage of the war, Kay and Eisenhower moved like actors on a stage, aware of what was unspoken between them and aware too that moments alone would be brief and liable to interruption.

That hardly mattered to her. She had rank in the American army and a badge on her shoulder that showed she worked closely with the supreme Allied commander.

Her mother was impressed. "You look so important, darling," she said. "I never thought my little girl would wear a uniform like that. But does it mean you'll go to America when the war is over? I wouldn't like that."

Charlotte was less impressed. She ran her fingers over the badges with one hand while drinking a gin and lime with the other.

"Well, well, doll, you really are in the army now," she said.

"Congratulate me, go on, be nice for once and don't tell me I'm being used."

"I don't have to, doll, you know you are. I suppose it's a fair trade. He gets to keep you and you get little gold stars on your shoulder. Women have been bought for much less."

"I think you're jealous."

"If I thought all those gold stars came with some high-powered fucking I would be very jealous indeed."

"I hate that word. You know how to make a girl feel good, you really do. What did you do in your last life, I wonder?"

"I was the Duke of Wellington's Thursday mistress."

"Thursday?"

"He had one for every day of the week. He saved the weekends for his wife. Randy bastard."

Christmas was coming, and beyond that lay hopes of an end to the war. Kay was in the staff mess at Reims drinking coffee and daydreaming about the day when Eisenhower would return to Washington, there to be appointed chief of staff. She would become an American citizen and she would join him there. She looked out of the window and saw it was snowing. The last Christmas of the war was just a week away. She picked up her coffee and slipped back into her dreams.

And Mamie Eisenhower, the wife who had waited for so long – what of her? Kay frowned slightly. The boss was finalising plans for a broad-front offensive early in the new year. The Germans had been retreating since the D-Day breakout and they would go on retreating all the way to Berlin.

Ike would finish the war by Easter. Then he would return in triumph to America and ask Mamie for a divorce. If he made up his mind to do something, he followed through. The Brits had been complaining about him behind his back and Montgomery had been sniping away as usual. Ike had stuck to his guns and refused to change strategy.

It was his military training, Kay knew that. He was pig obstinate and liked quoting an old military maxim: never change tactics while engaging the enemy unless your line breaks. She had heard him tell Montgomery that. The field marshal muttered and blustered but had no real answer. He knew it was Napoleon's favourite advice to his generals.

Ike wouldn't change his mind about her either. He would ask for a divorce. She was sure of that. They had never discussed it, but just last night, in a rare moment alone, he had taken her in his arms and given her a long bruising kiss. That kiss was a promise: *I will never let you go.*

There was an urgent tap on her shoulders. It was Mickey McKeogh.

"The boss wants you to take the car and get his clothes. He'll be sleeping rough here tonight. There's a big flap on."

"Why? What's happened?"

"The Germans have broken through, some place called the Ardennes."

16

January 1945

"A case of oysters, Mr President?" Steve Early, White House press secretary and the longest serving of all Roosevelt's aides, tried to keep the surprise out of his voice.

"A big case of oysters," corrected the president, looking with satisfaction at the bewilderment on his press secretary's face. Men in power enjoy being able to surprise those who serve them, especially people such as Steve Early who, although a remarkably able and loyal aide, lacked imagination.

"Right, Mr President, but where shall I send it?"

"To his headquarters in Versailles, of course. I want it there by tomorrow."

"Tomorrow, Mr President?"

"Don't repeat me, Steve. You're being a little slow today, if I might say so. Call George Marshall and tell him to ship a case of oysters to Ike. He's got planes going over there every day. It's my New Year's greeting, congratulations on the way he dealt with the Ardennes business and a little gesture to salute his fifth star."

"Right, Mr President," said Early, wondering where he was going to get a case of oysters in Washington. He did not like the molluscs himself, but he knew Eisenhower did. They were his favourite seafood but no longer obtainable in France; the invasion had wrecked the fishing fleets and most of the oyster beds in Brittany and Normandy.

Later that day George Marshall entered the Oval Office for what had become a daily meeting between the chief of staff and his commander-in-chief.

Marshall put down a file of papers and sat in the vacant chair opposite the presidential desk. "The oysters are on their way," he said.

The president smiled. "Good. He deserves them. It's been a tough time."

"I agree," said Marshall, looking grave. "But…"

There was a pause. Roosevelt watched Marshall's fingers twisting into each other as he sought the right words. The president admired and trusted this man like no other in Washington. He had vetoed Marshall's appointment as supreme commander of the European campaign two years earlier for that very reason. He had needed him here, by his side, close to the White House.

Roosevelt had just won an unprecedented fourth term and now intended to make more history. There was a major Allied conference coming up where Stalin, Churchill and he would draw up the post-war map of Europe. It was a long way to travel, halfway across the world to an unknown town called Yalta on the Crimean peninsula, but he had to be there.

At first he had wanted Marshall to stay behind in Washington, keeping that military mind of his focussed on the final weeks of the war in Europe. But his golden rule, one which had served him well at every stage of his political life, was to take a fresh look at any major decision the morning after it was made. Thus he had changed his mind. He would take Marshall to Crimea to allow Stalin and Churchill to understand and admire the man who was the real architect of the war in Europe.

Roosevelt's respect for his army chief of staff did not extend to personal warmth in their relationship. Marshall believed that men in high office, whether military or civilian, should adhere to, and were enhanced by, formal behaviour.

He did not approve of the casual camaraderie of Roosevelt's White House. The president used first names to address most of those around him, including servants, cabinet members and the press corps. He had once addressed Marshall in a similar manner back in 1938. The deep frown that followed ended such informality.

Marshall placed his hands on his knees and leant forward. The man he faced, the president of the United States, who had broken with constitutional tradition and won a fourth term, the man who held the future of Europe in his hands, looked old and haggard. His face was furrowed with deep lines and the eyes had sunk back into their sockets. He had lost weight and was said to be eating little. There was death in that face, thought Marshall. He wondered which would end first, the president or the war.

"Yes, general?" Roosevelt prompted.

"...but it shouldn't have happened," said Marshall.

Roosevelt sighed. "You know I don't like post-mortems. Let's look forward, the war will be over in a couple of months."

"I must tell you that big mistakes were made. We missed a lot of intelligence about the build-up in the Ardennes. The Germans switched six divisions from the Russian Front while no one was looking. A lot of good men died because of that."

"Are you blaming Ike?"

"Not me, Mr President. He blames himself. Intel that didn't fit the conventional wisdom was ignored."

"Conventional wisdom?"

"That the Germans would go on retreating and we would go on advancing."

"Go on."

"We had reports of a German build-up as far back as November. The Brits gave us Ultra reports saying that Hitler was stripping divisions from the Russian Front and switching them to the west. Eisenhower's people didn't want to believe them because the information didn't fit."

"Why are you telling me all this, general?"

"Because I think Ike is tired. His mind is not on the job. He's getting distracted."

The president lit a cigarette and waited.

"Go on."

"I'll be frank, Mr President. The Brits are beginning to lose faith in him."

"Really?"

"I'm sure you've heard reports from our people in London, but this is from me."

"And?"

"They think he needs a firmer grip on the ground forces. They use the Ardennes to make that point. The British want him to appoint a second-in-command to take charge of all front line forces. A Brit, naturally."

"Who are 'they' exactly?"

"It's Churchill. He's been pressing Ike to appoint a deputy supreme commander. And Ike seems to have agreed. That's the issue."

"Who have they in mind?"

"Not Montgomery. The Brits are not that stupid. Bradley and Patton would go mad."

"So who?"

Marshall had seen the president do this many times. He was a tactical master in such conversations, posing gentle questions to draw out the problem and find a solution. Everyone who faced the president in the Oval Office knew that for every problem they laid on his desk they had to follow with a suggested solution.

"It doesn't matter who, Mr President. We should resist any such suggestion. I hardly have to tell you that three-quarters of the troops fighting in Europe are American. We are producing half the world's armaments. I don't think Congress would stand for a Brit in command of their boys."

"Where is Montgomery in all this?"

"Bitching, as usual, but Ike shut him up. We need him. He'll take the fight to the Huns in the north."

Roosevelt placed one of his Camels, his favourite brand, in the holder and lit it. There was a picture of a camel in the desert on the pack above the slogan *A camel is worth a long walk*. He hadn't walked a step unsupported since stricken with poliomyelitis in the hot summer of 1921, when he was a forty-year-old successful lawyer and businessman possessed of a famous political name and the ambition that went with it – he was about to enter politics when the polio struck.

George Marshall had presented him with the problem and the solution.

"Go and see Ike," said Roosevelt. "Tell him he remains the sole commander of Allied forces in Europe. Tell him to stop those generals squabbling among themselves. We've got the Germans to beat. I'll talk to Churchill."

"Thank you, Mr President."

Roosevelt looked down at his desk diary. The meeting had overrun his next appointment. But Marshall had not risen from his chair.

"There's something else," said Marshall.

Roosevelt raised an eyebrow.

"I think Ike needs a break, a few days off somewhere, maybe where he can get a little sun."

"Sun in Europe in January?"

"Well, you know what I mean. He's tired. There are too many distractions in his life."

"What sort of distractions?" said Roosevelt, knowing perfectly well what his chief of staff was trying to say but interested to hear how he was going to frame it.

"He's got that English driver of his…"

"I know. I've met her. She's a charming young woman."

"He thinks so too. There's a lot of talk, but that isn't the point. Every night he ends up with her in his room, or in his tent if they're on ops, and they stay up late and drink, I guess…"

"That's gossip, general."

"I think it's a huge distraction."

"You mean you think he might have learnt a little more about German intentions in the Ardennes if he hadn't had the occasional nightcap with his driver? Come on, that's not like you. Where's the logic in that?"

Marshall didn't take the hint. He wasn't going to change the subject.

"He's made her a WAC and he's trying to get her American citizenship."

"I know. I authorised it."

"Aren't you worried he might be…"

"Might be what, general?"

"Well, bringing her to Washington. I mean, there's Mrs Eisenhower."

The president leant forward. "We've got a war to fight and a war to finish. A lot of young men have died and a lot more will go on dying until we complete the job. I sent Ike those oysters as a measure of my trust and my admiration for the man. I don't know what goes on between him and Miss Summersby, and frankly, I don't care."

"So you are going to give her citizenship."

"It's not my call."

"You could stop it."

"I have no intention of stopping it. Nor should you."

"It means he's going to bring her back to DC after the war."

The president put his cigarette holder down on an enamel ashtray, dropping a roll of ash onto his desk.

"Let's get to 'after the war' first before we worry about this, shall we? Frankly, I'm a little more worried about getting to Berlin before the Russians than whether Ike is sleeping with his driver."

Marshall wanted to remind the president that Kay Summersby was no longer the supreme commander's driver. Her recent promotion to first lieutenant in the Women's Army Corps meant she now occupied an even greater position of influence within Ike's tight circle of aides and advisors.

That raised some interesting questions. She had been checked out thoroughly by the FBI and nothing suspicious had been found in her background. If she had any political views she kept them to herself. Summersby's mother lived near London, while her father, who had served in a cavalry regiment in the Great War, lived out his life quietly in Ireland. The British intelligence agencies had said repeatedly that she was nothing to do with them.

Marshall believed them. Trouble was that everyone seemed to like Kay Summersby – except Mrs Eisenhower and her friends in Washington. Patton and Clark approved of her because they said it kept Ike sane. In any case, since

Patton had that Red Cross nurse of his around all the time, he was hardly going to object.

But Marshall's view was that Eisenhower was on the edge of a breakdown. He was exhausted as much by the political infighting within the Allied command as anything the Germans had thrown at him. He needed a break, a few days away from the front line – and more importantly from Kay Summersby, because there were other more dangerous implications behind the Allied Commander's rumoured romance.

Scandalous tittle-tattle in the salons of Washington was one thing, but any press story that speculated on a break-up of Eisenhower's marriage to Mamie would bring disgrace on the army while young Americans were dying in their thousands in Europe. It was unthinkable. Marshall resolved to stop it happening.

First he needed to get Ike back on his feet and fit again. A wealthy American expatriate had offered his villa near Cannes in the South of France for just such a purpose. The villa was perfect, with a heated pool, sea views, a good staff including a decent cook, tight security and maybe even a little winter sunshine.

He would send Ike down there for a few days by plane with orders to rest up and get some sleep. He would have liked to fly Mamie in to join him, but long-standing presidential orders were clear: no wives were allowed in the theater of operations – with no exceptions.

As for Summersby, Marshall considered himself a military man trained in a methodology that was almost a religion in army circles – the solution to all problems lay in careful planning. She was a problem, and he would need a plan. But first he needed the approval of the man facing him in the Oval Office.

"So it's okay if I fix for Ike to take a break?" asked Marshall.

"Sure, but go over and tell him yourself – and make sure he gets those oysters."

Like most women, Kay could gauge men by the looks they gave her. A man's eyes often told a story more clearly than his spoken words. Even a momentary glance, a sideways look or a full-beam stare over a pair of glasses could instantly communicate surprise, jealousy, lust, curiosity or sometimes a heady mix of all of them.

But she had never before experienced the cold look of distaste that George Marshall gave her as he swept through Eisenhower's outer office on a late January morning. The American chief of staff had flown in from Washington for a private meeting. No secretaries or staff were to be present. Those were the orders.

The way Marshall had looked at her seemed to suggest she should not even be in the same building. On reflection, she realised he had not in fact looked at her at all. He had simply looked through her as he passed without even a curt nod of acknowledgement.

The meeting had lasted for ninety minutes without a coffee break. The two men emerged looking grim. Kay had not heard raised voices, but the mood was obvious. She watched from the window as Eisenhower walked George Marshall to the front door of the building where they shook hands with only a brief a word of farewell. Minutes later he was back in the outer office looking serious.

"They want me to take a few days' break," he said. "There's a villa down on the French coast, apparently. Very fancy. I'm supposed to take only Tex with me and a small security team. They've laid on a plane. They want me to have time to rest up. Time alone. Time to think. That's what George said. What you do you think?"

"I think the rest will do you good. Let the war wait for a while."

Eisenhower smiled. "You're right, but I'll need company. Make travel arrangements. I'm taking General Bradley and Tex with me – and you."

"I thought you said General Marshall wanted you there alone?"

Ike laughed as he walked back into his office. Kay felt a surge of satisfaction. The chief of staff of the US Army had tried to cut her out of Ike's trip and probably wanted to cut her out of his life altogether. *Well tough luck, George Marshall*, she said to herself. *You can take that hard-boiled bully-boy act of yours back to the Pentagon. Just leave Ike and his team to get on with the war. And by the way, just remember the next time you come calling that I'm on Ike's team and he likes it that way.*

She lit a cigarette and smiled. She had been around Americans too long. She was beginning to think like them.

17

February-May 1945

Washington knew the president was dying. Death had stamped his face with the mask of a man not long for this world. The smile, the jauntily angled cigarette in its holder and the spirit that occasionally flashed from his dark grey eyes were still there, but the flesh was visibly failing.

At the end of February, Roosevelt returned from the Yalta conference to address the joint houses of Congress. The speech heralded a new dawn in world affairs based on a United Nations organisation that would discuss and arbitrate international differences.

Undertakings had been given by the Soviets at Yalta which would redraw the map of Eastern Europe. Nations such as Poland, which had been enslaved by the Nazis, would be free to decide their own future.

The response to this major announcement, framed in the characteristically optimistic language with which Roosevelt had inspired the American people for so long, shocked the White House.

An exhausted president had misread the mood of war-weariness across America. People were less concerned about

a new map of Eastern Europe and far more interested in
when the war was going to end, and above all when the boys
were coming home – the question that showed up most
frequently in opinion surveys of what the nation was currently
thinking.

Everyone could see Germany was beat and Hitler finished.
So when would the war be over and the boys on their way
home?

The answer from Eisenhower did not improve the mood
of the White House. The war was far from over.

Worn out by reports of Allied infighting and anguished
over the plight of his friend and confidant Harry Hopkins,
who was once again seriously ill in the Mayo clinic, Roosevelt
left for Warm Springs, Georgia, and the sanctuary and
comfort of his own home, known as the Little White House.
His motorcade left the White House on March 30th. He
would never see Washington again.

In the capital, Mamie Eisenhower waited, as she had for
two and a half years, for the end of the war and reunion with
her husband. In that time she had seen him for only those
few hurried days of home leave that had been ruined by his
calling her Kay.

Despite all the assurances of her friends and the inner
conviction that her husband would never throw away twenty-
nine years of marriage, nothing allayed the gnawing doubt,
nurtured by long absence and fuelled by regular evenings
when one cocktail rather too readily led to the next, that Kay
Summersby had won her man and taken her husband.

General Marshall, over tea in her apartment, had just told
her that Ike was tired and would take a break without his
immediate staff in the south of France. He had said that her
husband would be accompanied by General Omar Bradley
and one other member of the general's staff – no one else. He

had looked straight at her when he'd said those three words: *no one else*. He did not mention Summersby's name, but the meaning was clear.

"Where will Ike be staying?" Mamie asked.

"I wish I could tell you," Marshall replied. "It's a private house on the coast. Let's leave it at that."

"That's good – he really needs to rest, by the sound of his letters. But who will take the calls and do the admin down there? He's going to have to stay in touch with headquarters, isn't he?"

Mamie needed further reassurance.

"No," he said. "I made him agree: no cables, no telexes, no calls. Just peace and quiet."

Mamie leant forward to pour more tea. She was satisfied. Briefly she had thought of asking if she could fly out to be with him for a few days, but quickly dismissed the idea. Marshall would never agree. Army wives knew their place, and it was not at the husband's side in the field.

For a moment after that teatime visit she was reassured. Marshall was fiercely loyal to her husband. She knew from the Washington grapevine that he deeply disapproved of Kay Summersby and wanted Ike to drop her. But at the usual round of evening cocktails with fellow army wives, all the rumours resurfaced. The gossip clung like ivy, coiling tentacles of doubt into every fibre of her being.

Sous le Vent was a lavish villa outsides Cannes built in the 1930s by an American millionaire who wished to emulate the expatriate lifestyle on the Riviera caught so accurately by Scott Fitzgerald in *Tender is the Night*.

When Churchill heard that the Allied commander intended to leave his duties and take a brief vacation in the south of France, he was amazed. His view of a break from work was a longer than usual lunch.

Kay Summersby had been at Eisenhower's side for so long that her presence on the plane had not surprised Bradley. Like most of those who worked closely with Eisenhower, he supposed that the two were lovers – certainly her presence late at night in his sleeping quarters wherever they were based would suggest that – but it didn't bother him. The woman was important to Ike, she made him happy, and if she did so in bed at night as much as at his side by day, then so what?

Bradley shared the view that the imperative for the Allies was that a man careworn by overwork and stress should be restored to health in time for the last phase of the war. When Kay moved into the Sous le Vent villa Bradley raised no questions. Nor was he surprised when Eisenhower, after two long nights of sleep, asked Kay to join him every day for lunchtime drinks, usually chilled white wine on his private terrace. He invited no one else.

Her bedroom was on the floor below his, connected by a carpeted wooden staircase that creaked as she went up taking the steps two at a time. Ike had retired to his room for the night. Dinner had been served early that evening. Only Bradley and an aide had joined them and neither played bridge.

He was sitting in a chair by open French windows that led to a balcony. On the beach below men were folding deck chairs and raking the sand. On one side large yachts of the rich and smaller fishing boats sheltered in a harbour enclosed by stone piers.

A calm sea stretched to a horizon lost in the dusk. The war did not seem to have touched this part of the Riviera. The aroma of lavender, jasmine, rosemary, thyme and juniper, the timeless piny scent of the south of France, drifted in from the plants on the balcony and the garden below.

She wore the same black dress as at dinner but had taken off her make-up and jewellery. His jacket lay on the bed and his shoes lay scattered on the floor. He looked up as she entered and smiled.

"I came to say goodnight," she said.

"We could have a nightcap downstairs if you like, I'm not sleepy."

She picked up his shoes, placed them beside the bed and sat down.

"You look about ten years younger," she said.

"I feel it. Let's have a drink."

"No," she said. "It's too nice here. Let's enjoy the view. Breathe the air. You can almost taste it."

They stood on the balcony watching the beach, the boats and the harbour slide into the night. They lit cigarettes and breathed smoky plumes into the aromatic night. She put her arm around him and he around her. They stood for a while looking up at the first of the stars.

"That's the evening star," he said, pointing to the brightest in the constellation above them. "Lets raise a glass to him. There's a bottle of cognac downstairs."

"It's a she. Stars are female," she said.

"All the more reason for a toast."

"I've got a better idea," she said.

They made love quite differently this time, no scrambled shedding of clothes, no awkward fumbling on that leather sofa. It was a warm night for so early in the year. They lay naked on the sheets and kissed. He was relaxed at first, softer to her touch, surrendering slowly to the uncontrollable pulse of pleasure.

She felt like a hostage, held tightly in his arms, watching the unmistakable intimations of a man rising to climax and closure.

Later she tiptoed out of the room, holding her shoes, looking back at his sleeping figure. They had shared their satisfaction, he with a groan and she with a cry that must have been heard in the garden below.

She wondered if anyone had been listening, then told herself, as he had often told her, that it was only worth worrying about the really big things: life, death, victory and defeat. And what about love?

Lust has no contract with love. The white flash carries with it the seeds of life, not love. All that sweaty shuddering and juddering of flesh and bone leaves the human heart far behind, lost in the slipstream of desire.

She was no more than one of those birds that mate on the wing, two feathered creatures that meet high in the sky, fuse as one for a few brief seconds and then part, never to meet again. A one-flight stand, the perfect metaphor for ephemeral love.

They smoked afterwards and drank glasses of fizzy mineral water. He wanted her to stay at least until dawn. She knew they would oversleep. She didn't want to be there when the orderly came in with the breakfast tea. The possibility didn't worry him at all.

That was very Eisenhower, she reflected as she went back to her room. He felt no need to explain her presence, nor his decision to exclude everyone else from the lunches. Bradley accepted the arrangement and was gratified to be invited to join the general in the evenings when the whole party gathered in the big villa.

Everyone there could see that with the good food and the unseasonal sunshine, the man who had directed the Allies' armies across Europe and to the borders of Germany was recovering fast.

The visit lasted a week and was a closely kept secret, known to only a handful of people in Supreme Headquarters in England and in Washington. General Dwight Eisenhower had taken time out from the war to spend a week in a lavish Riviera villa in the company of one of his senior commanders – and a woman widely regarded as his mistress – it was not a story that would look good in the press; nor would the presence of Summersby have much appeal for the disciplinarian chief of staff in the Pentagon.

Eisenhower remained in the villa, refusing suggestions that he might dine at local restaurants or even play the tables at the nearby Monte Carlo casinos. As he recovered, Kay was at his side, arranging the menus, pouring the evening drinks, partnering him at two-handed card games.

Bradley thought they looked and acted like a married couple. But he knew, because he organised the secure communications from the Riviera hideaway, that Ike had been writing to Mamie in Washington, and had used the elegant Sous le Vent writing paper to do so.

He wondered whether he told his wife of the warm days and chilly evenings on the French coast, or of the grandeur of the villa, or merely remarked on the excellence of the cuisine. Perhaps he ended by saying how much he missed her.

Eisenhower seemed to see no incongruity between his obvious love and need for Summersby and his deep affection for his wife in Washington. Or perhaps it was the other way round. Perhaps Ike merely felt affection for Summersby and retained deep marital love for his wife in Washington. It was a puzzle that neither Omar Bradley nor anyone else at Sous le Vent that week cared to consider too closely.

Battles are the hinges on which the doors of history swing back and forth, said Clausewitz. Throughout the months of

April and May in 1945 those battles closed doors on the Nazi past and opened them to the victory that was finally achieved with Hitler's suicide on April 30th and the German surrender a week later.

It was two a.m. when General Alfred Jodl, the German chief of staff, walked into a small recreation room on the second floor of a school in Reims which had served as Eisenhower's war room for the last weeks of the fighting.

Kay bent over her desk to note down the words that would put the seal on the surrender.

"Do you understand the terms of the surrender you have just signed?" said Eisenhower.

"Ja," said the German.

"You will get detailed instructions at a later date, and you will be expected to carry them out faithfully."

There was a pause. The German bowed, then stared blankly at the wall.

Eisenhower said, "That is all."

Jodl turned round and left. Kay rose from her desk as he marched past. She looked at her watch. It was 2.41 a.m.

Ike poked his head out of the office.

"I want to send a message to Marshall. He'll still be at his desk."

Kay took out her notebook.

"Ready?"

"Yes, sir."

"'The mission of this Allied force was fulfilled at 02.41 local time.'"

"Is that all?" she asked.

"It's enough, isn't it? Get it sent straight away."

She turned to go.

"Oh, Kay…"

"Rustle up a bottle of champagne?"

He laughed and nodded. An army photographer was called to capture the moment as Eisenhower held up, in a V-shape, the two pens with which the Germans had signed the surrender. There, just over Eisenhower's smiling right shoulder, and between him and the British Air Marshal Tedder, was the equally smiling face of Kay Summersby.

It was a time of endings. The curtain had fallen on a play whose actors had been stripped of their lines. Roosevelt's death at his Warm Springs home on April 12th was followed on April 30th by the single shot that Hitler fired from his revolver in the Berlin bunker. It was an end of the horrors found in the concentration camps which left those who witnessed the aftermath of such slaughter lost for words and cursed with memories that would never fade.

Eisenhower had received the news of Roosevelt's passing at his Reims headquarters and was remarkably unmoved, Kay thought, by the demise of a man who had propelled him to the pinnacle of authority in a conflict that was nearing its end.

"I can't say I liked him or agreed with everything he did, but I admired him," she heard him say to George Patton. The two men were meeting to plan where and when the Allied armies would meet the Russians, and she, as usual, was sitting at a desk in the corner taking notes.

She noted the lack of warmth in Ike's comments about Roosevelt and not for the first time wondered at the cold, unknown interior of the man she had served and lived every day with during the long years of war.

She knew that the unwritten code of conduct for officers was that they never showed emotion in front of their men or their staff, and had sometimes wondered if her boss had any emotion to show. The only time he revealed himself was at moments of hot temper when he would bawl out a member of his staff. That was rare, and there was always a smile and a handshake afterwards. He would never shout at her, but there had occasionally been a roll of eyes to the ceiling and a voice raised in irritation saying, "For Chrissake, Kay, I ordered that up an hour ago."

That was Eisenhower. He did not ask, he commanded, and his commands demanded immediate action no matter that the person concerned was busy implementing a previous order. But for Kay there would always be a quick smile, a hand on the shoulder and "Thanks, kid," afterwards.

But his ungenerous words about Roosevelt surprised even Patton, who said, "I think you should do better than that when the press asks you for a quote."

The day after the German surrender, Winston Churchill phoned Eisenhower eight times offering praise and congratulation in language that become more effusive as the day drew on. De Gaulle sent a long message of praise in florid French. But the one man for whose words Eisenhower waited patiently was his immediate superior and mentor.

George Marshall did not disappoint him. The American chief of staff sent a message of congratulation that began, "You have completed your mission with the greatest victory in the history of warfare," and ended, "You have made history, great history, for the good of mankind and you have stood for all we hope for and admire in an officer of the United States Army."

18

June 1945

London in June 1945 was waiting to garland Eisenhower with all the celebration that a city diminished by six years of bombing, rationing, terrible food, bathtub gin, rocket attacks, endless casualty lists and false dawns could muster. Grief and mourning had become so commonplace that those attending funeral and memorial services in cold churches and chapels felt they were trapped in a never-ending cycle of the same prayer-book words of regret and remembrance.

The high human toll exacted in final battles across Europe that spring had shocked people on both sides of the Atlantic. In France, the first of the cemeteries that would hold tens of thousands of Allied dead were being prepared.

In Britain and America there was a palpable hunger for a hero to emerge from the wreckage of war, someone who could offer reassurance that the suffering had not been in vain; that a new Europe would rise from the ashes of the old; that rationing would end, that food would become more plentiful and that, well, everything was now going to be all right again.

There was no better person on whom these hopes for happiness could be projected than Dwight Eisenhower, no better person to satisfy the yearning for reassurance that the sacrifices had not been in vain.

Eisenhower agreed to make a victory tour of major cities in Europe and America. He crafted the itinerary with care. His first stop was the Allied city which had suffered most and in which he had forged the strategy that had carried the Allies to Berlin. He wished to pay his tribute to the city that had been his second home during the war – London.

As much as London wished to acclaim their new hero and rejoice in his victories, so Eisenhower wished to step aside from the horrors of war, especially those that were being uncovered in Germany, and have a good time. He had done his duty as a soldier.

The celebrations began on the plane to London. Ike and Kay partnered against Omar Bradley and another aide at bridge. They won a hundred francs and divided the money between them.

At the airport several cars were lined up to take the party to the Dorchester Hotel and then lunch at Number Ten Downing Street.

Eisenhower had other ideas. He told Bradley and the rest of the group to go on to London, explaining that he would join them later.

"Where are you going?" asked Bradley. "The whole of London is waiting for you."

"A little trip down memory lane – we'll see you later."

Bradley noted the "we". He watched them go, both sitting in the back seat of a Packard being driven by a woman chauffeur. He knew exactly where they were going.

Telegraph Cottage looked a great deal more attractive on a summer's day than when Eisenhower had last seen his woodland refuge in the dreary autumn of the previous year. The windows had been cleaned, the garden had been well kept and the small lawn had been mowed.

Before he went in, he walked around to the back to find the vegetable patch had been tended and was bearing runner beans, peas and what looked like marrows. He snapped off a string of beans and gave Kay an enquiring look.

"I asked them to look after the place," she said. "I knew you'd want to come back."

They walked through the house together, Eisenhower displaying schoolboy excitement as each room and its possessions provoked memories. The decks of cards and score pads were laid out on a sitting table waiting a bridge four; his riding breeches had been cleaned, pressed and were hanging in a bedroom wardrobe; his golf clubs were in their bag in the hall next to polished riding boots.

The nine months since he had been here might have been nine years. The D-Day landings, the battle for Normandy, the race across France and then the final climactic battles in Germany felt like events that spanned a lifetime.

The planning for the liberation of Europe had taken place in endless meetings in panelled rooms choked with smoke and loud with argument in London and Washington, but it was here that Eisenhower had brought every problem, every plan, every idea. It was here that he had been able to relax and find release in bridge, evening cocktails and golf, here that he had stumbled on that rare commodity in a commander's life – moments of personal private joy.

They walked outside into the small front garden.

"Goddamnit, I'd like to play that thirteenth hole again," he said suddenly.

"Go on, then. No one's going to stop you."

He slipped his arm around her waist and kissed her softly, and then again, and again, little kisses that quickened her heart.

Kay pulled away and looked around. They were screened from the golf course by trees, but anyone could have been walking in the woods that summer's day. Ike didn't care.

They walked out to the golf course, and to the surprise but willing agreement of the morning golfers, Ike was allowed to cut in and play his favourite hole, the 13th.

It was mid-morning by the time they'd completed their visit to Telegraph Cottage. London and lunch were thirty minutes away and their chauffeur was waiting.

As they went to the car, Eisenhower called Kay back, took her by the arm and walked with her to the wooden bench in a grassy grove hidden from the house by shrubbery.

"Come on, let's sit here for a moment," he said.

They had sat there many times before, talking about what he called the real things in anyone's life: the passing of parents, the first love at college, the death of a friend.

They sat in silence for a while, listening to the murmur of insects, the distant drone of a plane, an exclamation from the golf course, and feeling the growing warmth of the day. They had never sat like this before, peacefully. There had never been enough time or freedom from other people. They hadn't been alone even on those outings to the river pubs she had driven him to on his first visit. Mark Clark had always been there.

He took her hand and then said something so pleasing yet so ambiguous that she later repeated the words to herself to try and understand what they meant.

"Do you remember what I said when we talked here on this bench last summer, the day we got Telek back from the kennels?"

"You said a lot of things."

"I said that we made a great team – remember?"

"Of course I remember. We had drunk some good wine and we were fooling around."

"Well, we've got to think about our future."

There was a silence. The old cliché was true, she thought – the human heart beats faster at moments like this. Ike stretched back and looked up at spears of sunlight filtering through the tracery of leaves above. She watched him. He looked better since the end of the war; his body was still lean, his face was less jowly and had lost the grey pallor of fatigue.

She tried to work out what he meant. He had said "our future". Did that mean he saw them as a couple now the war was over? Or was there something sinister in the suggestion that their lives together had to be considered and weighed in the balance? She wasn't sure.

She kissed him lightly on the cheek and whispered, "I love you."

He pushed her gently away and said, "That's not a victory kiss." Then he held her, hugged her and kissed her without stopping until she broke away for breath and laughed.

"Come on, they're waiting for you in London."

They said nothing on the drive back, but the chauffeur had noticed her passengers were holding hands. Kay caught the driver's eyes in the rear-view mirror and smiled at her. This had been her way into his world and now another driver was doing the same.

Looking at him in the car, she could see the smile on his face and feel the pressure of his hand on hers. Perhaps he really did mean it. Perhaps now, in the glorious freedom from war, they could really find each other.

One thing was for sure, she told herself. General Dwight Eisenhower was about to make a big decision about the new life that awaited him. If she had caught the true meaning of his words he was thinking of their shared future. Together. A couple, married maybe?

She would be lying if she pretended she hadn't thought about marriage. He would leave the army and move to England. The wedding would be somewhere in Mayfair close to the embassy. A grateful British government would give them Telegraph Cottage as a wedding present; they would have a house somewhere in London, maybe Chelsea.

He would have his pension, but that would not be enough. Suitable directorships would be arranged with big companies in the defence industry. London society would open its heart to the conquering hero and his new English wife.

Ike could do all this if he wanted to, and she knew he did. Or rather she thought she knew. He had the willpower, the strength of character, to put his previous life behind him. After all, he had put George Patton behind him – he had sacked his old and much admired friend when he'd opened that big mouth of his and talked out of turn yet again. Kay had forgotten what the issue was, but Ike had exploded and stripped Patton of his command.

Ike was like that. The Eisenhower the world knew was a master of diplomacy, conciliating the warring generals around him, stroking the egos of Churchill, de Gaulle and Roosevelt, and listening carefully to those who served below him. But that had not stopped him having one of his own men shot for looting and rape in the final months of the war. Kay had seen him sign the papers. He had thrown the pen away right across the room afterwards.

Now he was facing another tough decision. But he would follow through, she was sure of that. Once married, there would be a new world waiting for them both. He would write his memoirs, play golf in Richmond Park. They would give dinner and cocktail parties; they would be the toast of London, General Eisenhower with Kay by his side. There would be honours, too, an honorary knighthood for the Allied victor. She would become Lady Eisenhower.

As for Mamie... well, Mamie had had her marriage to this man. And the man had changed; he had fallen in love. Eisenhower would act respectfully and act properly. But he would get divorced, she knew he would. He had said he would never let her go. He had said he wanted time to think about their future. He was a man of his word.

"Here we are," said the driver as they drew up to the Dorchester Hotel. She opened the door, giving Kay a conspiratorial smirk as she got out.

That night Eisenhower was granted the only request he made of the British government by way of a gift in gratitude for the Allied victory. The cabinet had been planning to offer lifetime membership of a famous golf club or a rent-free apartment in central London, but all he asked for was theatre tickets.

At the Prince of Wales Theatre in London's West End, Eisenhower settled into the royal box with his party that evening to see a light comedy called *Strike a New Note*. Theatregoers rose to their feet when they realised who had joined them and shouted "Speech! Speech!" Eisenhower bent over the rail of the box and said loud enough for almost everyone to hear, "It's good to be back in a country where I can almost speak the language."

Photographers clustered around the door to the box. Eisenhower agreed that one cameraman should be allowed to take a quick picture. The next day, to the immense satisfaction of the theatre's management, the papers carried the photograph of Eisenhower's first night in post-war London.

The flash-lit photo showed the Allied commander in the centre of the box, to his left General Omar Bradley and to his right Kay Summersby, with an unidentified elderly woman beside her. On enquiry the photographer was told that this was Kay Summersby's mother, Mrs MacCarthy-Morrogh, who had been invited to join the party.

Churchill was surprised to see the photograph in the morning papers. He had met Kay Summersby during his visits to North Africa and several times since when Eisenhower had brought her to dinner at Number Ten with other members of his staff. He liked her and admired her Anglo-Irish heritage.

The prime minister was even more surprised to learn that on the first night of his visit to post-war London Eisenhower had taken both Summersby and her mother to watch a West End play. It was perhaps understandable in the circumstances to take Miss Summersby along – after all, she remained officially his personal assistant and was also a member of the American armed forces – but inviting her mother as well?

"Are you sure?" he asked an aide.

"Yes, prime minister, it was her mother," was the reply.

"Well, that's Ike's business," he said, "but it's going to cause trouble."

Churchill's view was that a man might take his mistress to the theatre in London, but to take her mother as well implied a relationship rather more substantial than that involved in the business-like liaison between a man and his lover.

The photograph did cause trouble. It was widely reprinted, especially in the American press. All the rumours that had been submerged by the final months of the war resurfaced in fresh innuendo and gossip.

George Marshall, at his desk in the Pentagon, and Mamie Eisenhower, in her Washington apartment, were both in their separate ways dismayed, but neither uttered a word of reproach. Or rather, Marshall decided to say nothing at the time. The photograph angered him. His advice had not been taken. He would bide his time. Eisenhower was not just a national hero, he was the most famous American in the world; soon he would be coming home to a new life and a new career very different from the one on which he had embarked as a second lieutenant in the infantry. Then Marshall would act.

The visit to the theatre was Eisenhower's first public appearance in London since arriving three years earlier, and he intended to make the most of it. After the show, his party drove slowly through crowds of well-wishers to Ciros, a well-known supper and cabaret club where the band struck up "For he's a jolly good fellow" as they took their table.

Drinks were served, food was ordered and then couples took to the small dance floor to a slow jazz number. Eisenhower rose, offered his hand to Kay and took her onto the floor.

For the first time in public she was in his arms, dancing. Other couples on the floor pretended not to notice the celebrity in their midst. Over his shoulder, Kay could see diners slipping menus onto their table for Eisenhower to sign. He had already signed several for the waiters.

Normally he would have hated the attention and snapped at the autograph hunters; this was a man who had shunned the luxury of living in one of London's great hotels, turned his back on the limelight and had never sought to magnify his reputation with press interviews, unlike those showboaters Patton and MacArthur. Now he was basking in the admiration, indeed adulation, of journalists from around the world.

What's more, he was dancing, or rather hopping from foot to foot in time with some private rhythm of his own, and doing so quite openly with the woman widely regarded as his lover. Eisenhower didn't care.

At their table, the rest of his party finished the first bottle of champagne, ordered a second and seemed to find nothing odd in the attention that their host was paying to Miss Summersby.

Kay briefly wondered whether there was a journalist in the room who might make something of such a display of affection, but the thought quickly passed. The man she loved had encircled her in his arms while dancing in front of an admiring crowd in one of London's famous nightspots. Their photograph had been taken together in the theatre. He had insisted that her mother join them for this evening. This was her very own victory celebration and she was going to revel in it.

Mrs MacCarthy-Morrogh was quieter than most at the table. Like every mother who suspects her daughter of an unsuitable love affair, she was worried. General Eisenhower was married with a grown-up son. He was eighteen years older than Kay and had emerged from the exhausting conduct of a successful war to become an instant hero.

She had met him several times before, usually for tea with Kay at Telegraph Cottage and once at the Dorchester Hotel. She'd been proved right; he really had wanted to have an old-fashioned English tea with them and relished the break from the embassy.

Yes, he was charming and polite, and she could see he cared deeply for her daughter. He hardly cared to disguise the fact; at the theatre, where every opera glass in the surrounding boxes was turned on them and not the stage, he had shifted his seat towards hers.

When the curtain rose and the lights went down, she had seen his hand meet hers in the darkness and link for a few seconds before breaking apart. These emissaries of love had quickly been withdrawn to be laid discreetly on the armrests of their chairs.

But theirs had been a wartime affair, when life was different. Now all but the blind could see that a political career for Eisenhower was on the horizon across the Atlantic. The press were full of it. How could Kay possibly be part of that world?

She had gently tried to discuss this with Kay, who did not seem to doubt that Eisenhower intended to make her his wife. He had apparently told her he was worried about the eighteen-year age gap between them. She was thirty-six. He was fifty-four. Kay said that never mattered to those in love.

She told her mother that he had said, over and over again, that he would never let her go. This did not make Mrs MacCarthy-Morrogh any happier. Men in love did not need to say such things. They did so to convince themselves not others.

"I want you to be careful," she said to her daughter, "think about what you are getting into."

"Mother, I know you worry about me and I am very grateful, believe me, but I'm a big girl now and I know what I am doing."

"But that's just the point, darling! You may know what you're doing but do you know what he's doing?"

The conversation was circular, exasperating, and to Kay's irritation it took place in similar form every time she met her mother alone that summer.

The highlight of the London celebrations was to be Ike's speech to the Guildhall, where the great and the good of the business and political worlds gathered to listen to wise words from distinguished speakers. Eisenhower was not a natural speaker, but he knew he had to make the speech of his lifetime. He had worked on it for weeks. Kay had typed every draft, listened as he rehearsed it, made suggestions and timed him speaking every new version.

"No one else could do this for me, Kay," he told her. "I have to get this just right for the audience here and you have an Irish way with words."

The reception, both on the night at the Guildhall and in the press the following morning, bordered on sycophancy. Eisenhower was compared to Lincoln and hailed as a great orator and thinker. Even Churchill was impressed with his friend's powers of oratory.

The previous stream of requests for Eisenhower to give interviews, make speeches, open schools or hospitals and lend his name to everything from breakfast cereals (*"Take the fight to the day Ike's way"*) to a new model of car (*"Get there fast and get there first with Ike"*) now became a torrent.

It was time to move on. He would visit the King and Queen at Buckingham Palace and then return to Frankfurt, where he had established his new headquarters in the former offices of the I.G. Farben chemical company. There he would wrestle with the intractable problems of occupation.

Kay no longer had to be told that she would accompany him. It was simply understood between them that where he went she went too. He told her to put all the dates for travel, lunches, dinners and parties in her large leather-bound appointments diary and to make sure she was included in every one. His plans now included her for every hour of every day; with one exception.

"I've been invited to do a tour stateside – coast to coast, every major city, big receptions, ticker-tape, the works," he said one morning. He was holding up an itinerary that had come in on the teleprinter overnight.

"Congratulations! Home is the conquering hero," she said. "When is it?"

"Too damn soon, three weeks' time."

They looked at the diary and Kay began a list of appointments to be cancelled. Ike was excited; Hollywood was going to turn out its film stars for him; there would be ticker-tape parades, speeches to be made and honorary degrees to be accepted. Kay fell silent as he recited the roll-call of honours he would receive. He looked at her and stopped.

"What is it?"

"I'm not coming, am I?"

He lit a cigarette. She could see he hadn't even thought about including her.

"Not on this trip," he said.

"Oh," she said.

"What?" he asked.

"Well, you're going to be gone weeks and you'll be there with…"

"With who? Mamie my wife? Of course I will. This is an official tour, Kay. It's something I have to do. I've told you – you've just got to trust me."

Kay said nothing and looked down at her shoes.

"We can't possibly be there together – don't you understand?" he went on.

"Yes, sir."

"What would it look like if I was riding around America with an unknown Brit woman at my side?"

"I understand, sir."

"Do you? I sometimes think you think only of yourself."

"That's not fair, sir."

"Well, don't look at me like that. This is a great honour I am being given."

"I know, sir. I am pleased for you – and for Mamie."

"Yes, it's been a long time."

"Ike, has she ever…?"

"What?"

"Well… mentioned me in her letters?"

"Kay!"

"I'm sorry. I just wondered."

Ike put a hand on her arm and squeezed it gently.

"Don't wonder – and don't worry, it will be all right."

She stiffened to salute him.

"And don't salute me," he barked.

She saluted.

It was strange, she thought, that her famous lover did not seem to care how many photographs the cameramen took of the two of them in London, where they publicly danced and dined as a couple, yet once back home the photographers would be taking rather different pictures – Ike would once again be with Mamie.

Charlotte Montagu thought it was rather more than strange.

"Forgive me for repeating myself, doll, but you're being taken for a ride. A long ride, an enjoyable ride, but at the end you're going to come off the horse."

Kay lost her temper. "Stop saying that! You're like a bloody parrot."

"Calm down, doll, I'm just trying to help."

"Well, you're not helping. And I don't need lectures from someone who's had sex with a complete stranger against the railings of Eaton Square!"

"Wartime quickie, doll, you should try it sometime."

Nothing phased Charlotte. They were having tea in Fortnum and Mason's emporium in Piccadilly, where Charlotte had shamelessly invoked her mother's position at Buckingham Palace to secure a table.

"It's harder to get in here than any restaurant in London," Charlotte said. "The famous English tea has returned after its wartime absence – look."

Kay allowed her irritation to cool. She admired the way Charlotte would change the subject to avoid a row. She surveyed the crowded room with starched white linen laid on tables mounted with tiered cake-stands full of toasted crumpets, cucumber sandwiches and a variety of cakes and tarts.

"Charlotte, do you really think that?" she said.

"You can't get whisky for love or money, but the flour ration has been raised – wonderful, isn't it?" said Charlotte, loading her plate. "Come on, doll, eat up."

Whatever Charlotte did she did without pause, be it eating, drinking or talking, and sometimes she managed to do all three at the same time. Kay enjoyed their meetings for the simple reason that Charlotte reminded her what it was like to laugh. Her friend was selfish, outrageous and set no limit on life's pleasures, especially when it came to cakes at Fortnum's, or a stranger pushed against the railings of Eaton Square during the blackout.

"Charlotte, did you hear me?"

"Yes, yes. Shall I pour?"

"Well?"

"Well what, doll?"

"You think I'm being taken for a ride?"

"I think you see too many unicorns and rainbows. OK you're having fun but it has to end sometime. Rainbows are an illusion aren't they? And you don't see many unicorns around these days."

There was a pause. Kay sipped her tea and took a cucumber sandwich.

"You think I'm a fool, don't you?"

"Not at all. I think you're in love, and…"

"And what?"

Charlotte had just lifted a crumpet from the cake-stand and was about to take a bite, but she put it on her plate and looked at Kay in a way that suggested she was about to say something important.

"And good for you. It's lovely being in love, I imagine. I wouldn't know. And I don't think I'm ever going to know."

"Of course you are – don't be silly. Anyway, who said I'm in love?"

"I did, and don't deny it. It's just that I think the man you love is going to leave you sooner than you think. They all do. Trust me, I'm an expert. There, I've said it." Her eyes turned back to her plate. "Here, have one. *Carpe* crumpet!"

She offered Kay a crumpet smeared with jam on a small plate. Kay shook her head and Charlotte lifted the pastry off the plate and devoured it in two bites.

Maybe it was the sugar rush from all the cakes, or perhaps it was just being in such exuberant company, but Kay felt elated as she walked past the anti-aircraft batteries in Green Park towards Victoria Station. Charlotte was just plain wrong. Her warning was predictable and possibly motivated by jealousy. What filled her with a glow of happiness was the thought that she was in love. And he was in love with her, so why would he choose to throw away such happiness? It didn't make sense.

She wasn't sure she knew what love felt like. If it was the pulse and flicker of heightened emotion that refuses doubt and deals only in certainty, or the feverish state of mind that conjures up unicorns and rainbows, then it had certainly never affected her. As she often told herself, love was a mystery and long may it remain so.

She had hardly been in love with dear Gordon Summersby, had she? That was just lust, and very welcome too. As for her fiancé Patrick – well he was gone and there was little point in thinking of him. She loved her family, of course, but that was different. If love was supposed to be the passionate, romantic sort that had inspired poets and musicians for millennia, the kind which is supposed to lift you off your feet and make your heart turn somersaults, it had passed her by.

Until now. She thought of him from the moment she woke until last thing at night; there was hardly a moment in the day when she was not with him – working for him, listening to him, answering his questions and thinking of what he needed to do next.

The moment she entered a room and saw him she felt a pang of pleasure. These feelings had not just arrived, they had crept up on her, unannounced and unasked for. Was that love? She didn't know. It didn't matter. What mattered was that he felt the same way. She saw it in his eyes when she entered his office in the mornings or joined him at a meeting amid a crowd of other people.

It was always the same look, a nod and a brief smile that told their own story. They were never alone but always together. That was all that mattered. It was easy for Charlotte to say he was taking her for a ride. She didn't know him.

During his tour across America that summer of 1945, Eisenhower drew audiences of millions in Washington and across the nation, at concert halls, sports stadia and city parks. Mamie Eisenhower was at his side every step of the way, cheerfully wearing a succession of smart hats in the open motorcades. She looked radiant, if, as the fashion writers said snippily, in need of a little more *avoirdupois* on such a slender frame.

Tracking the photographs and TV newsreel film from Frankfurt, Kay at first felt proud of the way this man she had served so long, now the man in her life, had assumed the mantle of national hero. As the tour stretched into the second week doubts raised themselves. She could not shake them off. She began to wonder whether the ongoing gossip held a seed of truth – was Eisenhower unable to make up his mind between the two women in his life? Or had he simply subjugated his emotions to the media demands made upon such a popular hero to act out the role of the loyal and loving husband?

Perhaps Charlotte was right, she thought; perhaps she was being used as a wartime fling like so many others. But if so, why then had he promised to organise her American citizenship? Why had he given her rank in the US Army? It didn't make any sense. She shouldn't listen to any of it. She was the one. He'd said so.

On return to his Frankfurt headquarters after a hero's welcome in the US, Ike appeared to those around him to be moody, morose and depressed. He paid little attention to the praise, the press interviews and the hints of a political career that were circulating in Washington.

"Come on, tell me – why so gloomy?" Kay asked as they waited for guests to arrive and join them for an early dinner and a game of bridge.

"I'll tell you why," said Ike. "Someone once sat at the desk in my office and signed off production of the Zyklon B gas, knowing that it was to be used to commit mass murder in the concentration camps. Some person or persons had eaten a good breakfast in a smart suburban house one morning, kissed his wife and children goodbye, come to the office and called a meeting to discuss the production timetable for a toxic gas that could only have had one application."

"You'll go mad if you think like that," she said. "Look around you, there are guilty men everywhere. Be positive, think of the future."

"I am being positive. I positively want to see the bastard who sat at this desk in the hot end of hell."

Behind that comment lay the real reason for the angst that had descended on the Allied commander. As the horrors of the concentration camps and the numbers of those murdered became clear, a haunting question posed itself. Could the Allies have brought the war to an end more swiftly, should they have bombed the death camps even if by killing the prisoners they saved so many more?

Eisenhower's job as Allied commander in charge of a defeated Germany was in many ways more complex than his wartime leadership role. At a humanitarian level, the country was on the verge of starvation, industry was at a standstill, and power supplies were infrequent.

Every morning, Kay typed out new statistics that had arrived on the teleprinter overnight, a steady stream of impersonal numbers that threatened to overwhelm the newly created Allied Control Centre and its beleaguered, chain-smoking boss. Eight million foreigners had been found working as slave labourers in factories and farms across Germany.

These displaced people were now struggling to return to their homes in countries across Europe and especially to the Soviet Union. Tens of thousands of Allied prisoners of war, mostly British and American, many suffering from maltreatment, had been liberated and now clamoured to be repatriated.

Somehow Germany had to be rebuilt to allow war reparations to begin, and to avoid, as Churchill remarked to Eisenhower, "Europe being shackled to a corpse."

The problems of administering a defeated nation were as nothing compared to the complex diplomacy required when Eisenhower dealt with his Russian allies. Stalin had demanded immediate Allied withdrawal from the Soviet zone of occupation throughout Germany, while the British and Americans had countered by asking for guaranteed access to Berlin.

The name of the city burnt into every teleprinter message received at the Farben headquarters. "Berlin" became a code word for the rapidly deteriorating relations between the allies of East and West.

Kay sifted the reports when they had arrived and placed them in one of two in-trays on Ike's desk, one marked *Urgent*, the other *Very Urgent*. It was his little joke. Everything was very urgent.

It was while doing that one morning that she saw the letter. It lay open on Eisenhower's desk. A silver ivory-handled letter-opener lay beside it, partially concealed by an envelope which had been carefully slit open. He had clearly been called away while reading it. The address on the envelope was written in a neat curling script she had seen so often in his in-tray. She picked up the letter and placed it on top of the other mail. As she did so she saw the words at the top.

My Darling Ike
Kay paused for a second, then read the rest of the letter.

My Darling Ike,

The war is over and your tour of duty is almost at an end. I can't tell you how much I am looking forward to seeing you again. We had such fun in the summer, didn't we? As long as we remain apart even if briefly keep writing your warm and loving letters. You have told me how much you missed me and that is a blessing and a comfort.

It is wonderful and very moving to know our love is still strong and has survived the flames of war. That makes me very happy.

Someone slapped Kay hard in the face. That's how it felt. She let the letter drop and put a hand on the desk to steady herself. She felt faint and could feel her heart thumping. She sat down on a padded chair in front of the desk. The door opened behind her. She turned to look at him.

"Kay, are you OK?" said Eisenhower.

"I'm sorry, so sorry," she said.

"About what? What's the matter?"

"I shouldn't have."

She waved a hand at the letter on the desk. Eisenhower picked it up and scanned it briefly.

"Oh, Kay," he said. "Why did you open it?"

"I didn't, you did. And don't 'Oh, Kay' me."

She got up and smoothed her skirt. She always did this to stay calm.

"You've been writing love letters to your wife. You told her you loved her when you were in the states this summer."

Eisenhower picked up the letter and waved it at her.

"I write my wife letters, not love letters. I'm married to her, for God's sake! She's the mother of my children. What do you want me to say to her? How's the weather in DC and by the way I'm having a lovely time with my personal assistant here in bombed-out Germany?"

"Don't lie to me!"

"I'm not lying to you."

Kay seized the letter from him and read it out loud.

"*We had such fun in the summer, didn't we? As long as we remain apart even if briefly keep writing your warm and loving letters.*"

"Give me that back," he said, angry now and coming towards her. She quickly moved around the desk.

"*It is wonderful and very moving to hear how our love is still strong and has survived the flames of war. That makes me very happy.*"

They paused, staring at each other over the desk.

"Well, that doesn't make me very happy, sir!"

"You had no right to read my private correspondence."

"It was open on your desk. '*My darling Ike*' it began. How was I supposed not to read that? Anyway what the hell's that got to do with it? You've written a love letter to your wife. You probably made love to her in the summer on that hero's tour. Where does that leave me?"

"Come here, Kay." He opened his arms and walked towards her.

"Did you? Did you sleep with your wife in all those fancy hotel rooms you two were staying in?"

"Stop being ridiculous. Come here."

"No, I bloody well won't."

She picked up the letter-opener and pointed it at him.

"Don't come anywhere near me. You're a lying cheat."

"Stop it, Kay, I can explain."

"Know something? Every woman in history has heard that before."

"Put that knife down, come and listen to me."

She threw the knife on the table.

"Go on then. Explain. I'm listening," she said.

"All right, I do miss Mamie, why shouldn't I? I miss my boy. I miss my friends back home. I love them all. That's why I miss them."

"Nice speech. I miss my family too but that's not exactly what we are talking about here, is it?"

"Stop this right here." He leant across the desk. She could see the veins beginning to throb on his temple. The last time she saw that look on his face was when they had argued about the uniforms. But this was very different.

"Mamie has had a miserable war. She's lonely, depressed and she misses me. What do you want me to say? Sorry I don't love you any more, my dear wife. I love this Brit woman with blue-green eyes and a nice long legs and she makes me happy and by the way, dear wife, when this bloody war is over I'm going to kiss you goodbye and set up with her?"

"You think I'm going to fall for that old baloney?"

"God, you've got an Irish lip on you."

"And you've got a lying tongue in your head."

She was crying now and reached for a handkerchief.

"You told me it was all over between you two."

"I said no such thing."

"Well, you let me believe it!"

"Oh for Chrissakes, Kay – you're making a mountain out of this."

"All I want to know is whether you love me."

"Of course I do, I've told you that. You're in the army, you're an American citizen, what more do you want?"

"But Mamie, your letter to her…"

"I write to her all the time. You know that. I love her but it's different. I wouldn't be much of a man if I didn't have feelings for a woman I've been married to for God knows how many years. Mamie has done nothing wrong. Why should I hurt her?"

That was true, she thought. Maybe he was in love with them both although in different ways. Maybe he did have a right to pen loving *billets doux* to his far away wife while taking her in his arms here in Germany and covering her with kisses. That was a lot of maybes.

She blew her nose, aware he was watching her.

"I need a drink," she said. He came around the table and tried to put his arms around her. She stepped back and shrugged him off.

"That very nice cognac you've got locked away in your drawer will do. Make it a double with ice."

That was when she should have walked away. She should have resigned, gone back to England and started a new life. But he had reassured her, explained himself. A woman in love will believe anything, that's what Charlotte had said.

Looking back, Kay could see she really did believe then that her boss, the Supreme Commander General Dwight Eisenhower, was preparing to seek permission to divorce his wife.

A few days later she prepared to mix their evening drinks. The row had not been forgotten but she persuaded herself it had simply been a silly misunderstanding, an overreaction on her part. "How about a game of bridge with some of the boys – twenty cents a hundred?" she said.

This was the only way she could get him to take his mind off the secret cables, the complaints, the commands, the pleading letters and all the other wreckage of war and occupation that washed up on his desk.

She poured the cocktails, just one each to ensure a clear head if they played later. Sometimes these bridge games went on well after midnight if Ike was in the mood – and when he was wound up he was usually in the mood for bridge.

He lit a cigarette. He was on to his third pack that day.

"No thanks, and no bridge tonight. But I'll take that drink."

She passed him the cocktail and sat down to listen. He was in that that sort of mood.

"I think if you spend a lifetime in the army, you believe that every problem can be solved," he said. "That force, or the threat of force, can be used to obtain the objectives given to you. Life is clear-cut. You have your orders and you obey them. But once you leave the army…"

"But you haven't left," said Kay.

It was the first time he had mentioned leaving the military. Kay suspected there was some truth in all the gossip about a political career back home. She had come to realise that he would never accept the generous offer of a London home from the British government, nor seek a comfortable career as an author and speaker in England. That was a silly daydream. Her man was going home, but as what? And when she went with him, how would she survive as a Washington wife?

"No, I haven't, and I'm not going to," he said, "but my point is that the military creates a world for every man jack in uniform, from the ordinary grunt to top brass like me. Once you step out of that world and look around, you see that life isn't really like that. In a world where there is no control, no order and no one seems in charge."

"You're talking about politicians."

"No, I'm talking about people generally – you can't prescribe for them. You never know what they're going to do next."

"You mean it would be better if we were all in the army?"

Eisenhower laughed, sipped his drink, and smiled in appreciation at the mix of gin and bitters as he lit another cigarette. She could see he quite liked the idea.

"That's the first sensible idea I've heard in a long time," he said.

She waited for him to pat the sofa and say, "Come here." She would sit down beside him, feel his arm slide around her. They would undress, not quickly as that first time but slowly, stroking and teasing each other. In the sweet clemency of sex they would both find forgiveness.

But he didn't do that tonight. He just lay back with his cigarette watching the smoke rising to the ceiling. It was as if she wasn't there.

19

October 1945

Eisenhower celebrated his fifty-fifth birthday on October 14th. He had remained in Frankfurt with a reduced staff since the wartime "family" had returned to the US, all except Kay, who stayed on as his personal assistant.

Ike hated the Frankfurt headquarters and the tedious bureaucracy that went with administration of the US area of occupation. His days now began with a refrain familiar to those who worked with him.

"Anything to get me out of this goddamn city! Anything. Christ, this place is enough to drive a man mad!"

The histrionics were not necessary, but neither Kay nor anyone else felt able to point this out. They knew he had been told by President Truman that he was to succeed George Marshall as chief of staff. He just had to wait for the formal appointment later that year. Then he would shake the dust of Europe from his feet, turn his back on the rubble of war and fly home where he belonged.

Kay could see that the weathervane of his mind had swung from Europe to Washington. There was no doubt that he would take her with him. The only issue was that of her citizenship.

"I think we can fix that this fall," he said. He had just opened an envelope containing a cable from the Pentagon. "It looks like I'll have to go to DC and see Marshall. Perhaps I could push it through then."

"That would be great," she said, "but try and be back for your birthday."

"You'll have to go to DC yourself to sign all the papers," he said. "You do know that?"

He looked up, smiled briefly and returned to the paperwork on his desk.

Ike's birthday had been circled in her diary for months, but she began to make a note of other dates, too, especially his flights to Washington and return to Frankfurt. Time and place had begun to matter. She wanted to hurry the clock forward to get to Washington. Once she had citizenship, she'd never have to leave him again.

Kay had wanted Ike's birthday present to be two of the finest steaks she could find in Frankfurt, but such luxuries were only a memory in a city of half-starving people. Every food shop was either closed or had long queues outside. She had some dried pasta in the cupboard; spaghetti would be an unusual birthday dinner, but it would have to do.

It was Friday, the end of a long week, and this was Ike's birthday dinner. She baked a small cake and decorated it with the numerals 55 picked out in bright red pins. She placed just one candle on it and propped a small framed photograph of Telek against the cake. That was her present to him. He would want nothing more.

She had found tomato ketchup and onions to make a sauce and a hard cheese to grate on top. Once that was simmering on the stove she opened a bottle of red wine from a case donated by a liaison officer with the Free French Forces.

The birthday supper would be little different from what had become almost a domestic routine at the end of every week – drinks, dinner and then long talks together sitting side by side on the sofa after the servants had left for the evening. Outside, as the temperature dipped towards freezing, soldiers patrolled around the house.

In all the time she had known him, there was no greater surprise than when her boss put his arms around her that Friday evening and said, "Close your eyes. I have a present for you."

"Just a minute – it's your birthday. I have a present for you."

"I was first. Close your eyes."

"No, I'm first."

"Close your eyes, that's an order!"

She closed her eyes, held out her hand and opened them to find an envelope in her palm. She opened it to find a single slip of embossed paper. It was a travel warrant stating that Kay Summersby was officially authorised to fly on the Allied commander's personal plane, a Flying Fortress, to Washington two days hence on Sunday evening.

At first she thought that some strange practical joke was being played. She took a large sip of her drink. Ike was not a joker.

"Washington? But I thought you–"

He put a finger to her lips. "You're going first. I discussed this with the president in the summer. He agreed, but it has taken a while for the paperwork to come through."

"But to do what?"

"You're going to become an American citizen – that's what you wanted, wasn't it?"

She turned around once, put her drink down, swirled around again, opened her arms and flung herself into his, sending his drink flying from the glass.

"You're wonderful! Thank you!"

"Whoa!" he said, brushing down his jacket sleeve. "First things first. You've got to write a nice letter to Secretary of State Byrnes. This has to be done by the book. I'll write a covering note."

There and then he dictated the letter that would open the doors to her American citizenship. That's when she knew she was safe.

Until now it was as if he had felt unable to complete the circle he had so patiently drawn around them in their years together. He could say, as he did, that he never wanted to let her go, that what they had found in each other felt so right, but the end of the war and the pull of his next big career move had placed the word *perhaps* between them.

"It's too bad we didn't meet years ago," she had said to him once, and he had nodded.

"Trouble is, when you're in the army you don't see the world outside. You don't sometimes see what is more important. Perhaps…"

Perhaps what? she wanted to say. Perhaps if we had met earlier in our lives you would have married me and we would have been man and wife by now? Perhaps if there had been no war I would have emigrated to America as I had planned and we would have met and fallen in love?

Now there was no perhaps. The doubts in her mind had been banished. She was going to Washington on his personal plane. Secretary Byrnes would reply to the letter and set the wheels in motion. American citizenship would allow her to work at the Pentagon with him.

She wondered whether she would be stationed outside Washington to start with. He would have to start divorce proceedings and that might be awkward. He would want her assigned somewhere else, maybe in the Midwest, to avoid the gossip. There would be a firestorm of scandalous talk and condemnation.

She knew, and Ike would well know, how the American press would react. But he never seemed to mind that. He had nothing but contempt for newspaper chit-chat, as he called it. In the years she had known him he seemed impervious to the gossip he trailed in his wake. When Clark and the others openly called her his shadow in front of him, he paid no attention.

As he had said so often, he was a soldier living the military life and nothing penetrated that world other than training for the next war and learning the lessons of the last one.

With her flight authorisation in her handbag signed by the man she loved, Kay's life became a blur.

Two days after the birthday supper she flew with a number of officials in the supreme commander's personal Flying Fortress to Washington. There she spent days waiting in line, signing forms, producing this document and that, watching the wheels of bureaucracy grinding through the formalities of becoming a US citizen.

The press were unaware of her presence in a modest hotel, and no one else knew she was in Washington. In between the long waits in government departments she became a tourist, marvelling at the sights she had heard so much about but never seen. It was a warm autumn but she knew the winters were harsh and the summers steamy in the capital. She would need a new wardrobe, light colourful dresses for the summer and warm well-lined coats for the winter. After the war years in London the big department stores offered an Aladdin's cave of riches. If only Charlotte could see her now.

She would wait before writing to her. She could just imagine Charlotte's reaction. Her friend would be sitting in a swanky bar with yet another married man, pointing to a photo in a newspaper and saying, "See that woman with Eisenhower. She's my best friend, Kay Summersby." Charlotte would conveniently forget, of course, that she had predicted a swift and sorrowful end to her relationship.

At the end of her four days' stay, a story in the *New York Times* caught her eye. Citing White House sources, the report said that President Truman was about to appoint George Marshall, chief of the army staff, as a special envoy to China. That meant only one thing.

The job that Ike knew was coming his way was about to be formally announced. He had never expressed great enthusiasm for the role. Indeed he had told her that the idea of a desk in the Pentagon – in overall control of the sprawling defence bureaucracy – would be a shock after years of movement and action in the European theater of operations.

On the overnight flight back to Germany, she couldn't sleep. There was a headwind and she found herself drinking cup after cup of bitter instant coffee and willing the plane to fly faster. It was November and they would be landing at the military airbase outside Frankfurt in what the pilot had announced would be a heavy rainstorm.

She had arranged to meet him at his house. A car picked her up and drove her straight there through the pouring rain. She had a present for him to make up for the failure to cook him a proper birthday dinner. Ike had said nothing about the simple pasta supper and had loved the framed photo of Telek, but he was an impossible man when it came to choosing proper grown-up presents.

The only gift she had ever seen him receive with real pleasure was the box of oysters that Roosevelt had sent from

Washington the previous Christmas. She had bought him a book of poems by the English war poet Wilfred Owen. He had probably never heard of him, but she felt he would like the elegiac words of a man who so beautifully and painfully captured the futility of trench warfare, in which he was to lose his own life.

As they drew up outside the house, Kay saw the official car with the driver standing ready to open the passenger door. The engine was running and he was looking at his watch. Her heart sank. Ike would be flying off to another award ceremony in Europe. She was tired, but she would ask to go with him.

An orderly was bringing two large suitcases out of the house. They were the big leather ones with brass locks and D.E. stamped on the side that had followed him to France after D-Day. They held all the clothes he possessed; almost everything he owned, in fact.

Eisenhower came to the door, stopped, surprised, then smiled and said, "Hi, Kay. Welcome back."

"Where are you going?" It was all she could say. No other words came to her. She had just arrived, and he was leaving.

"I'm going back to Washington."

"Right now? But I've just got back!"

He saw the look on her face as her features crumpled into tears beneath recent make-up.

He walked round the car towards her, put his arms around her and led her back into the house, kicking the front door shut behind him. He held her close.

"Orders. Immediate return. The president has appointed me chief of staff."

She began to cry. She couldn't help it. "I know. I saw it in the paper. Congratulations," she said. "I'm sorry. This is a bit sudden."

"Kay, we knew this was coming. Don't worry – I'll send for you. Be patient and look after Telek."

"But… when? It won't be long, will it?"

"No. You'll be over in a couple of weeks with the rest of the gang. We're all going back."

"Put your hand on my heart and say that."

He looked at her, puzzled. "What?"

"Like you did with that captain."

"Who?"

"The officer who didn't want to fly on D-Day. McMichael. Remember?"

"Oh, him. Sure."

He put his hand just above her left breast and she covered it with hers.

He opened the door and gestured at the car that was taking him back to the airfield she had just come from. They were like two ships in the night flashing semaphore signals at each other as they passed. She felt sick and faint, as if someone had punched her hard in the stomach. It was the same feeling as when she had seen that letter from Mamie. Then he kissed her softly on the forehead and was gone.

It was afternoon when she woke in her apartment. She made scrambled eggs, breaking two into the pan and whipping them up with butter, then put coffee in the percolator and watched it bubble through the filter. Women would sell themselves for coffee and eggs on the streets outside – there was hunger, fear and anger in this and every German city.

In the womb of the US Army, however, with its canteens and commissariat, little was lacking and there was nothing to be afraid of. But she was a little afraid. He had left so quickly. She realised she had not had time to give him his Wilfred Owen poems.

She sat down to drink her coffee and go through her post. Telek was whining and growling for a walk. She put the post aside, put on his lead and took him round the block.

Sitting down with the post on her return, she came across the US Army magazine *Beachhead News*. Ike was on the cover and on almost every page inside: there were photographs of him with Bradley in Paris, him on the Normandy battlefield posing with Montgomery, both men looking stiff and awkward, and him holding up the two pens after the German generals had signed the surrender document at Reims, with Bradley, Tedder and Clark alongside him smiling.

She flicked the pages forward, and then stopped. There was something wrong with the surrender photograph. Something was missing.

She turned the pages back. Ike was smiling in the centre of the photograph, holding up the two pens with his officers on either side of him. They all looked so happy, she thought, even though it was three a.m. Then she saw it. She was not in the photograph. She knew with certainty that she had been there when it was taken. The army photographer had checked with her afterwards to get all the names right – he hadn't had to ask for hers; everyone knew Kay Summersby.

She went to her bureau and got out the original photo, one of a file she kept of pictures of herself with Eisenhower. There she was, standing just behind Ike, smiling as the camera flashed, and very visible. She looked again at the photo in the magazine. She took a deep breath. She had been airbrushed out. George Marshall must have ordered that, probably at Mamie's suggestion.

Mamie would have hated that photo. The Pentagon brass wouldn't have liked it either. It would have been embarrassing to have the new chief of staff pictured with his mistress beside him at the moment of victory.

She wondered if Ike had agreed to the deception. No, he wouldn't do that. He probably hadn't even seen the magazine. She would tease him about it when they were together again.

20

November 1945

Eisenhower's crowded programme in Washington began with an appearance before the Senate armed forces committee. The senators were deferential in their questioning about the conduct of the war to the point where the hearing almost became a eulogy, which both embarrassed and irritated him. Immediately after the two-hour hearing he was summoned to meet George Marshall for the first in a series of handover meetings at the Pentagon.

Marshall stood to greet him as he walked in. There was a handwritten letter sitting face up on his desk. They shook hands. Neither man sat down.

"Before we go any further, you wrote me a letter concerning your personal life," Marshall said matter-of-factly.

"I did."

"In that letter you sought my permission to file for divorce."

Eisenhower sighed, looked out of the window and said nothing.

"That's right, isn't it?" Marshall spoke slowly without raising his voice but emphasising each word so that they sounded like an accusation. Eisenhower turned to face him.

"Yes," he said.

"And you got my reply?"

"I did."

"Is there any more to be said?"

"I don't think so."

"You don't think so?"

The two men looked at each other in silence. Marshall, a steely-eyed disciplinarian who exuded more than a whiff of New England sobriety, had done more than anyone, including the late president, to promote the man who stood before him.

Eisenhower, exhausted and finally feeling the burden of the European campaign, began to cough. He reached for a handkerchief in his trouser pocket. His chest felt tight and a sore throat was beginning to pain him. He didn't even want a cigarette, not that Marshall allowed smoking in his office.

"You've been a fine commander in one of the greatest wars ever fought. You gave us a great victory over the forces of evil. You are a hero here, and I hardly have to tell you that your future may well extend beyond the military."

"Thank you."

"So let me make sure I've made myself absolutely clear."

Marshall picked up the letter on his desk and held it briefly in his right hand, not looking at it but showing it to the man he faced across his desk. It was handwritten in three paragraphs, with a scrawled signature at the bottom. Eisenhower didn't look at the letter. He didn't have to.

Marshall spoke slowly with a voice lowered to just above a loud whisper.

"If you seek a divorce, the army will not stand for it. Nor will the people of this country. You will be finished here. Most likely you would have to make a home for yourself abroad, in England. You would not be wanted here. You understand?"

"Yes."

"I repeat – you would be finished here. Do you get that?"

"You have made that very clear."

Marshall paused, fiddled with something on his desk and said, "I take it therefore that in accepting your new role as chief of staff you have made a clear choice in this matter."

"That is correct."

"Good. Now, let's get down to business. By the way, you look awful. Have you seen a doctor?"

After a week of speech-making and giving evidence to various senate committees, Eisenhower was taken to hospital with bronchial pneumonia. It was the 22nd of November. Kay learnt of his illness in the Frankfurt office canteen, where she overheard a conversation at the next table.

The words "Ike" and "hospital" floated across to her.

"Excuse me," she said, "did you say something about General Eisenhower being in hospital?"

The two men at the next table looked up from their coffee.

"Yes," said one. "It was on the wires this morning. Pneumonia."

"Do you know which hospital?"

"A clinic in White Sulphur Springs, apparently."

"Did the report say anything else?"

The man shook his head and returned to his coffee.

Someone should have told me, she thought. After all, I have been working closely with him here in Frankfurt and I am still doing the job, and there he is seriously ill in America. People die from that, don't they? Why didn't they tell me?

She wrote the date down in her personal diary when she got home. Dates mattered more than ever to her now. She was counting not just the days but the hours now until her return to Washington.

Of course she knew why she hadn't been told. She also knew she couldn't send Ike a message. Mamie would be with him at his bedside, caring for him, reading the letters and cables of goodwill that would be pouring in, and the American and European newspapers, who had been following his every move, would have reporters waiting outside the hospital.

The next entry she wrote in her diary consisted of two exclamation marks underlined in red crayon. The corrugated texture of the page suggested it had been splashed by water. The movement orders for the remaining members of Eisenhower's headquarters staff in Frankfurt had come through in a long telex. Their names and ranks were listed with details of departure times for the military aircraft taking them home.

No one was given much time, two or three days at most to pack up and leave. Kay Summersby's name was not on the list. She had cried at first, then told herself she was not surprised. She knew that there would be a separate movement order for her.

It was obvious, really. Ike didn't want her to be seen travelling with the rest of this staff. For discretion's sake he would want her to fly back after the main airlift. There would be crowds and a lot of press at the airport in Washington when those planes landed. Her flight might well be routed via New York or Philadelphia.

She smiled at the thought that the man who had never bothered to conceal her presence in his life in Europe was now becoming so discreet. It would have been nice to have received a message from him, even if he was in hospital recovering from pneumonia, but she understood. She wished she could be there with him. She would read him some of his westerns, maybe even a few poems from Wilfred Owen. He would like that.

Two days passed. The other members of the team, including orderlies, cooks and communications people, were beginning to disappear. Eisenhower's rented house was locked up and the blinds drawn. The headquarters' offices in the Farben buildings were almost empty. The cleaners that remained moved among rows of desks, past empty water-coolers and phones that never rang.

There must have been a mistake, confusion in the flight orders that explained the delay. He had placed his hand on her heart and said that she was to join him, had he not?

The next telex that arrived was addressed to all remaining Frankfurt headquarters personnel and pinned on the main staff noticeboard. There were a series of announcements about the times of flights and about medical checks for those staff who had been working in camps for displaced persons in the city, a list of names of those eligible for the remaining flights to the US, and a further short list of those "not eligible for repatriation".

Kay Summersby. Not eligible for repatriation. It said exactly that. The telex didn't carry the signature of any person but merely cited the authority of the Pentagon department responsible for the transportation home of foreign-based personnel.

She hadn't been overlooked. She'd been deliberately excluded from the airlift back to America of Ike's headquarters staff. Ike had obviously decided to get her to the US by other means. There could be no other explanation. They had both known that her return to Washington could cause problems.

Kay took the day off and went riding. It was what he would have done; she could almost hear him saying, *Don't worry, Kay, it will be all right, just a snafu. You'll be here soon – I promised you that, didn't I? Have you ever known me to break a promise?*

She said goodbye to the girls who had shared her flat and all her other friends on the staff. They all hugged and kissed and promised to meet up for celebratory drinks in Washington as she watched them pack their bags into the transport bus and leave for the airport.

She wondered how long it would be until she followed. It was just her and Telek left now. What was it he'd said when people asked about the name? *It's made up of the two things that make me most happy, Telegraph Cottage and Kay.* She just had to be patient.

The letter ended all her hopes. Kay prided herself on her emotional maturity, her ability to deal with the hard knocks life dealt to the credulous and unwary. She knew about men and their ways. After the pain of a divorce and the loss of a fiancé to the war, she had promised never to give herself lightly to anyone. But to her dying day she would tell those close to her that this letter broke her heart.

The official white manila envelope was handed to her in her office with the other official mail. Next door, Ike's large office had been locked and sealed. She was almost the last one in the building now except for the security guards.

She saw that the letter had been stamped and franked by the War Department in Washington. At first it gave rise to the faint hope that this was it, that a note inside, handwritten in Ike's inimitable scrawl, would apologise for the manner in which things were happening and for the delay. But a moment's thought told her this could not be. Ike wouldn't write; he'd call with such happy news.

She sat down at her desk, lit a cigarette, slid a nail under the rim of the envelope and opened it.

The typewritten note on War Department stationery read:

Dear Kay,

I am terribly distressed, first because it has become impossible to keep you as a member of my personal official family, and secondly because I cannot come back and give you a detailed account of my reasons.

In this letter I shall not attempt to express the depth of my appreciation for the unexcelled loyalty and faithfulness with which you have worked for the past three and a half years under my personal direction.

I am sure you understand that I am personally much distressed that an association that has been so valuable to me has to be terminated in this particular fashion but it is for reasons over which I have no control.

Finally, I hope you will drop me a note from time to time – I will always be interested to know how you are getting on.

Below his signature Ike had written a postscript in his own hand:

Take care of yourself and retain your optimism.

Kay felt faint. She took a huge breath as the room revolved slowly and then breathed hard and fast, shaking her head to stop the world spinning around her. She crumpled the letter into a ball and flung it at the door, walked to the door, scooped up the balled paper and flung it harder at the window. It bounced back and rolled towards her as if a reminder that bad news was not to be so lightly dismissed. She walked across and kicked it into a corner.

She needed a drink badly. In the old days there would have been half a pint of whisky or vodka on a sideboard. Not now. They had even taken the pictures off the walls.

She picked up the crumpled letter, smoothed it out and read it again. The same words stared back at her. So it was true. She'd been literally airbrushed out of history. Their love affair – and what else could you call it? – had become an "association"; she had shown "loyalty and faithfulness" as if she had been a long-term secretary rather than the woman he had held in his arms and covered with kisses, and with whom he had stripped off his uniform.

He had kept her at his side from the summer days of 1942 right through to this moment. He had introduced her to Churchill, Roosevelt and all his top generals, especially Bradley, Patton and Clark. They liked her. Why? Because they knew Ike could not do without her, and the imperative of the war overrode all else. More than that, they thought he loved her, that they were having an affair.

That was what Bradley and the others gossiped about, wasn't it? Ike hardly concealed the fact. He had even insisted she stand in line to meet King George VI in North Africa despite the objections of royal aides. That cold, crowned fish had looked right through her and moved on without a word.

And after all that, she had received a typewritten note on Pentagon paper. The cold, hard tree-trunk of a man she had held and hugged so often was just that – cold and hard. He was a career soldier who had taken the ruthless step of dismissing her from his life when she was of no further use. He had done so to reclaim his marriage and embark on the next stage of his career. Could she blame him? Was that not what great men did? Use others around them to climb to the next level of the mountain?

How right Charlotte had been. A woman in love will believe anything.

Kay went out that night looking for a bar, anywhere to get away from the Farben building with its vile past and now its grim association with personal betrayal. Normally she would join the few remaining staff in the headquarters' hospitality suite, a coy name for a shabby bar in the basement, but not tonight.

She waited a few minutes for a taxi she knew would never come. There were few in the city, and most didn't work after dark.

She would walk in search of a bar if she had to. The streets weren't safe, but she wasn't afraid. The Beretta was in her handbag as always. She would occasionally take it out and marvel at how such elegant craftsmanship could be the agent of death.

She wanted to take it out and use it on these dark streets, to hold it as he had showed her and pull the trigger, watching the robber, the rapist crumple to the ground. The boys on the range had said the Beretta lacked stopping power, but Kay reckoned that a couple of .25 bullets at close range would stop anyone intent on harming her.

She was enjoying the fantasy when an unmarked car clearly cruising for passengers drove slowly past. She hailed it. This was against all military rules. She didn't care.

The driver was an old woman with rheumy eyes that made her look as if she was crying. The woman stank, the car stank, in fact the whole filthy city stank. The stench of death, shit and unwashed bodies pervaded the streets and invaded every building. She hated the place and everybody in it. Soon it wouldn't matter – she was going to get drunk.

Within fifteen minutes she was in the bar of the Metropole Hotel. This had once been one of the city's favourite meeting places, famous for its long marble bar and picture windows overlooking the river Main. Now the windows were boarded up and the marble bar had been replaced by plywood. The hotel was off-limits to all Allied staff because, as Kay had been warned, it was a base for hustlers of every stripe, mostly black marketeers trading in

US dollars and stolen medical supplies, usually morphine, and pimps trading in human flesh.

But like the city itself, the Metropole was doing its best to forget the war and get back to business. A scruffy woman on the door was turning away people who seemed to be dressed no better than she was, but waved Kay inside without a glance. She walked into a babble of noise and a low cloud of smoke that hung over tables crowded with drinkers.

To Kay's surprise, most people were young and dressed in smart new clothes, mostly leather jackets. This didn't look like the thieves' kitchen she'd been warned about, not that she would have cared. She just wanted a drink. The tables were all taken, but she squeezed through the throng and took a seat at the bar. The second surprise were the shelves behind the bar. They contained every type of whisky, gin or vodka, all brand names in new bottles.

An old woman with the crevassed faced of a drug addict who looked remarkably like the driver who had brought her here nodded wordlessly at her.

"Scotch – Highland Park, please, large one," Kay said.

The woman had no difficulty in understanding her English. She swivelled, reached for the bottle, swung round to the bar again, flipped the top off and poured a large measure into a glass which had somehow materialised in this balletic manoeuvre.

"Wasser?" asked the woman.

Kay nodded and a carafe of water appeared on the bar. She mixed her drink fifty-fifty and decided not to ask for ice. She told herself she would drink the first in a hurry and take time over the second. She wanted to talk to someone – anyone, really. She wished Charlotte was there and smiled to think of her friend in a place like this. Charlotte would have understood. She would have reminded Kay of her warning and then said, "Get back on your horse, doll. You're not Humpty Dumpty. We can put you back together again."

Kay lit a cigarette and drank deeply. It was very good Scotch, probably stolen from a bonded army warehouse. The peat taste of the Highlands and the kick of grain spirits burnt her throat. Ike would have liked this whisky, she thought. He always said he preferred Scotch to bourbon. What a bastard he had been. Not even a handwritten letter but one typed up by some secretary. Kay wondered who she was. She would have another Scotch and she wouldn't cry. The bastard wasn't worth her tears.

"Can I join you?" said a voice.

Kay turned to see a woman not much older than her wearing horn-rimmed spectacles, a smart dark suit and hair tied tightly back in a bun. She recognised her from the office but couldn't place the name or department.

"Of course."

"It's Marjorie. From the office."

"I thought you had all gone home."

"There are a few of us left. Special duties."

"Of course. I'm Kay Summersby."

"I know who you are, Kay."

The woman sat down and nodded to the bartender, who produced a tall glass of vodka, orange and ice without being asked.

Kay looked at her in surprise. "You know this place?"

"Sure. I come here sometimes – business."

"Business. Here?"

"Best not to ask, Kay. Cheers."

They raised their drinks and Kay remembered that Marjorie was one of a small group of people at the headquarters with vague job titles who worked in a series of rooms that were off-limits to all other staff.

"Drowning your sorrows?" said Marjorie quietly.

Kay looked at her sharply. "What are you talking about?"

"Let's just say that I work in communications. My job is to know who and what goes in and out of that office and who's talking to whom."

"Why would that mean I am drowning my sorrows?"

"Because I know you got some bad news today and that you might need a little company tonight."

Kay looked at the woman properly for the first time. The horn-rimmed spectacles and the suit looked strangely out of place in a black market bar.

"Just who do you work for?"

"It doesn't matter. Have another drink."

The woman was right. It didn't matter. Nothing except the next drink mattered right then. They drank and talked of Marjorie's family back in Vermont, and how she had got a degree in modern languages from Richmond University in Virginia and angered her family by joining a new government department in Washington. Her father had wanted her to become a lawyer and her mother had wanted her to come home and get married.

They talked of men, friends and their favourite pets, especially horses, and agreed that the latter were more loyal and loving than the former, and drank some more.

Kay described her Irish childhood and her arrival in London in 1938 to become a model. She skipped quickly over the early marriage but described life as an ambulance driver in the Blitz, the relief at becoming a government driver and then her role with the American embassy. It was then, through the blur of alcohol, that Kay realised she was telling Marjorie what the woman already knew.

Marjorie didn't seem to mind, and nor did Kay. The numbing effect of the whisky and the relief of being able to talk to somebody who was prepared to sit and listen was deeply satisfying.

They talked of the American commanders around Eisenhower, Patton, Bradley and Clark, and how they had fought among themselves, fought the British and finally fought the Germans. They laughed at that joke, and then Marjorie said she had heard they had called Kay Ike's shadow. That was a surprise. Marjorie seemed to know everything. Then the whole story of the final letter from the Pentagon came tumbling out in long incoherent sentences washed with tears.

Marjorie put her arm around her, ordered more drinks and whispered kind words of consolation. "Most army men would have said a warmer goodbye to their horse than you got in that letter," she said, and Kay laughed.

Finally Kay found herself being unsteadily but gently ushered through the door of her apartment building.

Marjorie gave her a hug goodbye and said, "We won't meet again, but good luck. You have a strong heart. You will come through this, but a word of advice – don't talk to the press. They'll come for you when this gets out." Kay nodded, fumbled the key in her front door and stumbled to bed.

Kay didn't go into work the following day. She drank copious quantities of water and took aspirin to dull a hangover that had settled in like a rainy day. It was a Friday. The long weekend stretched ahead like a desert that had to be crossed to get to the oasis of Monday morning, not that Monday would bring any relief. The week after that there would be no office to go to. The headquarters was being closed.

Only Telek made any sense now, and he kept her sane. She decided that she and Telek would take long walks through the ruined city. They would snuggle up together in the evenings and she would read aloud to him from her book, a detective story by Agatha Christie. Together they would kill the weekend.

Ike had adored that dog, probably more than her, and he would want to see him again. Well, he would. But she would be there too. She would see him again. She deserved an explanation. She wanted at least a conversation and an answer to the question: *Why did you promise me so much? I wasn't dreaming, was I? I have citizenship and a stripe on my American army uniform to prove you loved me, haven't I? That proves I didn't make it all up, doesn't it?*

21

December 1945

Within days of receiving Eisenhower's letter, Kay was assigned to a new job working at the visitors' centre for American VIPs in Berlin. There was no consultation: she was in the American army and under army orders. She was promoted to captain and found herself working for a pleasant middle-aged man called General Lucius Clay.

The general greeted Kay when she reported for duty with a remark that he obviously thought would please her: General Eisenhower had personally recommended her in a note that said she was very good with people. He announced this as if conferring a great compliment on his new member of staff. He was puzzled by the look he got in return.

The remark stung Kay, but not as much as the fact that she had been sidelined to a junior hospitality role as far from Washington as it was possible to arrange. She had just spent three years witnessing great decisions taken by men who were making history, men who treated her as a friend and ally: Roosevelt, Churchill, Patton, Bradley, Clark and Eisenhower. These men were giants. She had served them well and loved one with abandon.

Now, at the age of thirty-seven and a captain in the US Army, she was required to meet and greet every Congressman, Senator and other supposedly important person from every walk of American life who wanted their photograph taken in the ruins of Berlin.

These men thrust their cameras at Kay, wanting their pictures taken amid the rubble of what had once been the Adlon Hotel against the backdrop of the Brandenburg Gate. What they really wanted was a tour of Hitler's bunker, but that lay in the Russian sector of a city now divided between the occupying powers.

Kay numbly accepted her role. She watched the months pass in a state of narcosis as handshakes, dinners, drinks parties, photographs and potted history talks merged into a seamless garment with which she clothed herself against the bleak reality of betrayal.

Telek, although barred from her office, was at her side every evening when she returned to her apartment and would bounce along beside her when she went riding at weekends. Apart from him, she was always alone. She saw nobody and turned down offers from the visiting dignitaries of dinner, drinks or sometimes just a walk among the ruins.

Wherever she was and whatever she was doing, she went over and over in her head what had happened. She knew why he had done it – for his career, for the power and glory that awaited. There was a brutal logic to such ambition that was at least understandable. But it was how he had done it, how he had behaved towards her that was so wounding. Why had a man who had loved her once consigned her to this lonely exile in the rubble of Berlin? Why had she believed him?

There was no answer to that question unless it was to be found in the sad story that Berlin would tell those who walked through its ruins. She did this every day, sometimes wandering through the bomb-cratered Tiergarten Park, hearing the burnt and shattered trees whisper their regrets.

The most famous zoo in Europe, beautiful buildings housing great offices of state, the opera house and art galleries had all crumbled under the bombs. Yet people in this city and across the country had believed only a few years ago that they were being presented with a golden future. They had had no reason beyond irrational optimism to believe the mad National Socialist party mythology and the demonic dreams woven by barbarians.

Perhaps she had been just as blinded by hope as had the people of this blighted country. Once again she wished Charlotte could be there with her. The dirty jokes, the indiscretions about the latest lover and the morning cocktails would cheer her up, but travel to Berlin was impossible. In any case her friend would find little of interest in the ruins of the Third Reich; except men, of course.

Charlotte would find a man anywhere. And what would Charlotte have advised her to do? Kay could hear her voice: "Stop feeling sorry for yourself, doll. Find a man, give him a good time. It's always the best revenge."

Charlotte moved through life like one of those characters in the cheap romance stories that filled women's magazines. Aching hearts and throbbing loins, or was it the other way round, led to romps in four-poster beds, love, marriage, betrayal and revenge.

Kay didn't want revenge; what was the point? She had just been a bubble in his glass of champagne. She had stupidly allowed herself to dream of – believe in – a future that was never going to happen. A moment of caution would have told her that. The bubble had burst.

"Stop being so bloody miserable, doll – so intro... intro..."

It was Charlotte again, a voice in her head that would not go away.

"Introspective?"

"Exactly. Self-pity is so, well, selfish. You're better than that. Look around you – people are starving, they've lost everything. So stop feeling sorry for yourself. Live a little."

He looked as if he was in his mid-forties and was wearing the uniform of an army major when she saw him at breakfast, forking scrambled eggs into his mouth. She had gone, as she did twice a week, to the same heavily guarded hotel to meet the visitors she was guiding around the city. That hotel and a few bars were the only places in the city where foreign visitors could meet.

She liked the look of him. Major Charles E. Burrows. His teeth were white, his uniform smartly tailored. It wasn't difficult to catch his eye on the tour that morning. He asked the most interesting questions. He didn't want to know where Hitler's bunker was or whether it was true that Goebbels had poisoned his wife Magda and four children before taking cyanide. He wanted to know what was being done for the women of the city, how to get them food, clean water and blankets.

"Why just women?" she had asked.

"Because if you hand out supplies to the men, they'll sell the stuff on the black market. The women will get this city back on its feet if you give them a chance."

"You mean give them all the food and fuel?"

"Why not? They've got children to feed. It's happened throughout history. Did you know that women rebuilt Rome after the barbarians sacked it back in the sixth century?"

"No," she said, and laughed because he was being serious. Of course she didn't know what had happened in ancient Rome after the barbarians left.

At the end of the tour that evening he said in the straightforward American way, "You look like you could do with a drink. I know a place. The food's not much but the wine is good. There's music too."

She liked him immediately. No sidelong glances, mumbled compliments and vague enquiries as to whether she might be free. That was the English way. This was different.

Kay had made a point of turning down all such offers. They usually only meant one thing, and she didn't have the energy to slap down wandering hands. But Burrows was definitely different from the rest. She was also curious to see where he might take her in a city whose few restaurants served only tinned meat of dubious origin and ersatz coffee.

They walked in silence for fifteen minutes, following the beam of his powerful torch through deserted streets until they arrived at an old three-storey schoolhouse in the Charlottenburg suburb. The building had been badly damaged, but the school crest and Latin motto hung over a makeshift front door of barbed wire and wooden slats. Inside, a dark passage lit by candles on the floor led into a large room which must once have been the assembly hall.

She looked around in wonder – it was as if she'd walked into a witches' grotto. Candles provided the only light. On one side, what looked like white bed sheets had been laid over a row of packing cases to make them into a bar. There were bottles and glasses on top. The brick walls glistened with damp. An assortment of bedclothes had been hung over the windows.

Several people were eating at a dozen tables crudely fashioned from old school desks at the end of the room. The straight-backed chairs had lost their varnish to generations of school children. In the centre there was a small circular wooden dance floor. Next to it, on a low table, stood a wind-up gramophone.

At the far end of the bar, where charcoal fires burnt beneath mesh grills, two women were tending pots, stirring the contents with long wooden spoons. They presented ghostly figures in the low light, wearing dresses made of what looked like stitched sacking. They only needed pointed hats to complete the effect of the entire room.

"What is this place?" she whispered.

Burrows nodded towards the women.

"They're Polish. They used to work in the kitchens of the Adlon Hotel. Slave labour," he said. "When the hotel was bombed right at the end, they escaped, taking everything they could lay their hands on – bedding, food, kitchen stuff, including much of the wine cellar, and even that dance floor."

They were seated without a word by one of the women at a table on which were carved childish initials. There was no menu and without being asked they were served pasta with tinned tomatoes on fine china plates that carried the monogram *AH* entwined in gold letters.

He had brought with him a bottle of red wine whose label showed an impressive turreted French chateau. "You know what they say?" he said. "The grander the chateau on the label, the lousier the wine in the bottle."

He didn't ask the usual questions about her background and upbringing, nor did he tell her anything more about himself than that he was part of a delegation that would report to a Senate committee in Washington.

That was the unspoken pact between them. They were going to remain strangers. Kay was relieved. He didn't want to know more about her than the little she was prepared to say, and he, in turn, had no desire to spill out his life story to her. He talked instead of the authors he liked, Henry James and Ernest Hemingway, both American writers who had fallen in love with Europe, he said – James with London, Hemingway with Paris.

He stopped then and said, "You know the problem with us?"

She looked at him with a frown, searching for a meaning in the question. She was beginning to enjoy herself and feared that he was about to bring the evening to an end.

"No."

"You Brits forget how young we are and we Yanks forget how old you are."

She smiled, relieved, and raised a glass. "To the New World and the Old."

He was curious about which books she read and raised his eyebrows when she said she preferred films.

"Which ones?"

"I love Garbo. She has that quality of mystery about her in every film she's made."

"Such as?"

"Oh, you know – *Queen Christina*, *Grand Hotel*, *Mata Hari*. The camera loves her – that's what makes her a star."

"You're right," he said. "She never shows so much as an ankle in any film, and yet there's an eroticism there, wouldn't you say?"

"I think that's a man's view, isn't it?" she said.

"Not at all. Women find other women sexually attractive, don't they?"

"Maybe," she said. It was all she could think of.

Then he bent over the table and kissed her gently without a word, their lips touching only briefly. Before she could react, he had stood up and offered his arm. "Shall we dance?" he asked.

They walked to the deserted dance floor. He wound the gramophone handle vigorously before lowering the needle onto a crackly version of a fast-tempo Viennese waltz.

"How did you find this place?" she said as they began to dance.

"I passed it one day on a walk, looked in and was amazed at what those two women have managed to do here. That took guts. I've told you, it's women who are going to rebuild this city."

He held her at a respectable distance, turning them both through the steps with confidence. Over his shoulder, she could see admiring glances from the other diners. He changed the record and the tempo slowed to a slow operatic aria. He held her close, his hand linked with hers, their bodies moving almost as one. She remembered Charlotte's story about the advice given by her dancing teacher.

"It's hot. Shall we have another glass of wine?" she said.

It felt quite natural that he should slip his arm into hers on the walk back to the hotel. When they got there he asked her if she would like a nightcap.

"I'd love one, but where?"

They looked across the lobby at the iron grill drawn down to the counter of the bar.

"How about my room?" he asked.

She said yes without hesitation. She had met him only a few hours earlier, but he was an interesting, attractive and unusual man. She was going to sleep with him the moment they got into his room. No, that was not right, she thought. They were not going to sleep with each other or make love. The euphemisms were decorative but meaningless.

This man was a stranger. That was the beauty of it. She was going to fuck her stranger. All night long. She repeated the word to herself. Fuck. She had always hated it – until now. It was a clenched fist of a word, brutal in its brevity and exquisite in its capture of an act, not of love or lust, but survival. She was going to survive. There would be no clemency to be found in the night ahead, only the sweet taste of what – revenge? Why not?

In his room he offered her a whisky, raising a bottle and two glasses enquiringly. She shook her head, slipped off her coat and lay back on the bed, feeling light-headed and dizzy.

He loosened his tie, took off his shoes and walked to the bed. He leant over and kissed her. She slid a hand between his legs and squeezed gently, listening to a long slow sigh in response.

"Get undressed," she said.

He took his clothes off without embarrassment and faced her naked, erect and with a glass of whisky in his hand. Kay suddenly wanted to giggle. She wished Charlotte could see her now – her friend would have warmly approved. Kay swung off the bed and undressed.

She faced him as she bent forward to slip off her dress and then turned her back to remove her underwear. She looked over her shoulder at him as she had done in front of the cheval mirror all those years ago. He was watching every movement, his eyes moving over her body. He drained his whisky and put the glass down. She turned and slipped quickly between cold damp sheets.

"Come here and fuck me," she said.

They had coffee and hard brown bread with American marmalade for breakfast in the dining room the next morning. The shared intimacy of the night left little need for conversation. Both were comfortable with small talk about the weather and the knowledge that they would never see each other again.

That was the whole point, Kay realised. Charlotte had been right.

"Thank you," she had said as he rose to go.

He kissed her again. "There's one small confession I have to make."

Her heart sank.

"The women of Rome didn't rebuild the city after its destruction. I made that up. But they could have done, and they will do here."

With that he gave her one more quick kiss, a light touch on her lips. Then he was gone.

She returned to the breakfast table and finished her coffee. It was over. She knew she must leave her job and put Berlin behind her.

When Kay put in for a transfer to the US in early 1946, General Clay forwarded the request to the Pentagon with relief. He was glad to get rid of her.

22

February 1946

On his first day as chief of staff of the American army, Eisenhower lunched in the Pentagon commissary. He ate alone by choice, having explained to his staff that he wanted time to read the morning papers and reflect on a series of depressing meetings. Afterwards he got disorientated in the honeycomb of corridors and failed to find his way back to his office.

When bemused officials realised that their new boss was not walking around on a lightning inspection tour but was actually lost, they guided him back to his office. The story was leaked by a helpful underling and made headlines in the next day's papers.

Constant Washington gossip about his supposed presidential ambitions interested Eisenhower only in that it exposed what he had always thought was the real business of that hothouse world inside the beltway – endless chatter about who was in or out, up or down. He wanted no part of it and told everyone he was a soldier, not a politician.

The sharp-eyed Washington press corps noted, however, that in negotiation with President Truman the new chief of staff had carefully limited his term to two years. This would mean his release from the army in 1947. The next presidential election was scheduled for 1948. The timing did not look like a coincidence. "Ike for President" campaign committees began to appear across the country.

In response, Eisenhower insisted that all he was thinking about was the tough job he now faced. Millions of men had to be demobilised and brought home. Defence spending cuts voted by a Congress looking for a peace dividend meant battles with other service chiefs over reduced budget funds.

A lifetime in the military had left Eisenhower with a mind that could swiftly assess the risks and rewards of any given action. The methodology had been hammered home since his cadet days at West Point: a commanding officer drew up a balance sheet weighing the risk of sending men into battle by listing the pluses and minuses.

There were always more minuses than pluses, as there had been at D-Day, when the weather, Rommel's ability to move the panzer divisions to the beachheads on day one, and the strength of coastal defences in Normandy had posed real dangers.

The plus side of the D-Day balance sheet lay in command of the air, superior numbers and the element of surprise. The logic had pointed clearly to delay. But that itself posed an unacceptable risk, which swung the balance to action. Eisenhower had taken a gamble that had triumphantly paid off.

The balance sheet he drew up in the early months of 1946 seemed very largely favourable. Mamie, now at his side, was in the process of furnishing and decorating their large if not lavish army quarters with an impressive address: No 1, Fort Myer, Arlington. Virginia.

Across the Potomac River from Washington DC, in the traditional home of the renowned 3rd US Infantry regiment, he and Mamie were surrounded by staff and servants. From their new home she travelled with him to meetings across almost every state in the Union, greeted everywhere by crowds that told their own story. His marriage, cruelly tested by three years' absence and scurrilous gossip about Kay Summersby, had been restored.

There was, however, one item on the balance sheet that did not lend itself easily to risk analysis.

Kay Summersby was due to return to Washington. Her request for a transfer had been successful. Since administration of the visitor centre in Berlin was about to be transferred from the army to the state department there was no way of avoiding her return to the US.

Eisenhower knew she would wish to see him, and he knew he would agree. It would be difficult not to. She would bring Telek into his office and place that faithful dog on his desk as she had done in the old days. She would stand there in his office looking at him, smiling the way she always had done, and that would be enough to make him go red in the face, partly with embarrassment and partly with irritation.

There was nothing he'd feel able to say to her beyond the usual civilities and good wishes. They would talk about Telek, of course. He loved that Scottish terrier, although giving the dog that name had been a mistake. But dog talk would not be enough. Kay Summersby was not going to go quietly.

He knew his letter had been cold. He knew it would have been a hurtful shock her. But it was better for both of them, he had argued to himself, to end the relationship that way than let it linger on.

He had found a new life, a new world away from Europe. Three years of war, three years of fighting the Germans, three years of dealing with the endless clashes of big personalities under his command and the titanic egos of de Gaulle and

Churchill, had isolated him from reality. He looked back on his time in the European theater as one remembers a dream. It seemed like a past life on a distant planet.

The anguished wait for the first reports from the D-Day beaches, the headquarters in the Normandy apple orchard, the shock of hearing that captured Canadian paratroopers had been bound then strangled with their own harnesses by a Hitler youth unit, the anguish of the Ardennes breakthrough, the dinners with Churchill, the unimaginable horrors of the death camps – they were all experiences far removed from his new life at Fort Myer. They had become folk stories, to be remembered with affection or with anger, but stripped of meaning in the now of a new life.

The heart of the problem was that Summersby belonged to that old world, the world of Europe and war. He didn't deny he had had feelings for her. They had been deep. She had given unstinting service and more. She had been someone to come home to when he wanted to shut the door on the world outside.

In a moment of euphoria after the German surrender, when the liberation of Europe seemed to herald a new beginning, he had thought that he too might find a new beginning – with her.

He could not deny that he had written that letter to George Marshall and that he had, briefly, thought of divorce. His excuse was that he had been exhausted. He had let naturally affectionate feelings for that woman assume an unwarranted importance in his life.

Perhaps, in truth, he had become a little obsessed with her because she was... well, she was Kay Summersby. She had drawn him into a moment, not of madness, but of weakness. In those frantic days after the German collapse, anything had seemed possible.

Of course he had desired her. When she sat across from him on the sofa with drink in hand on those evenings they enjoyed so much her skirt would be drawn up high over those long legs and she would unbutton the jacket of her uniform, allowing him to see the shape of her; he knew that shape because he had held those breasts in his hands and kissed them with his lips; yes, he had desired her. Any man would have.

The truth, he told himself, was that he had needed her because just having her around had kept him sane, given him moments of private joy. That was what Kay Summersby had been for him. A partner in the great adventure that was World War Two.

And now he had a new life and Kay could not be part of it. It was as simple as that. He would never close the door on D-Day, or the grinding battles after the Wehrmacht's surprise Ardennes offensive, or the final surrender – those were rooms in his mind he would enter with pride for the rest of his life. But there was no room for Kay Summersby.

Kay entered Ike's office in the Pentagon with Telek on a lead. The sight of the dog in the corridors of the Pentagon had surprised the staff. Ike looked no less surprised as he rose to meet her. He hadn't been looking forward to the meeting, but now he was strangely pleased to see her. She was looking well. She had somehow managed to make the drab green uniform of the Women's Army Corps look stylish.

She bent down, unleashed the dog, straightened up and saluted. The salute was returned. They shook hands formally as Telek ran to his old master, stretched his paws up on Ike's uniformed leg and growled a soft greeting. He bent down to pat the dog. Telek obligingly rolled over and allowed his tummy to be tickled.

A secretary who had been taking dictation slipped out of the room. The meeting had been requested, agreed and put in the diary. Even so, Kay's first impression was that her old boss was surprised to see her. He looked well, but older, she thought. As usual, when he was embarrassed or irritated, he had gone red in the face.

It was two weeks before Christmas 1946, well over a year since she had last seen him during the hurried departure from Frankfurt. She remembered those moments as one remembers a famous scene in a film. He had held her in his arms briefly. He had said he would be back. But he had not come back. He had sent for everyone on his staff except her. Instead he had consigned her to a job taking political hopefuls and has-beens to the Brandenburg Gate to deliver a brief talk on the fall of the city to the Russians and the four-power occupation that followed.

Thus passed a long and wasted year. In that time she had not received a single word from him, not even by way of a greeting passed on by a visiting army colleague.

She smiled and said, "You're looking well."

Eisenhower nodded. "You look fine too. How have you been?"

"Berlin was a bore, but it was a job."

"Have they given you something here yet?"

"I'm in the pool, waiting for deployment."

"I'll see if I can help out there."

"That would be nice."

She knew he wanted a cigarette. So did she. She wasn't going to ask unless he offered her one.

There was a silence, broken by a whimper from Telek demanding attention.

"He's well, isn't he?" said Eisenhower.

"He's in great shape. He kept me sane, if you must know."

"Ah. Yes. Those long Berlin winters."

"It wasn't the weather, Ike…"

She had always called him Ike, or "the boss", when they were alone, except during moments of intimacy when she had occasionally whispered "darling", but he had always flinched when she'd said that. She doubted even Mamie was allowed to call him that.

"I know. I realise it must have been difficult."

"Do you?"

"Do I what?"

"Realise how hard it has been?"

They looked at each other.

"I had no option, Kay. I don't control my life here. You did a great job for me in theater and I hope I thanked you."

"You did. You sent me that letter."

Ike frowned and grimaced at the same time.

"I know. Maybe it could have been worded better, but I was under a lot of pressure."

"You said you would be back, remember. You said that you would send for me…"

Her voice rose and the words tumbled out. For a moment they became almost a waterfall of regret, anger and accusation. She felt tears brim in her eyes. She had promised herself she would not do this, not lose control, not become emotional. She would stay calm, just have the conversation and leave.

But it was hard standing here in front a man who had taken over three years of her life, violent years of war in which history had been made and unmade, years that magnified emotion so that fear, joy, sorrow and horror had become feelings of exquisite intensity.

Above all they had been years of promise – the promise of victory, the promise of a new Europe, the promise of prosecution for the Nazi criminals and the promise of love.

Now those years, like the war, were over. Victory had been achieved. Justice was being delivered at Nuremberg, a new Europe would arise from the ashes. But one promise had been broken.

She went quiet.

"Kay?"

"Yes?"

"Are you all right?"

Eisenhower had fished a handkerchief out of his pocket. She sniffed, shook her head and opened her handbag. She took out her own handkerchief and blew her nose.

"Yes. I would like a cigarette, please."

He walked to his desk, opened a drawer and flipped a cigarette out of a pack. He lit it for her. She inhaled deeply, feeling calmer.

"Aren't you having one?"

"I'm trying to give up."

"It's difficult, isn't it – giving up?"

Ike bent down to pat the dog.

"I really appreciate you looking after Telek."

She wanted to scream at him. *Damn the dog, Ike, what about me? I'm the one you loved, I'm the one you kissed, the one you made love to in front of the fire at Versailles, not the bloody dog.*

But she didn't. Instead she said, "You remember his name."

"Of course I do."

"You chose it."

"Yes, I know."

"No one could ever work it out, could they?"

Eisenhower shifted uncomfortably and looked down at the dog.

She laughed then, and felt a little better. There was silence.

"Kay – it's impossible. You know that."

"What if I said I don't know that?"

"What?"

"What if I said I just don't understand why you behaved like that?"

"Like what?"

"I'll never let you go – remember?"

"Kay, that was then, it was wartime."

"And this is now and it's peacetime – is that it?"

"Kay, it's different now."

"You mean you never meant all those things you said to me, that… you… that…"

Her voice rose as the words trailed away. She blew into her handkerchief.

"I was under a lot of pressure. You know that. You were a huge help. You kept me going. I owe you more than I can say, but…"

"But what?"

"Things change. You must understand that."

There was a long silence in which Kay held his gaze until Eisenhower bent down to pat Telek.

"Yes, I do. I do understand. I understand very clearly," she said. There was an angry edge to her voice. The room seemed colder. Telek whimpered.

"I've still got the gun, you know."

Eisenhower straightened up. "The gun? Oh yes, the Beretta."

"Do you think I should hand it in?"

"Well that's up to you, Kay. I mean you don't have to."

"It was a personal gift, wasn't it?"

"Yes, it was personal. For your protection."

"I think I'll keep it then. Old times and all that."

"Of course. Kay, I'll look into your posting. Drop in again, but right now I have–"

"A meeting."

"Yes."

Kay walked to the desk and ground out the cigarette, twisting the butt until ash spilled onto the shiny wooden surface.

"Goodbye, sir," she said.

She saluted again, the snappy salute he had taught her, then turned and left. At the door she turned back. Telek had planted himself at Eisenhower's feet and showed no inclination to move.

"Here, boy," she said, patting her thigh.

Reluctantly, the dog ambled slowly cross the room. Eisenhower stood motionless, watching them leave.

A week later Kay Summersby was given orders to take up her new posting. She had hoped to be assigned somewhere in Washington to a role in the hospitality or public relations departments, where her contacts and her knowledge of the European theater background could be useful. She was ordered to report instead to an army press relations unit in San Francisco.

The typewritten order came with a warrant for air travel and information that shared accommodation would be available with another female member of the unit. Kay smiled as she read the orders. The US Army was nothing if not obvious. Her new posting was as far from Washington as it was possible to be while remaining in the continental United States.

Within two weeks of arriving on the west coast, she resigned from the army and booked a flight to New York.

If General Eisenhower could shake off the past and find a new life in America after the war, so could she.

23

Spring 1947

Kay Summersby had never been to New York. In the spring of 1947, the city seemed to be gripped in a frenzy of excitement for which there was no apparent reason. Perhaps the end of the hard winter or the return of some of the troops from overseas had made the neon lights in Times Square seem brighter and more colourful; perhaps that was why everyone moved faster, talked louder, ate more quickly, drank more deeply, blasphemed more openly, dressed more colourfully than anywhere else she had been. Or perhaps this was just the way New York had always been.

Kay's mother had written often to tell her of the misery of rationing, power cuts and lack of transport in bombed-out London. Everyone was saying that life had got worse rather than better after the war, her mother reported, almost happily, Kay thought. Her mother was never one to see the bright side of life.

In New York no one ever saw anything else. The city moved to a rhythm dictated by happy, greedy, money-driven people. From the first cup of coffee in the morning to the last groggy yawn at night, everyone was in a hurry. *Get up and get ahead* was the unofficial civic motto.

New Yorkers moved through the day with a brash self-confidence born of the knowledge that the rest of America was looking to their city for news of the latest fashions, the most popular Broadway shows, the most sought-after restaurants and the latest celebrity gossip. Marlon Brando wasn't filming in Hollywood, he was on Broadway in *A Streetcar Named Desire*. After the show he was often seen at El Morocco, the city's most glamorous nightspot.

America's most celebrated editor, Harold Ross, didn't correct page proofs in a newspaper office in Washington or Los Angeles; he could be seen every morning hurrying into the Fifth Avenue offices of the *New Yorker* magazine he had founded and edited for twenty-one years.

Famous for his business feuds, his failed marriages and his obsession with commas, Ross had become as well known as the magazine he had created, as much a celebrity as the writers, critics and wits he made famous.

New York loved them all. To satisfy the city's delight in its nationwide celebrity, and to feed the craving for hot news and gossip, ten daily newspapers in and around the city churned out new editions almost every waking hour.

The sheer excitement of her first days in the city lifted Kay. She felt, like Judy Garland in *The Wizard of Oz*, as if she'd been caught in a tornado, plucked from the ground and whirled around.

In her case she found she had been giddily deposited in a small second floor walk-up on a narrow street in Greenwich Village. She liked the address. Wooster Street sounded very English and grandly foreign amid the grid of numbered streets in Manhattan.

The apartment was not as comfortable as her old army quarters in Frankfurt, but that didn't matter. She had swapped the cold grey ruins of Europe for a city that painted with its own colours, made its own music and rejoiced in nothing more than the sight of Benjamin Franklin on a hundred-dollar bill.

The Wooster Street apartment had not been easy to find. The difficulty was Telek. Even the cheap-rent landlords on the Lower East Side would not allow a resident dog on their premises. In the end she simply smuggled Telek into the apartment in her handbag and agreed to pay more than half the rent to the woman with whom she shared.

Once again she wished Charlotte could be with her. She would love New York. She would become the cocktail queen of Fifth Avenue, dressed in designer silk and trailing admirers in a slipstream of French perfume.

The fact that with so many troops still overseas single women outnumbered men in Manhattan by a factor of ten to one would not have bothered Charlotte. She would have acquired and discarded lovers as if trying on new clothes, always moving on when the new man in her life showed signs of falling in love.

Kay longed to hear the news from London, but Charlotte had never written a letter in her life and Kay had heard nothing from her for months. The letter from her mother one morning in May, therefore, was a shock. It contained a newspaper clipping from the *Daily Express*, across the top of which was written, "I thought you would be interested. She was a good friend of yours, wasn't she?"

Kay sat down in amazement. There was a picture of Charlotte Victoria Montagu, of Eaton Square, Belgravia, leaving a church beneath an arcade of swords held aloft by army officers with her new husband, the Right Hon. James Arbuthnot Wilberforce of Thornberry Hall in the West Riding of Yorkshire. The wedding had taken place at St Peter's Church, Eaton Square, London S.W.1.

Charlotte married? It seemed so unlikely. Kay looked at the date of the clipping. The wedding had taken place a month earlier, April 16th. What a shame they'd lost touch. She would have loved to have been there. And who was James Arbuthnot Wilberforce, and how had he managed to pin down "this most exotic specimen of London's social butterflies", as a gossip column had once described Charlotte?

Kay examined the photograph closely. Charlotte looked exactly the same, laughing as she left the church. Kay read the piece again. The honeymoon was to be spent at the Grand Hotel, Nice, in the South of France. The happy couple would make their new home at the family estate in Yorkshire, it said.

Charlotte living in the country surrounded by servants, dogs and horses? Charlotte waking up for the rest of her life with the same man by her side? It didn't seem possible.

It was just further evidence that the world had turned upside down since the end of the war: there was a socialist government in London, Russia had the A-bomb and was blockading Berlin, the Middle East was giving painful birth to the new state of Israel, and Charlotte Victoria Wilberforce, née Montagu, had settled for matrimony. Whatever next, thought Kay: a man on the moon?

Kay had little money, but she didn't have to look far for work. The years of snickering mentions and pictures in the newspaper gossip columns opened the door to several publishing houses. They wanted a book that would tell the inside story of her life with Eisenhower.

A substantial advance of ten thousand dollars was offered, together with the services of a ghost writer. The message from every publisher who approached her was clear: the more Kay revealed of her relationship with Ike, the higher the price they'd pay.

The photographs of Kay and Eisenhower together in Britain and Europe had been widely published. There were two that had caused most comment. The first was taken at the Prince of Wales Theatre in London when she and her mother joined Ike and his party in the royal box. The second showed Kay walking side by side with Ike through the ruins of Frankfurt. Once the New York press discovered that Kay Summersby had moved to the city, they happily reprinted such pictures over the objections of the Pentagon press office.

The newspapers hadn't yet stumbled on the fact that the official army photograph taken moments after Eisenhower had signed the German surrender document had been doctored. America saw a photograph of a group of smiling military faces at the centre of which, with the biggest smile of all, stood Eisenhower holding up two pens. The original photograph, showing Kay standing just behind him, had been released and published in Europe. No American journalist had yet made the connection between the two.

"Welcome to the programme, Miss Summersby. You have resigned from the US Army after a long tour of duty as General Eisenhower's driver and, what shall I say, his personal assistant in Europe during the war. Can you tell us about those years?"

Kay was sitting in the studio of a local New York radio station in the first of what would prove a series of broadcast and newspaper interviews. They said they wanted to hear first hand what life was like as a member of Eisenhower's wartime family.

She knew that what they really wanted was rather more personal. She had planned her response to the inevitable questions about her relationship with care.

"I would like to tell everyone in New York what they, I am sure, already know: General Eisenhower is the greatest soldier in American history and led the alliance with Great Britain to a great victory. But the war is over and I would like to talk about the future."

Kay shifted in her chair, pressed the large headphones firmly against her ears and glanced briefly through the glass window of the studio to where her agent was sitting, together with an executive from the Prentice Hall publishing company.

"And what is your future here, Miss Summersby?"

"Well, thanks to the general, I have American citizenship, and I plan to make my home here in New York."

"Any other plans? We hear you might be writing a book."

Kay laughed. "You are well informed. Yes, I have been commissioned to write a book."

Kay could see her agent waving at her through the glass. She couldn't remember if she was supposed to reveal the commission or not. What the hell, she thought – just tell the truth.

"Can you tell us more?"

"A publisher here in New York has asked me to give an account of my time with General Eisenhower during the war – three and a half years."

"You were his driver, I understand."

"That's how I started, yes."

"And he promoted you?"

"Yes, but I would rather not say any more. My publisher has asked me to be discreet."

"Wow! Is there much to be discreet about, Miss Summersby? You know, I guess, that there's been quite a lot of talk about you two in the papers here?"

She looked at her interviewer, a young man who was reading from a file of typewritten notes.

"I have the greatest admiration for General Eisenhower and worked closely with him, but those years are over."

"With respect, that doesn't answer the question, Miss Summersby."

"With respect, if anyone is looking for tittle-tattle in this book, they will be disappointed."

"Does the general know you are writing this book?"

"No, but I am sure he will after this programme goes out."

"Can I ask the title?"

"Sure: *Eisenhower Was My Boss.*"

Kay looked through the glass again. She could see her agent and the man from Prentice Hall smiling.

The news that Kay Summersby was to write a book about her wartime experiences was not well received in the Pentagon. For Eisenhower it was just another reminder that there would be no easy way to put the war behind him. He did not wish to become trapped in endless talks and lectures about tactical triumphs such as D-Day, the fall of Paris and the final assault on Germany.

For one thing, the inquest into the failure to take Berlin was beginning to raise questions. It was Churchill and Patton who had urged the Allied commander to seize the German capital before the Red Army did so, and it was Churchill in Fulton, Missouri in 1946 who warned that an "iron curtain" had fallen across Europe from Stettin in the Baltic to Trieste in the Adriatic.

The inference was cruel but clear. If the Allies had taken Berlin before the Russians, the iron curtain would have fallen farther east than it did, and millions would have been living in freedom rather than under communist dictatorship.

Eisenhower had perfectly good answers to those questioning his strategy and his failure to take Berlin. He planned to lay his reasons out, and to refute critics, in his own memoirs.

Eisenhower knew his own account of the war years would be matched by those of his staff. He'd been told Kay Summersby would join Mickey McKeogh, Harry Butcher and others in his wartime family telling their story. Kay was a free agent now that she had left the army. He was sure she would do nothing to embarrass or hurt him. Others close to him, especially Mamie, were not so sure. His wife had warned him that Summersby would seek to profit from her presence in his team and would distort their relationship to help sell her book.

In due course, Eisenhower planned to make clear in his own memoirs exactly what Kay Summersby's contribution to his European command had been. He wouldn't address the continuing rumours and the gossips; he'd ignore them. But he would record that her service had been that of a loyal, hardworking driver and aide, someone on whom he depended for the efficient working of his office, just as he had been helped and supported by others in his team.

There would be plenty of people to suggest there was more to it than that. He could hardly deny it to himself; but why admit it to others? There had probably been an emotional involvement not quite in keeping with a professional relationship, but hell, he was fighting a major war, launching millions of men into battle. He had very nearly broken under the strain.

Marshall had understood that when he'd organised the trip to the South of France.

That was then, back in Europe. The world had changed. He would make that clear. He needed to put Summersby and the war behind him.

Now his army career was over, a political career beckoned. Eisenhower had weighed up the prospect and, for public consumption at least, had said that he did not find the prospect especially appealing. As he had told a reporter when asked about his presidential ambitions, "Any man who wants to be president of the United States is either an egomaniac or plumb crazy – maybe both."

The seemingly casual remark had been crafted with care. The old army rule was never to reveal ambition for promotion because it created enemies among one's peer group and did not impress superiors. Allow facts and actions to speak for themselves, that was the army rule.

He just wished he hadn't written that letter to George Marshall. It had been a mistake, a rare moment when his heart had ruled his head.

But nobody knew about the letter. Except George Marshall. After Marshall's angry and contemptuous response, the letter would surely have been destroyed.

He had never told Kay Summersby about it. He had planned to surprise her. But that was in the past, back in the war. And the past, they say, is a foreign country to which you can never return.

24

Autumn 1948

Morningside Heights on the Upper West Side of Manhattan had been potato fields before the first of the great modern buildings of Colombia University were built in 1895. The Low Library was designed in neo-classical style with steps rising steeply to ten fluted pillars above which a granite lintel carried an inscription:

> *Kings College founded in the Province of New York by royal charter in the reign of George II. Perpetuated as Columbia College by the people of the State of New York when they became free and independent. Maintained and cherished from generation to generation for the advancement of the public good and the glory of Almighty God.*

Kay knew the words by heart. She knew just how many steps it took to reach the Doric pillars and the entrance to the Low Library. She knew too that the building that many called the heart and soul of Columbia was no longer a library. The university's archives and books were now housed in a larger, more modern building that had been built before the war.

The Low Library was now a series of offices from which one of the world's great universities was administered. The president of the university worked from a suite of rooms on the ground floor. Every day of the working week, usually just before nine in the morning, the president walked through Columbia's iron gates, crossed the large forecourt, climbed those steps and walked past the pillars into the beating heart of the university. He would go to his office and the academic day would begin. It was a familiar routine welcomed by students and staff because it spoke of both great tradition and open governance.

Kay knew this, just as she knew the location of every classroom and lecture hall on campus. For weeks since the appointment had been announced she had taken the subway from Greenwich Village to 116th Street every day in those autumn months of 1948 to walk the campus, take coffee with students and listen and learn about the workings of the university.

She had ignored the advice of close friends and given into a desire so deep in her being that it defied rational explanation. She was obsessed – an obsession born not of love or loss, she told herself, but of certainty. Kay was certain that General Dwight Eisenhower, who had taken up his position as the new president of Columbia University in the fall of 1948, wished to see to her again.

She knew he would be glad of the chance to remind himself of what they had known together and what they had lost. She knew also that it was only force of circumstance and the rigorous code of army conduct that had made him turn his back on her.

Now he was free of the army and unconstrained by the stifling conventions of high military office. He was married, of course, but he had also been married in the years they had spent together during the war. He had been married when he told her he would never let her go. He had been married when he promoted her, gave her a position in the US Army and arranged American citizenship for her. He had been married when he sent her a four-leaf clover pressed into a greetings card. A well-wisher in Ireland had sent it to him and he had given it to her with a note saying it would bring them both luck. She knew his feelings couldn't have changed deep down. No man could deny such elemental emotions forever.

Ike had come to New York to become the top administrator and fundraiser for a major university. This was so far out of his area of expertise that there had to be another reason why he had accepted the post. After all, Kay had read in the papers, like everyone else in America, that the famous General Eisenhower was inundated with offers of well-paid corporate positions, all of which would generously allow him time to write his memoirs.

It must be because he knew she was in New York. He would have read the stories about her book contract and the impending publication date this autumn. He would have heard about the many speaking engagements that had been planned, and that there was so much interest in the book that a nationwide tour had been talked about.

She had been careful not to say anything that might embarrass him – the book was a fair and accurate record that showed him as the victorious commander of Allied military forces in a hard-fought war. If anyone wished to draw inferences from the fact that the book showed how closely they had worked together, how she had been promoted from his driver to his secretary, and then to his personal aide, well let them. Why should she care? That scuttlebutt had been going on for years anyway.

It was clear to Kay, beyond doubt, as it would be to any reasonable woman, that when Ike had decided to move from Washington to New York, he had done so not just to accept the mortar board, gown and hefty salary from Columbia but with a more subtle design in mind. His arrival was a sign, whether he consciously recognised it or not, that they were destined to be together in the end. He had come to New York because somewhere deep in his heart flickered the desire to see her again.

The ten-thousand-dollar advance she had received for her memoirs had enabled her to move into a larger apartment and rent a cottage in Long Island. Men were anxious to take her out, and one man in particular, a stockbroker called Morgan, seemed intent on deepening the relationship. She spent nights at his apartment. He was caring, kind and rather boring. He said he liked Telek, but she could see that wasn't true.

New York knew all about Telek. The black Scottish terrier was well known in all the good restaurants and the nightclubs, too, where he was allowed to stay in the coatrooms while she drank, dined and danced with her admirers. She made sure that the press stories mentioned Telek. When reporters asked what the name meant, she said it was a private matter between her and her old boss. She said she had given him the little puppy as a mark of her esteem and he had chosen the name. That was all.

And now, this autumn, she had decided the time had come to redress what was clearly a wrong done to both of them. It was asking too much to expect him to initiate contact. She would do it. She would arrange an encounter somewhere on the campus, a casual chance meeting that would bring together two old friends.

She had her story ready. Her sister in England had a cousin who was studying at the college. She had asked Kay to look him up. She knew Eisenhower would never believe it, but that wouldn't matter. What mattered was that he would see her again for the first time since that terrible forced parting in the Pentagon. And it had been forced. He would never coldly have turned his back on her like that if he had not been forced to do so.

Their chance meeting would give her the excuse for a conversation, just a few warm words of surprise and affection that would lead to a meeting for tea in one of the great hotels. There they would talk about old times. Telek would be there and would make much of his old master. She would bring a present for him. A box of luxury chocolates like the ones he had given her when he'd left London for the first time back in 1942. He would remember that. He would remember everything.

She saw him the moment he walked through the gates in a long gabardine raincoat. He was wearing a trilby hat that looked so different from the peaked braided army caps of the past that it seemed out of character. He was holding a briefcase in his hand and looked stern. It had been raining in the night and there were puddles on the paving. His polished brown shoes splashed into them, but he didn't notice.

Students laden with bulging satchels were crossing the forecourt in that aimless manner of those who wanted to be doing something else, almost anything else, other than going to a class.

She walked, head down, as if deep in thought so as to cross his approach to the library steps.

She heard her name. "Kay!"

She looked up. Eisenhower had stopped, a look of total surprise on his face.

"Ike! Hello!"

"Kay! What are you doing here?"

"How are you? Congratulations on the new job."

"Kay... why are you here?"

She began to tell her story, garbling the words, and stopped. She could see disbelief on his face. He had gone red in the face again with a familiar look of anger and embarrassment.

"Kay, you shouldn't be here."

"But I thought..."

"Kay, I can't do anything for you."

"...we might just talk."

"No, Kay. It's not possible. We talked about this last time. I wish you well, but... I'm sorry."

He stood there and shook his head. Around them students streamed towards the steps, some turning to look back at the famous face they had passed.

"Ike, can't we just talk – old times and all that?"

"It's not possible, Kay. There's nothing I can do. You know that."

She felt a sudden urge to throw this man the snappy salute he had taught her. A small gesture of defiance that would embarrass him in front of his students and probably make her look like a mad woman. Well, maybe she was – maybe this is what it had come to. The woman who could not let go of a man who had long left the stage. There she was, the last of the cast in a darkened theatre. Everyone had gone home.

She watched him turn and walk away up the steps of the library. The inscription above the entrance he passed through might as well have read "THE END".

But it wasn't the end. How could it be?

Everybody knew that Eisenhower would become president of the United States of America. That's what all the smart columnists in Washington and New York kept writing and the radio commentators kept reporting. They said he was being very clever in biding his time and not running against Truman this year but waiting until '52.

Then he and Mamie would move into the White House, the president and his First Lady. She would watch him greeting foreign leaders with that familiar smile and frowning at press conferences as reporters threw curveball questions at him. He would play golf just as he had done at Telegraph Cottage and maybe go riding as they had every day in Richmond Park. He might even try his hand in the White House kitchen at one of the favourite stews he had made at the cottage. It would be very Ike to move the White House chef aside and say, "Let me show you how to do this."

He was the kind of man who would do that. He would gather a new family around him in the White House, men and women who would work hard for him, look after him, and some of whom would maybe lose a little of their hearts to him.

She watched him disappear into the library, then turned and walked back to 116th Street. She knew now what she should have known the moment those movement orders were placed on the board in the Frankfurt office. She had been cut out of the life of a man who she thought had loved her.

The sky was turning dark; it was going to rain. She wanted a cloudburst to drench the streets and calm the rage rising within her. Let thunder roll over Columbia's ancient buildings and lightning strike the Low Library. She had been stupid of course, guilty of falling in love with the man who had just humiliated her. The humiliation lay not in the abrupt way he had walked off. It lay in her own stupidity. She had been credulous, allowing emotion born of make-believe to swell into the fantasy that flowered in cheap romance novels and corny love songs.

It began to rain, a light shower which opened umbrellas along the street. Heavy traffic was moving in both directions. Soon the street would be pedestrianised in a deal that had been struck with the mayor. It had been Ike's first act as Columbia's president. The announcement had made him very popular with the students. He'd always liked to show his troops he was on their side, that he cared, that he could make a difference to their lives. Those were the people he really loved.

She walked down the steps to the subterranean world below ground and caught the subway for the sixteen-stop ride down to Greenwich Village. In the womb of the transit system she felt calmer. Manhattan was so eye-catching, so unlikely, so startlingly original above ground that the fetid warmth of the subway was like a counter-reality, the real world of New York City.

Every stop on the subway added to the architecture of this dark world. She knew them all now. After Central Park North the line would swing south towards the Hudson River and turn again to run beneath the Upper West Side and Columbus Circle. The track would slide deeper after 50th Street, then run closer to the surface at her stop near SoHo.

The familiarity of this underground world, the warmth and safety far from the shiny, traffic-choked streets above, the symphonic rattle of steel wheels on iron tracks, calmed Kay and sent her into a sleepless reverie.

She closed her eyes and drifted back to her last days in Germany. She wondered why she had never thought to ask what the E in Charles E. Burrows stood for. Ernest perhaps, it suited him. He would be back home now with his wife and family. Would he remember, as she did so clearly, the night they had danced in a ruined school in Berlin? Would he recall, as she could, every moment in that hotel room when two naked strangers had collided and clung together between damp sheets?

She thought of Charlotte, now the lady of the manor on a country estate far from her wild days in London. The thought was so improbable that Kay spun the story forward. There would be babies and nannies. Charlotte would become bored with her husband and the country. There would be a brief fling with a younger man, an under-gardener perhaps.

This would be a deliberate act on Charlotte's part, a bid for freedom, but James Arbuthnot Wilberforce would not notice the indiscretion or choose to ignore it. Charlotte would then begin an affair with one of his friends, maybe another Yorkshire landowner, that would be too obvious to ignore. After a terrible row she would move to a flat in London.

A divorce would follow, made much of in the society press. Charlotte would revert to her maiden name and resume life as a social butterfly. But she would be older. She would have the responsibilities of motherhood. It would not be the same. And that, Kay reflected, was the bitter truth. Nothing, especially happiness, stays the same.

When she surfaced it was a brighter day than she had left at Columbia. Low clouds carrying the promise of rain had shrouded the skyscrapers uptown. Here in the village there were no high-rises, and the sun shone fitfully as the clouds continued their leisurely journey to nowhere. It was quieter and calmer in this part of the city.

She walked slowly, not hurrying, thinking of the decision she had come to somewhere on the subway ride beneath the city. She hated the idea but knew she had to do it. She walked briskly the few blocks to a small green park alongside the Hudson River. Beyond the trees and lawns lay a walkway with railings bordering the river. She looked over the railings at the mud-brown waters flowing imperceptibly to the sea.

She looked around but saw no one nearby. She reached into her handbag and took out the Beretta. The gun fitted so well into her hand that even a passer-by would not notice it. There were a few dog walkers in the distance and a pair of lovers coiled around each other on a park seat.

Otherwise there were no witnesses. He had given her the gun five years ago in North Africa. It had stayed with her ever since, a faithful companion and talisman of a mythical past. She raised her arm and threw the gun as far as she could, watching it fall in a silver arc into the dark waters. She turned and walked away.

Telek would be waiting impatiently for his walk. That night her stockbroker would take her to a candlelit dinner in an Italian restaurant they both liked in the village. A silver-framed mirror ran the length of one wall. An older and wiser woman would be watching her that night. There would be flowers and champagne on the table. He would propose to her, if not that night then very soon. She would say yes; they would kiss and she would cry, long pent-up tears that wouldn't stop. She was a long-lapsed churchgoer marrying a protestant of good Scottish American stock. They would find a church somewhere in the village where they would celebrate their vows with a discreet ceremony.

She would send an invitation to General Dwight Eisenhower and Mamie. She would receive a polite typewritten reply. He would decline the invitation but offer his best wishes for her future happiness. He would mean that, just as he had surely, in his heart, meant every word he had said to her on the long road they had travelled during the war.

She knew he would never forget.

Historical Note

This is a historical novel based on careful research which I hope lends credibility to the extraordinary stories played out by the main characters, almost all of them real people living and fighting in what was a very real war.

I have drawn on the many accounts of General Eisenhower's wartime service in Europe and his immediate post-war life in the US. The story of the man he faced across the Channel in 1944, Field Marshal Erwin Rommel, is also based on voluminous records. Kay Summersby, Eisenhower's driver, who became his secretary, personal assistant and wartime companion, has told her story in two books. The first, *Eisenhower Was My Boss* (Prentice Hall, New York, 1948) was a factual and detailed account of her work for the wartime commander. The second, *Past Forgetting* (Simon and Schuster, New York, 1976) was dictated as she was dying in 1975, and revealed her wartime affair with the man she called "the boss".

Many of Eisenhower's biographers have cast doubt on Summersby's account of the relationship, although I note that almost all of them quote from *Past Forgetting*. It is easy to see why. Although colourfully written in breathless prose, the book has the stamp of truth. One reason is that Summersby makes clear that although her relationship with Eisenhower was on occasion sexual, it was never fully consummated. If a dying woman was fantasising about her affair with a man who was to become president of the United States, she would hardly detract from her story with such an admission.

The real controversy about Eisenhower's relationship with his driver is whether or not in the immediate aftermath of the war he wrote to the chief of staff, George Marshall, asking permission to divorce his wife Mamie with the obvious intention of marrying Summersby. This story surfaced in *Plain Speaking: An Oral Biography of Harry S. Truman* by Merle Miller (Victor Gollancz, London, 1974), based on a series of taped interviews. Truman, then in his late eighties, was categoric that Eisenhower had written the divorce letter to Marshall and that the chief of staff had furiously refused the request. Truman went on to say that although he disliked Eisenhower, he had the letter removed from the Pentagon file and destroyed when he left office in 1953.

Again, most of Eisenhower's biographers have gone to some lengths to dismiss the story, claiming it was no more than a malicious tale invented by an old man. However, the distinguished historian Jean Edward Smith in his recent biography *Eisenhower in War and Peace* (Random House, New York, 2012) not only credits the divorce letter story as the truth but goes to considerable and convincing lengths to justify that assertion.

Tellingly, Professor Smith cites another distinguished academic, Professor Garrett Mattingly, the Pulitzer prize-winning author of *The Armada*, as a source for the divorce story. Mattingly, who was Professor of History at Columbia when Eisenhower was president there, had been a junior naval intelligence officer in the war with the job of monitoring outgoing cables from senior commanders for censorship purposes. According to Professor Smith, Mattingly told colleagues at Columbia that he had seen Marshall's cable to Eisenhower in May 1945 in which he threatened to force him out of the army if he went ahead and divorced Mamie. Professor Henry F. Graff of Columbia is cited as the source for the Mattingly story.

Since many real people are portrayed in this book it might be helpful to explain what happened to the leading characters.

David Dwight Eisenhower, the 34th president of the United States, died from heart failure in Washington in March 1969 aged seventy-eight.

Kay Summersby died from cancer in January 1975 aged sixty-six. She spent her last days in Southampton, Long Island. Her ashes were scattered where she grew up, at Innis Beg, Co. Cork, Ireland.

Field Marshal Montgomery died aged eighty-eight in Hampshire, England. His post-war years were beset by controversy not least over his criticism of Eisenhower's conduct of the final stages of the war.

General Omar Bradley died in April 1981 aged eighty-eight. His successful post-war career included a fine memoir, *A General's Life*, co-authored with Clay Blair and published posthumously in 1983. In the book he criticised Field Marshal Montgomery.

General Patton died on 21 December 1945 after a car accident in Germany. He was sixty. He was buried in a military cemetery in Luxembourg alongside men of his Third Army.

Apart from the books mentioned above, I found the following useful in my research:

Carlo D'Este, *Eisenhower: Allied Supreme Commander* (Henry Holt and Co., 2002).

Michael Korda, *Ike: An American Hero* (Harper Collins, 2007).

David Eisenhower, *Eisenhower at War 1943-45* (Vintage Books, 1987).

Stephen Ambrose, *Eisenhower: Soldier and President* (Simon and Schuster, 1997).

Susan Eisenhower, *Mrs Ike: A Biography of Mamie Eisenhower* (Farrar, Straus and Giroux, 1996).

Norman Gelb, *Ike and Monty: Generals at War* (William Morrow and Co., 1994).

Mark Perry, *Partners in Command* (Penguin Books, 2007).

Ed Cray, *General of the Army: George C. Marshall* (Simon and Schuster, 1991).

Omar Bradley and Clay Blair, *A General's Life* (Simon and Schuster, 1983).

Harry C. Butcher, *Three Years with Eisenhower* (Heinemann, 1946).

Acknowledgements

Never have I written a book which has required more help and advice from friends, colleagues, editors, and my long-suffering agent Annabel Merullo. To her I owe a debt of thanks that only the success of this book will repay. To my first editor Juliet van Oss I owe warm thanks, and more so to my colleague Karen Robinson of *The Sunday Times* who has a critical editorial eye and never lets friendship interfere with some hard but vitally helpful judgements. My final editor and friend Sue Robertson showed me the light at the end of the tunnel.

No book goes to press without a copy-edit to remove all the small but embarrassing mistakes that inevitably creep into the text. The fine eye of Deborah Blake did just that for this author and he is profoundly grateful.

Gesche Ipsen, who then headed the Duckworth office in London, supported the book from the start, as did that grand old man of British publishing, the magisterial Peter Mayer who has guided three of my previous novels into the bookshops. Thank you, Peter. I am also grateful to Matt Casbourne, now publishing manager of Duckworth, for answering my endless queries.

Mrs Deborah Keegan, who fills the role in my life of a cross between matron and mother superior, could not have been more helpful and encouraging even if she disapproves of my sending her emails in the middle of the night.

Katherine Raymond Hinton has been wonderfully generous in taking time off from her busy life with her husband, Les Hinton, in New York to read and comment kindly on my previous books. Her praise has always been the light that shines through the dark moments.

It is an invidious task to thank friends for just "being there" in the course of writing a book, because inevitably one cannot name them all. However, to Colin Adamson, Alex Shulman, Victoria Silberbauer, Graham and Sue Paterson, Mrs Yash Patel and the late Chris Buckland, who I hope will read this on whatever celestial perch he has alighted – thank you. I may not have seen much of you in the course of writing this book but trust me – you helped.

To Dotti Irving, counsellor, friend, critic and a lady who bestrides the London PR scene – I owe a lot, including another lunch.

Finally to my children Emily, Elizabeth and Nicholas, my gratitude and my love for doing more for me as a writer and father than they will ever know.

James MacManus is the managing director of *The Times Literary Supplement*. After studying at St Andrews University he began his career in journalism at the *Daily Express* in Manchester. Joining *The Guardian* in 1972, he became Paris, and then Africa and Middle East Correspondent. He is the author of several novels including *On the Broken Shore*, *Black Venus*, *Sleep in Peace Tonight* and *Midnight in Berlin*. He has three children and lives in Dulwich, London.

Also available

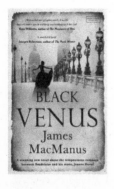